TOKYO THREE

Paul Lefley

Published in 2023 by FeedARead.com Publishing

Dedicated to Stanislav Yevgrafovich Petrov who on 26 September 1983, saved the lives of my children.

Thanks to my brother Roy for his support, to Chris Richards for his enthusiasm and to Chris Shone for detailed help.

As always great thanks to my wife, Diane. For? For everything.

FOREWORD

Before the core of this tale begins there was another in which none of its personnel took part and yet every soul on the planet was involved.

1945 August 6th to 9th.

An adapted B29 and its cargo were on their way to Mount Fuji. Japan hadn't yet surrendered. The Commander-in-Chief gave his reasons and had given the order. The bomb onboard had a special casing of high-grade stainless steel which was stronger than that of its two counterparts. The effect of the blast of the uranium 235 explosion over Hiroshima was known and that of the plutonium 239 over Nagasaki would be known. That of a subterranean explosion wasn't. This bomb wasn't as rotund as those two but at eleven thousand pounds it was heavier than its stable mates. It was aerodynamic and able to exceed the speed of sound if it was dropped from high enough. This time it could have little more than a thousand metres to fall. It had what looked like a standard handlebars style arrangement of a single bridge wire detonator. This one, however, was different. This trigger was a back-up, only coming into play in the event of the failure of three main devices, a forty-five second delay switch, a pressure gauge and radar depth sensors. Carved skilfully into one of the main bomb fins and painted in a red antioxidant was Tokyo 3. It looked like it had been there when manufactured.

Hiroshima and Nagasaki's explosions were higher above ground than this craft might fly towards the end. Having left the airbase at Tinian Island in the Pacific way behind them the crew came to see late on that this mission was dipping dangerously close to a mountain, heading almost straight for it.

The pilots were the best, the very best. They knew what their target was, but their crew was told only shortly prior to boarding. It was a natural phenomenon, unpopulated, nothing like the targets of Enola Gay and Bockscar. Hours earlier the mission plan had to be altered. The B29s meant to be flying an hour ahead as weather scouts had come back damaged from the previous mission and there were no parts immediately to hand for repair. An additional B29 which would have been for instrumentation and photographic support had not even made it to the island.

For a bomber of this sort, the operation would have it virtually skimming the terrain immediately beneath it, a strain on its superstructure. The ordinance it was carrying wasn't an airburst bomb, it was a special form of bunker buster. There was a chance things wouldn't work out. It was a secret that might remain a secret both because there would be nothing substantial to tell and because it would reflect badly on all involved.

There was plenty that was different about this mission but for its crew one aspect in particular stood out: its unique bombardier. The bombardier they knew solely by the surname Cassidy. Cassidy had non-regulation long hair and sloppily worn fatigues that gave little idea of shape or stature. Those fatigues were spied slipping in and out of the plane and all over it time and again, particularly around the specially built new bomb bay prior to any crew ever getting close to it. Rumour was the outlandish hair was seen at night just above a blanket in the bay from the second day the bombardier inspected the plane. It was said that behind a curtained off area in the hangar Cassidy was regularly pacing out the distance from one end of the bomb carcass to the other, then of the bay and then from the cockpit control panel along the entire fuselage. For safety it was standard the bomb's contents had been disassembled. What wasn't standard was that Cassidy handled almost every individual part.

The men knew little of the Cassidy. They hardly saw more than glimpses of a hunched figure pouring over the bomb while holding its blueprints. They always knew where that figure had been because it left behind a sweet smell of deodorants. They preferred the ubiquitous odours of grease and gasoline. Mystifyingly in a rucksack strapped to the bombardier's back was what looked like a set of artists paint brushes.

Doubts concerning the bombardier were multiple but there were no doubts when it came to the immense experience involved. Cassidy had been engaged in some of the heaviest combat in Europe, the D-Day invasion and the Battle of the Bulge while serving with the B26 marauders. The record was there. No target was too small, no terrain too complex. Once in a while in the armed forces mavericks can be tolerated when they deliver handsomely.

Eyebrows were raised almost above foreheads when Cassidy commandeered and locked away the regular Norden bombsight. Because genius was involved it was accepted, as was the failure to salute or acknowledge salutes. The captain, his number two, the navigator and a senior member from the rest of the crew confronted Cassidy, coming from the hangar one night. They demanded information on the methods proposed. All they got back was a look. If looks could kill, a mass grave would have been started there.

Once near the target it was the norm that the bombardier took charge of the aircraft, became the commander. Its speed, its direction, its altitude, its incline were all the prerogative of the bombardier. Whilst this included supervising the loading of the bomb, it was the operations officer who was charged with re-assembling it. That was Cassidy's sole concession to convention.

Tokyo was eighty odd miles distant from Mount Fuji, way beyond the effects of an atomic blast. But the volcano lay on one tectonic plate with two others subducting from it to north and south. When Laki erupted in Iceland its effects spread as far as Africa and India. The question was if man-made weapons exploited natural phenomena how powerful would they become? Without practical application that couldn't be known. Where better to aim than driving ordinance deep into a volcano? Penetrating the cone would be optimum and the only hope for that was Cassidy.

The craft was stripped of any weight it could be. Gun turrets and armour plating had been removed and it was down to a skeleton crew. Everyone knew of the dangers of the shockwave. A plane not built for acceleration would have to be light to escape the consequences of the blast once it dropped its cargo. The crew understood this well, having seen the condition of the two planes grounded back at base.

The mission was very nearly aborted. Tested, the pump for accessing the fuel reserves in the tail of the plane wasn't functioning. Regulations were clear, the mission had to be cancelled. Everyone was ordered off the plane. The crew stood around shifting from foot to foot. The brigadier general had them called to attention. He spoke to the captain and marched into the hangar to use the radio. The men were not at attention when he came back but he let that go. He told them in a cheery voice, that they were fast losing the weather, that the Hiroshima flight had been a milk run, with zero problems and not a drop of reserve fuel had been necessary. History was there to be made.

Hour after hour the plane battled head winds, using more fuel than had been reckoned on. Six hours plus into the flight and heavy cloud was assembling alongside huge smoke trails and a storm began. The crew stared out of portholes at a craft engulfed in St Elmo's fire. It writhed along the fuselage and the huge wings. It draped itself completely across the cockpit window, making visibility worse. The co-pilot slowly shook his head and said,

"Do you think nature's trying to tell us something?"

"I don't think the smoke is from any volcano, you know. I think it's from Hiroshima," the captain noted.

"They've fucked us here, they surely have. They're useless. They've called this Tokyo Three.

It's either Tokyo One or Japan Two. And does that lunatic in the bomb bay even know what he's doing? The captain guffawed,

"He? You think Cassidy is a he?"

"Impossible. It wouldn't be allowed… You think he's a 'she'?"

"I don't know what Cassidy is. There's no way of knowing."

The co-pilot gave no further response, recalling the bombardier was never seen in the mess, in the bar or in the restrooms.

There wasn't long to go. Cassidy was laying down on a bench wearing earmuffs put on to guard against the shriek of the four eighteen- cylinder engines on take-off noise. The bench was a couple of yards from the bomb. The bombardier was woken by the operations officer.

"It's all wrong, gone crazy. We got a red light going off like the bomb is about to explode right now. Armed, it's armed, fully armed, look at it, look." When Cassidy looked a red light that had been blinking steadily suddenly sped up.

"Holy fuck some of these bombs can pre-detonate if we drop below a predetermined level. It shouldn't happen with this one, but lights shouldn't be flashing either. Pass me the blueprints."

As the operations officer unrolled the blueprints, Cassidy ran to get a long kitbag. While the officer prised the bomb casing off, the bombardier plunged a shaking hand in, using the other hand to shine a torch at the switches. After five full minutes, Cassidy spotted a mistake in the arming process and cursed. The bombardier flipped two tiny switches and the red light stopped blinking. A huge breath was let out slowly followed by a grin and a kiss planted on the picture of an angel with outspread wings painted in black and grey on the bomb's carcass.

In the cockpit they were unaware of this close call. The officers there had other concerns. The fuel gauge was being temperamental and vision was bad. Spotting Tokyo was hard enough, let alone Fuji. They were flying mile after mile searching for it. The first officer wiped the inside of the front screen. He knew it was pointless. Both pilots stared and stared, rubbing their eyes as though the smoke was getting into them. Twenty minutes of searching and they believed they had found it. Twelve thousand feet and Fuji's summit looked impossibly tiny, if indeed that was the volcano and not another mountain altogether.

All the calculations had been done. They had had the go ahead. They slowed trying to get the initial approach absolutely right.

"Draw back, draw back. Fast for fuck's sake,"
the bombardier hissed on their headphones. The approach was too low, they were on course to hit the side of the mountain. The bombardier took over, but thermal currents were dragging the plane this way and that. There were shouts asking what the hell was happening.

"Leave it to Cassidy,"
was all they heard in reply. The plane's engines were roaring. Given the poor visibility the bombardier should have used radar, but he didn't. The plane was circling at speed, like it was trying to whisk the cloud away. After fifteen gas guzzling minutes a break in clouds came and Cassidy guided the plane in a swift descent.

Thermal currents once more hit the craft making the wings quiver and tilt. Crew not strapped in tumbled to one side of the fuselage and then crashed against the other. The single person on the plane not remotely shaken was the bombardier. This was a Zen focus. Things were not going to improve, the bombardier had rarely experienced perfect conditions, usually having to adapt. Being decisive counted for a lot. Gazing down, the mouth of the volcano's cone looked more than big enough and the volcano itself immense.

Cassidy whispered,

"It's on its way,"

instantly followed by

"Hold, hold,"

so no movement of the B29 influenced the bomb trajectory. But the plane had already been suddenly jerked upwards as the bomb was exiting. The instant it was leaving the aircraft the captain had sharply yanked the controls and accelerated the engines. The bombardier craned round and back and forth to keep the bomb in sight.

Both pilots knew they had gone a fraction early. The bomb rocked and was lifted on yet another thermal current. It was thrown sideways and then spiralled and then was spun, propelled both by its own design and further currents around it. Neither pilot so much as glanced at the other. Had anyone truly expected them to penetrate the cone? They hadn't asked for the maverick lunatic bombardier. The bomb was built with the ability to burrow into the side of the volcano. That would be mission accomplished. They were relieved to be on their way and desperate to have enough time to escape safely. The altimeter was playing up whilst the fuel gauge needle was swinging left to right like a windscreen wiper. They dare not go for altitude because of the fuel. They had been briefed that the Enola Gay hadn't flown much more than eleven miles when it was caught by the shockwave. They waited but the shock never came.

If it had they wouldn't have known it. As they reached the ocean the plane flew too low, grazed the water twice and as the pilot frantically yanked at the controls it bounced and then hit waves that might as well have been brick walls. Just where the continental shelf ended the B29 dropped, plunging headlong into the depths.

Like the plane the bomb never made it to where it was intended. More gusts had caught the bomb's fins, whooshing it an entire half circle around the volcano. As it spun it slowly got lower and lower, flattening out. Almost horizontally gliding it narrowly avoided a clump of Japanese Red Pines. Just above ground it coated itself in chalk powder as it swept through the side of an industrial pile deposited there. Still spinning it finally dipped into a couple of tons of sand that had been laid out in a tadpole shape on a golf fairway. There it burrowed its way metres underground, finally subsiding to form a twenty kiloton plus primed ammunition dump. It was there waiting to strike for the surface to be hit by the head of a golf club or anything hard.

Whilst the bomb near Tokyo wasn't buried deep its secret was. Over a period the decreasing number of those who knew of it and endured were encouraged to forget. Unlike the bomb itself the secret decayed and deteriorated until a handful or less would be able to recognise it. Like the bomb the secret remained a mortal threat.

C1 1966 January 7th

Lightning flashes lashed out from one cloud to another. Two English men sat behind the streaked dusty window of an ornately tiled tapas bar they had dashed in to. The difficult teenage years were past, Junior having been deemed everything from a 'tearaway' to a 'wide boy'. His father quietly thought him a rebel which was a plus by his reckoning. The son was now a man. They weren't exactly peas in a pod, the father was completely bald whilst the young man had a scalp bursting with follicles, but the pair were close. The father was a taxi driver, the son was in the process of becoming one.

Rain was pounding a canvas awning which dripped almond size drops from its corners. A tiny waterfall began from a dip in its front. Neither of them was concerned although the younger man kept showing the hours that had passed on his watch to his father. They supped San Miguel and chatted about everything and nothing in a heartfelt way. They had driven there in a car belonging to the owner of an apartment they had rented. The father told his son to take over the driving on the grounds that he "needed the experience". In truth the older man didn't like driving on the wrong side of the road or with a right-hand drive vehicle. The son had ribbed him,

"Oh and on which side of the sky did you fly captain?"

"I was an engineer and that was donkey's years ago."

The son knew that well. His father had told him many times of a last flight in the early fifties intended for the Royal Aircraft Establishment in Suffolk. It was a secret. As a boy he had loved the sound of that.

Chas Senior had guided his son along what was really no more than one serious road with the odd track coming off it. They had driven from basic lodgings where they were staying in Nerja. They had never been abroad before and didn't have a good grasp of the weather but were lucky with better than normal temperatures. What was about to happen, his son recalled later, "became the news that didn't make the news." The two men were a little tired of the town, whilst Chas Junior's wife and his mother were happy to amble around its white painted cobbled charm.

With one hand Chas Junior held the shaky steering wheel of a clapped-out Fiat 600. His other arm rested on the ledge of an open window through which warm aired streamed. Father and son had driven on past Roquetas de Mar and as far again through Almeria. To the two Chas', Senior and Junior, the sea to one side and mountains way over to the left on a road virtually traffic-free was like breezing through a tv adventure. It wasn't exactly a convertible Corvette on route 66, but they would never get closer to it. They had no idea of how the weather could change dramatically.

After a hundred miles plus, they were ready to return when a storm started up. The lights on the car hardly worked, the day had become dark and a wind began blowing dust at them. The rain came and it wasn't like anything at home. It was impossible to see beyond the end of the short car bonnet. The father thought it was so heavy it could break the wipers or crack the screen. They were forced to pull in to the first break in the road they came across. The tapas bar was a gift - they were obliged to have an early drink. After two beers each the storm halted and the winter sun shone. They had a final beer and knew they should head back.

In the car were the father's old scratched and chipped RAF field glasses. A loud droning had him fetch them, tilt them skywards, hold them there and focus. They were ancient heavy things, but the lenses were 'quality' and this wasn't to be missed.

"That's a B52 G, I think and a KC-135 fuelling tanker."
They were with the U.S. strategic air command.

"Yes. Yes, it is,"
the younger man heard taking up the glasses.

"Despite what happened on your final flight, you're still lovin' it, aren't you."

"This is a real treat. You're going to see something truly top draw."

His father knew flying, especially the military sort. Chas Junior focussed on two sparkling craft closing on each other. Having navigated there the old man knew the two planes were above a village called Palomares.

"Ruddy hell one of them'll be loaded with nuclear bombs, the other fuel."
"Ruddy" was about as strong as his father's language got and then he would plead, "Excuse my French". That was true even when he was flying with a bomb which was part of Britain's atomic weapons program when it had had to be dropped.

Wiping hair blown by a breeze from his eyes the son saw through the lenses a pipe dangle from the fuel tanker craft, stretching for the other plane.

"Watch, son, they're going to re-fuel in mid-air. Can you believe it? It's classic."

"The other plane's got to attach itself to the end of that pipe? You're having me on? No way."

"Son, this is for real, hundred per cent."
Using the binoculars he gazed, stuck to the spot whilst the sun warmed them.

As the fuel tanker kept a steady line the B52 G flew towards it. To the younger man it looked nigh on impossible.

"Surely once they start it's going to spill fuel

everywhere."

"No, no it's a good bit of kit. There's a poppet valve on the end of the boom and toggles on the other plane that hold it in place. We're talking flying within inches."

Junior gazed on. To him it looked dicey, but his father told him,

"The pilots keep within what they call an 'envelope'. And that's at thirty thousand feet and five hundred miles an hour."

"Wow, that's travelling. Unbelievable."

While they continued to watch the last patches of water around them disappeared and the ground was drying. It was time to go but they were rooted, they weren't going to miss this.

"Think, one false step and it'd be fatal," the father said.

The two planes edged ever closer.

"Dogs sniffing each other don't get…that close."

It started off light-heartedly, but the son swivelled sharply to look at his father, the tone changing completely. He looked back to the sky. It didn't look right, the angle surely was wrong. They were too close. Any second they'd be into each other. The son thrust the binoculars into his father's hands, to hear,

"I'm not sure. This is either something very special, or …bloody hell, I don't like it…"

The tanker boom smashed into the B52. One of its wings tore off and all thirty thousand tons of fuel were set ablaze in the tanker. A huge explosion threw the two planes apart. The KC-135 tanker became an airborne furnace, cremating its entire crew. The older man couldn't watch any longer and passed the glasses to his son. Jamming the binoculars against his eye sockets he watched as the B52 G shattered into chunks of flaming metal. Initially the two men saw it, then they heard it and then they felt it. Soaring above the warmth of the day, the heat of the sky borne furnaces caught them. Three huge zeppelin shapes dropped towards the ground while a fourth headed out to sea. What was left of the crew was also parachuting down.

Those on the ground near to where the bombs crashed would need help, including the airmen who made it down.

"Wait here, son. I'll join you shortly."
Chas Junior shook his head. His father often talked calmly when there was danger, but he wasn't a boy anymore and he wouldn't let him go alone. He said he'd have none of it, only to be told,

"It's Armageddon, it's a bloody holocaust. I've seen it."
He had indeed seen it. A few months earlier he had watched the War Game and been appalled. The son didn't budge.

Suddenly keys jangling Chas Junior ran to the car. The father raced after him, ripping the keys from his hand.

"It's got to be me alone son."

"No way. It's not a film and you're no technicolour hero, dad."

"You've got a young family. They'll depend on you for years to come. The area'll be plastered with radioactive dust."

"But there's no mushroom cloud, no shockwave. Those bangs we heard couldn't be nuclear."

"Bombs weren't primed, but the detonators went off, so plutonium'll be all over the shop."
Chas Junior knew his father was talking sense, but some things overrode sense. He was going too.

"Alright but first get them to ring for help in

the bar."
As the son entered, they were already on the phone but when he got back outside his father had gone.

By the time Chas Senior got to the site most locals had fled and the uniformed men who had parachuted down warned him off. It was military business exclusively. He didn't listen to them and went to knock on the door of a crumbling stone dwelling a hundred yards away. Somehow, he convinced the mother and child there of the emergency. He was going to take them to his digs in Nerja but they wanted to be left in the bar where his son was waiting.

The son would remember forever his father's words when he came back.

"The dust'll be a killer for hundreds of years. Nobody should go near there. Those bombs are appalling."
Bundled into the car like an infant, Chas Junior was told dozens of square miles would have been poisoned for a generation. In reality little more than 500 acres of the fishing village were showered with plutonium 239. If the father overestimated the area affected, he underestimated how long it would last. It's half-life, the son later learned, was twenty four thousand years. By the time he received his pension he was vaguely aware that the fifty thousand cubic metres of contaminated earth had still not been removed.

Racing away in the car, crashing the gears Chas Junior heard his father retell his tale of being the engineer aboard a Vickers Valiant in the early nineteen fifties. He took his eyes off the road to see his father looking unwell.

"You alright, dad?"
Whether or not Chas Senior was well the tale continued, his son listening with more respect than for years. He heard again the story of his father's last

flight. A five ton single piece of atomic bomb engineering had swung loose from its moorings and had to be dropped into the sludge of the Thames where to that day it lay. He firmly believed that his father was key in preventing it falling on a populated area. On the first occasion he heard it he was asked,

"Can I tell you what the most important thing about this story is, son?"

Of course, he must, he usually did.

"It's true. Gospel."

Between the dummy bomb carcass bedding down in the Thames and the death of his father, Chas read and saw nothing of that flight. He knew the old fellow could spin a tale and began to doubt it ever happened. One way and another he would have his doubts about the conundrum of the Tokyo Three bomb when he first encountered it. Those doubts took some working through – at a cost. What he didn't doubt after Palomares was the source of the acute myeloid leukaemia that killed his father. He knew exactly where to place the blame.

Although he felt that strongly, it couldn't match his regret at having told his father he was no hero.

C2

Chas, he was no longer Junior, was little more than ten years older than his father when he himself was pronounced dead. At the scene his skull had smashed into a rock outside a country pub after he was felled by his wife's young lover. Friends and family tried to revive him and finally a doctor from inside the pub shook his head. He was gone, they were shattered to hear. It was a corpse being carried off in the ambulance. Within minutes of arriving in the hospital morgue his groaning had him transferred to intensive care.

Not much more than a day after losing consciousness Chas awoke in a hospital bed with a bruised lump on his forehead. All his mates had visited his bed side where eyes closed but ears open, he registered the wonderful things they said of him. His wife had also been there and whispered he needn't worry she would behave herself from then on. Later he appreciated this promise was made under emotional duress.

It was towards the end of September and a rare dry hot day. In spite of a headache he was 'chipper'. Discharging himself he went out into the world not so much as if it were new but as though he hadn't been there for a long while. He popped into an optician's where they were pleased to fit him with trial contact lenses awaiting a prescription. Next, he strolled into the nearest barbers to have his head shaved, getting rid of a rascal of a comb-over. That done he breezed onto a bus simply telling the driver he had forgotten his pass and plonked himself at the back. The driver would normally have had it out with him, but the brown misshape on his forehead had him decide otherwise.

Chas then called in on a local woman who ran a back street tooth whitening parlour – no appointments needed. After ninety minutes of illegally strong bleaches he emerged with white teeth and scorched gums. He was on his way to see the most important person in his life, Eamon. He hadn't gone far when he heard some angry hollering and what sounded like forlorn pleading. It was coming from the recess of an empty shop doorway diagonally across the road. Closer up he saw a man back a woman against the door and punch her. That simply wasn't on, a man can't hit a woman like that - it was basic with Chas. He shouted,

"Whoa, there's no need. Cut it out,"

and began to trot forwards. He wasn't going to stand for that any more than his father would. The woman beater, paused, looked him up and down and then turned back. The assault was going to continue. The wretched woman was groaning but not screaming as though this beating wouldn't be her first. Chas hopped across the road, narrowly missed by a car as he went. The look on the woman's scarred face wasn't of terror but resignation. He wasn't having it. At the bus stop opposite a woman was ringing - the police, Chas hoped. He was sure they would be there promptly.

There was no point in appealing to thugs, they had to be deterred. Chas started shouting,

"Police are coming, police are coming. Be here any second."

There was no response. He was sprinting forwards, shouting again,

"The police are coming, the police are coming…"

followed by a more definite lie,

"I heard the siren. Best to make your getaway."

Within a few yards he was shouting louder than ever when the big man turned to face him. He was mid-thirties, roughly six two and fourteen stone with panoramic shoulders.

"Best to make your escape, mate, while you can. The police are coming."

It was a quiet persuasive voice, meant to sound like helpful advice. The big thug swivelled back and head butted the woman. She was slight but he held her up, preventing her from crumpling. Chas had never dealt with anything like it.

He screamed,

"You can't hit a woman. You can't bloody do that. You bloody can't hit a woman."

Glancing around there was no sign of the police, no sound of a siren. The thug had switched from the woman and was now coming for him. He half swallowed the words but still managed to get them out,

"The police are coming."

"Yeh, because you called them, you little arsehole. He'd brazen it out, put the frighteners on him until the police got there.

"Too right, I'm not long retired. My old colleagues, the boys in blue, are on their way."

The brute was a twenty four carat bully. He wouldn't dare hit a former policeman.

The woman beater spotted the remnants of a head wound on Chas' head. He was about to get more of the same. Chas read the way things were going. He didn't mind the idea of a broken nose, some cuts and bruises. It was possible to get over those so he would take his chances. While it was happening, the woman might be able to get away. But it suddenly dawned on him the fashion had become to leave victims at death's door – and he had only just begun to get his life back.

From his jacket pocket the huge thug drew out a pair of scissors and these were no ordinary scissors. They were the size a seamstress would use, six centimetres longer than a household pair. And this man was no seamstress. Was Chas going to get a severed artery? Running in this situation was no good, he'd be on top of him in seconds. Death? It was a possibility. Chas became calm. He held up his fists bare-knuckle style.

"Come on then. I went to the Olympics with these. Any lie had to be a big lie to work. There was no way the woman beater could know for definite it wasn't true. Did he have the guts?

The hulk paused. Rather than running or cowering

or leaning away the little old man leant towards him fists forward. Half smirk, half snarl the thug turned his shoulders and drew back an arm on the end of which were the scissors. Those blades would go in and then out the other side of him. Adrenaline got the better of Chas.

“Fuck it, fuck that, fuck it and fuck you!”

He wasn’t going to take a hiding with absolutely nothing to show for it. He’d have a go, hope to leave a bruise at least. In for a penny in for a pounding. The giant was taking his time, savouring it. His arm remained held back. He wanted the victim to see what was ready to be unloaded on him. Chas stepped closer and threw a punch. He had gone early but managed to hit the target right on the chin. He waited, thinking he could hear something like the sound of an incoming missile. But something strange was happening. His would-be assassin swayed back and was making a whistling noise as he took in air. He teetered, looked at Chas as though seeing something he hadn’t seen there before. He swayed again and careered off. He didn’t go far and that was towards the woman to re-start his assault.

Chas called out to him. The brute’s head had cleared and back he came. He had hold of the scissors afresh, this time like a dagger. Even when a bomb was dropped his father hadn’t walked away. You did what you had to do. Chas understood well he wasn’t going to escape with a few stitches. A siren that went off in his ears in intense moments was howling. In that instant the old taxi driver saw into the future, he knew what happened next. He had had recent experience of being killed.

C3

Chas was no soothsayer. There was a siren but it was the police arriving. He and the woman beater were arrested. He was let go, the woman beater wasn't. A young reporter from the Herald, the local paper, exited a police van to get the story. She liked the upbeat Chas, humouring him and his ear catching version of the 'battle'. Big as the hulk was, he was bigger in Chas' version. The scissors, he told her, had missed by millimetres as he deftly side-stepped and the blow he struck had toppled the giant. His knuckles would need bandaging. That's not quite how Ashley reported it, but he was a local character, so she wrote her number and address on a newspaper card and gave it to him in case he was caught up in any more newsworthy antics.

Chas resumed his journey soon getting to the doorstep of his closest friend, a man who had lost his job and who had begun to show signs of losing his way. A curtain shifted and then a door flung open.

"You, you're a lunatic."

Eamon meant not the fight Chas hadn't long had but the one he had lost badly to his wife's young lover.

"Still, it had to be done. Me hat's off to ya."

Eamon took a look and then another at a shaven headed Chas wearing no glasses, teeth whitened.

"Bejasus death's been good to you."

The Anglo-Irishman stared and scrutinised. He hadn't reached the point where he could no longer trust his own senses, but that was coming. Things had begun to look different, nothing was quite so familiar anymore.

"Don't stand there, come in and plant your arse on a seat."

Chas laughed, got out his phone and, summoned up an image.

"What do you think?"

Eamon didn't know what to think, except that the phone screen was ancient and cracked.

"I think you could do with a blessed new phone."

"It's a black cab. I'm buying it from an old contact. The job's got too much for him. He's booked for a long schlep out of London which he doesn't fancy. He's tired, giving it all up."

Chas was buying the taxi with a built-in first fare.

"I'm naming the cab after my dad."

"Mother of God. A cab, to do what with?"

"Finance my new zest for life. This fare is a good earner. Sheer stroke of luck to have got it on a plate." Having been 'retired', Eamon believed they were both past it.

"You're ancient enough to be grade two listed. Sit back and look good. That's all there is."

In that minute Eamon's wife had finished a phone call from their son who rarely asked to speak to his father. Having overheard a little of their chat she called Chas into the kitchen. Her husband had been doing poorly, ever since he was forced out of teaching.

"He's become terrible maudlin. You say you've got a trip, take him with you. Say you need him."

When told they would be going to Cheltenham, Eamon was keen. He loved the races and then he found out where precisely they were going.

"Feckin' GCHQ? Spies and assassinationists. It's not for the likes of us."

"No, no, no. They check on industrial espionage and keeping us all safe."

"You're a feckin' dreamer. They've put eyes everywhere and they'll be on me and you, given half an excuse."

"It'll pay well. There's the two passengers, yanks and some old boxes."

"So, it's the CIA if not MI5 although they'll be in on it together. And boxes eh – packed with what, Semtex, bombs? Never mind what it is it'll be no good for the likes of us."

He had a talent for ranting, but he seemed to be

getting worse. Chas knew then it was right to take him. He needed to be distracted but persuading him wasn't going to be easy. Eamon did, however, agree, because he didn't think a friend should be left to face such perils alone. That decided Chas produced a bottle of Jameson's.

"Ah, you the blessed zombie, back from the dead. I shouldn't, it wrecks me head, these days. I can never remember a thing after a drink or two."

Three doubles each and they were drunk. Chas told his old friend he was going to rekindle his own life with his errant wife. She had committed to him.

"What on your near-deathbed? She'd say anything. What shade of rose are those new lenses of yours tinted?"

Chas looked hard at his friend. Raucous, riotous though he could be, often was, a little of the fun had left him. Maybe it was the booze. The pair were sat on a decaying settee and a frayed old leather armchair opposite each other. They were gently dozing off.

Coming round Chas, declared,

"I'm off to my gaff. Tomorrow it's Cheltenham. You should check the route on your phone for us."
He pretty well knew the way he was simply giving Eamon something to occupy his mind.

Once he closed the front door Eamon opened up to his wife on his fears about going to a British spy house. She simply told him not to be an "eejit", it wasn't like the old days. It was now all computers and what-nots. Guns and bombs were of the past. He had no counter arguments to offer but doubted that.

Chas picked up the veteran taxicab on his way home. No sooner had he opened his front door than he smelt it. Perfume. In recent years his wife was using it a lot. Every room, including the kitchen and the downstairs toilet exuded it. He trod quietly, not wanting to disturb whatever might be going on. He believed she could be turning a corner but wasn't sure he wanted to be there if she hadn't yet made it. Upstairs in their room the pillows and mattress were both crumpled and hollowed. It still looked like this was a bed in multiple occupation. He knew what to do. He wasn't going to live where he was second choice – on a good day.

From a set of drawers he collected a little white clay badge with its split upside down 'Y'. His father had explained semaphore to him and he knew in particular what the shapes on this CND original stood for. He had been thinking more of his dad recently. He hadn't worn the badge for ages but Ban the Bomb once more sounded good to him which it hadn't for a long while. He packed clothes in two suitcases. Prior to leaving, he rushed back up to the bedroom to collect a letter given to him by his father all those years before, just prior to flying home from Nerja. It would be occasional bedtime reading for him.

Arriving at Eamon's with his baggage he was welcomed, as though expected. They had room. Siobhan didn't approve of Chas' wife and guessed why he had come back there. She rolled her eyes when he came in, nodding in a direction where her unshaven husband was slumped in a chair. Chas knew he had a job to do.

"Have you ever wondered why we journey so feckin' hard simply to reach the edge of the abyss?"
He ignored it, instead saying,

"It's surprising how far you can get with a bright idea. I'll earn with this taxi. I want to travel. We can go together, see the world while there's time left."

"Travel the world. You mean this one or the next?" What had gotten into him?

"Time, you say time. We're ancient, decrepit…Bejasus, time's the trapdoor that opens when you're born."

"Cut it out mate or you'll convince me soon."

In truth nothing would ever convince Chas of anything at all like that. Eamon stood and left the room and Chas wondered if he had the jitters. He generally did around anything military and that's how he would see GCHQ. Eamon had gone to consult Siobhan but got no support there.

She merely told him he must go with his mate. He knew that, of course he did, wherever it was. That didn't stop him telling Chas again they were past it, it was too late for them.

"It's never too late. Tomorrow morning get on board. Read the map for me."

"You need a blessed celestial map, your hopes are that high."

After breakfast Eamon slumped into an armchair. Chas called out,

"Wakey, wakey,"

and pulled back the curtain to reveal the cab.

"I'll get an electric one for the future. What do you think?"

What Eamon thought was Chas didn't have his experience of spies and the military or of supposedly well intended people and how dark things could get. He grinned and said nothing like that because he saw the single word on the side of Chas' cab. He knew the story and how Chas felt about it. The old cabbie had picked up his vehicle fresh from the sign writers. On the black doors in white letters was, 'Palomares' and he understood why. Yet they were beginning a journey which would take Eamon and Chas far beyond Cheltenham and GCHQ and even beyond Palomares. Not unrelated to bomb fragments in the Thames riverbed and in the soil of the Costa del Sol, it would lead to Mount Fuji's slopes and a bomb with its detonator intact. They were literally to end up there with the consequences of Tokyo Three.

C4

Leaving for the intel headquarters in Cheltenham the two old friends stepped over a copy of the Herald that was left on the doorstep. Its headline read,

"OAP Sees Off Woman Beater".

The young hack, Ashley, had done justice to the tale.

Days later at eleven a.m. Ashley was in bed. Her partner, Billy, was a teacher but it was school holidays. She was waiting for Ash' to wake for a serious conversation she hoped wouldn't become a row.

Billy had looked at IVF hoping before too long to have a child, children. Ash' on the other hand thought it was too early in their relationship. She never said but she actually agreed when Billy said that a reporter's work hours didn't go well with raising a family. She was in no hurry. The mood in their flat was currently tetchy. Billy began with her partner's job. For her it was too dangerous. She feared for her future co-parent on the police raids. Ash' was brave, it was one of the things she liked about her but at times she was too brave. She sometimes went to crime scenes, which were 'live.' Unlike the police she wasn't armed or trained to handle that sort of danger.

"I know what's behind this. I want a baby too, but childcare costs are scary and if you are to go part time I have to be on more money – I am getting there."

Billy had heard it before and knew Ash' was thought highly of at work. She could wait but not forever.

When a row loomed, the pair had a tactic: they would go to their favourite pub and let alcohol sink in to soften the edges of their differences. One craft beer each and one glass of Malbec later, Ash' announced she was now the senior crime reporter for the Herald, although she had covered for her predecessor there. Ashley should have saved the news until after their lunch and another drink.

"Does that mean more going out in the back of vans on raids?"

It did but it was relative. The area they themselves lived

wasn't the safest. Nowhere was these days. She recently had to write up an event where a big lump had tried taking a pair of shears to an old boy because he tried to stop him beating up a woman. It was a few hundred yards from their flat. She was having to report on break-ins galore. There was one in which the burglars were spotted by neighbours. After they shouted they were calling the police,

"The thieves ran off leaving behind an axe and a machete – both abattoir sharp."

Ash' maintained she was safer than most.

"Safer than you. I'm in the back of a vehicle until there's an all clear and I'll have a stab proof jacket. The police truly look out for you in these situations."

Billy wasn't convinced.

The first time Billy met Ashley she had in a frame on her bedroom wall a list of 'heroes'. These were all journalists who died doing their jobs, from the Amazon to the middle east.

"Yes, but they were nearly all killed in conflicts."

"But you'll be taken to all sorts of conflicts. There'll be knives and guns there. Look at that journalist in Derry. It was accidental but that doesn't mean she's not dead."

That was the exception but a hard one to argue against.

"I've spoken to the editor. He likes me and has old contacts in Fleet Street. A year from now and I could be on a national daily. It'll be much more money."

"How does that work? The nationals are letting people go. Why would they take you on?"

"They took up my story on the pensioner bruiser. Herald editor's instinct is the old fellow is special - the sort who'll come back with more."

"Instinct! Come on."

"I've got the same feeling. Did some delving and he's got an interesting background. Unusual goings on."

Billy shook her head.

"It's an iron in the fire and hopefully it'll be too big

for the Herald. A year and we might be able to afford going in for a baby. It'll be his story or somebody else's."

"Why would he come back to you?"

"Gave him my card, home address and all. He's mine."

It sounded less than likely but Billy let it go for the moment.

C5

By the time they were ready to set off for Cheltenham Eamon wasn't really up to navigating, but it wasn't this that was bothering him. He was nervous – Chas could see it.

"What's the problem, old friend?"

If the Anglo-Irishman had any wits at all he would be keen on keeping himself busy on this trip. Eamon came out with a jumble concerning Belfast, police and agents.

"These people are feckin' intelligence. They've got bullet chambers where everybody else's got heart chambers. The only feeling they've got is the impulse to pull the trigger on you."

"Look, I know you had some experiences when you were a lad, but this is the new millennium and GCHQ's a world famous venue."

"It's national security – which means some people know some things and they don't want us to. If you don't want to be a casualty steer clear."

Although it was a life-long worry it was clear it had got worse for Eamon.

The old taxi driver gave up the argument. There was a job to be done and what's more Eamon had to be kept occupied. He moved him on.

"Did you check the route?"

Eamon hadn't. He was about to say 'they' hung you up by your thumbs or water boarded you, but Chas pre-empted it.

"As fares go this is a long one. It'll feel endless if you carry on like this pal."

Eamon knew his wife had asked Chas to take him along. Regardless of his misgivings he wanted to rein himself in, but it was beyond him. Chas would keep trying to perk him up.

"Taxi trade, a new trip - c'mon. tomorrow's looking bright,"

"What if tomorrow never appears, eh?"

"Then you've overshot it. Pick it up on your way

back."

"Y' buck eejit."

"Buck eejit yourself"

They both laughed. The pair got into the taxi and hardly stopped bandying opinions and insults and laughing throughout the journey. It drowned out the noise of the engine as it wheezed out cloudy fumes whilst they chugged along. Chas thought he had bought a bargain, but the vehicle needed pensioning off almost as much as the two men inside it.

Chas had a fair idea of the general route to most towns from the 'Old Smoke', he called it. He drove generally towards Cheltenham, whilst Eamon was supposed to be referring to the route map.

"What was all the ULEZ stuff?"

Eamon said he didn't know despite Siobhan having explained it to him. The big blue motorway boards were clear enough, so they arrived on time at the outskirts of the town. Chas glanced in his mirror and his friend wasn't looking at the map at all, he was gazing out the window. He swore quietly so it wasn't heard.

"I'll pull over, you jump out and ask where the old spy place is."

"Will I feck. Should I do that they'll come looking for, us not the other feckin' way round."

Chas looked in his rear-view mirror at his old friend and saw plummeting satchel size dewlaps, shoulders sagging towards his hips and a sharp mind blunted by the years or by recent inactivity or both. Since he left teaching, he had gone downhill. On this day he simply drew into the kerb and waited for his friend to relent. Resolve was never Eamon's strong point, so he soon got out and asked passers-by the way. All gave directions, one suggesting they follow a particular bus route. Chas rolled his eyes when told,

"They know where it is because they understand they need to avoid it. It's not meant for the likes of us, you a working man and me a Catholic."

In spite of his wariness Eamon called out the number of a bus they should follow, changed it and then changed it again. Chas wasn't thrown by this; he would follow the bus that came along that had the nearest to that combination of numbers. He was helped on the way by several road signs showing the route to GCHQ. They weren't going to the Doughnut shaped building itself in Benhall. That was a staging post, not their destination. Once there he would plot their route to what was left of its former partner facility in Oakley where his passengers should be waiting. There was time enough.

Where that facility used to be had become a housing estate. What was left of it wasn't difficult to spot with its barbed wire sidling up to a school playground and a rusted old sign on which could faintly be read,

"This is a prohibited zone within the meaning of the official secrets act."

"For Jasus' sake, will you just look at that. It's barbed wire and a warning. I'm telling you it's not meant for the likes of us."

Parking up Chas ignored his friend, leaving him in the cab as he got out. When he saw his passengers he frowned. There were three, not two. What looked like the lead was a grey suited middle aged woman shaped like an electric guitar, flat back to front, with big hips and a long neck. Her hair was swept back so tightly it dragged the wrinkles from her brow towards the crown of her head. She was accompanied by a short lad and a tall slim young man whom she obviously liked. The short lad had a ponytail and implausibly white teeth. The good looking lad had a small shoulder bag with the Australian flag embroidered on it and something inside it that moved.

Chas folded his arms and looked. Seeing his friend had stalled Eamon got out of the cab and looked in particular at the woman. He then looked at Chas as much to say can't you see military when it's right under your nose. He had noticed a bulge in her jacket where he believed she carried a gun. Senior though she was, the woman wasn't heading up this task. The pony-tailed youth signalled Eamon should fetch their luggage, but Chas was bristling, stuck out an arm and held him back. The woman understood and offered,

"Please."

To her fellow American she said,

"I'm here for the ride, this is all yours."

She may not have been wearing a uniform but Eamon was right, she exuded rank. On her lapel was a small stars and stripes badge topped with an image of the statue of liberty. The pony-tail lad checked and answered.

"Ready to go, Jess..."

The young Australian shook his head. Jessica didn't see the lad as qualified to be familiar. It wasn't nerves, the young American brimmed with unjustified confidence and felt he should be on more than first name terms with her. She generally liked young people but not this one. He had no idea, wasn't directly CIA and in her opinion was under-schooled. He had flunked at Harvey Point and yet gone straight to a cleared contractor, where the pay was better. She happened to be visiting in Cheltenham and was simply on a free ride back to London. Normally she was in charge of people who were in charge of people who allotted tasks like this.

There were five boxes to be brought in all. The pony tailed lad asked,

"Do we need the old disintegrating one? It's a left over from the second world war. It's got weird arrow heads and SOS on it."

"OSS, OSS! Your decision,"

but she relented.

"Maybe we do. Of course we do."

Neither Chas nor Eamon moved. The ponytail lad froze.

"Please,"

Jessica said it winking at the Australian.

The two old friends fetched the five boxes to the taxi boot and two large cases. Eamon sat with his back to the direction they were going, opposite the woman officer but refusing to look at her. The younger American was trying to impress her with garble about "humint", "sigint" and the like. She clearly glared, 'shut up' at him and shifted round, to engage the handsome young man. He didn't notice because he was waving out the window at a woman he appeared to know. The junior was silenced. The Australian wished Eamon, "G'day". Eamon liked Aussies. The Australian told him he had relatives in Ireland. He seemed personable. Eamon generally abhorred a social vacuum, so this was an invitation to fill it. He relaxed.

"Jasus it's a long way to come for those dusty old boxes."

The ponytail was texting on his phone and wasn't drawn in and the woman was checking through a folder of papers. Eamon concentrated on the Australian. From then on the cab was full of his sociability. Initially there were observations regarding clouds, rain, the occasional sunshine and varying temperatures. Neither American was interested. In the front Chas chuckled, knowing his mate wouldn't be subdued. His skin could be thicker than a pachyderm's. He gave virtually no space for others to begin chat, not that there was much competition. Getting some responses from the Aussie he regaled him with rebel songs, folklore and old Irish witticisms. Chas liked the one about Catholics staying in bed Sunday mornings for,

"Three hail Mary's and one how's your father, a bit of unholy communion."

The Hackney carriage man drove on to the A4, M4 and Heathrow. He didn't know if his friend was irritating the other passengers much but was entertained by the thought he might be. The Australian was dropped off. He was meeting some friends in Philomena's bar, he said, for a "few cans". The woman officer was taken to the Biltmor hotel across from the statue of F.D Roosevelt in Grosvenor Square.

"Full of potentates and ponces", was Chas'

unspoken opinion of the place. The last time he was in that area was in the seventies at a demonstration – where he met his future wife. While Chas fetched out the woman's case Eamon ducked down in his seat. He knew that spot would be festooned with cameras and had no desire to be a star of CCTV. The hotel doors were opened for Jessica, but she had changed her mind. She too wanted to go to a bar, Philomena's sounded good to her.

The ponytailed lad was to be dropped at the airport. There were no trolleys to hand, so he tried to stack the boxes on his luggage case. Chas told him to "hold on" whilst he brought some string from his boot to help tie them up. He wasn't allowed to touch the boxes himself and it was taking time. Eamon wandered off. As Chas was readying to fetch him, he returned struggling with a trolley that had a wheel impediment. Chas looked skywards. In a prophetic moment the son of a Falls Road man said,

"There's bound to be feckin' venom there. Sooner we get rid of this blessed spy stuff the better."

The old cardboard box toppled off several times, refusing to stay. There wasn't enough string. It was in a bad way, spilling papers on the terminal paving. The young American shrugged. The contents were for geriatrics, a total pain in the butt. He paid the fare, held out the old box and told them,

"Dump this pile of crap."

He believed the papers would not be missed. Neither of the old men moved but for different reasons.

"Please."

He was a poor learner, but he had learnt that much. It didn't do the trick. They didn't budge. And then he thought he understood. Reaching into his wallet he fetched out a small wadge of dollars.

"That'll do,"

Chas said taking the currency and reaching for the box. Eamon leapt between the taxi driver and the dusty cargo, but Chas pocketed the dollars and began picking up the frontispiece papers that had fallen to the floor. Shaking his head Eamon joined him gathering up the rest. As the pair stuffed them into the disintegrating box Chas read aloud,

"Hmm Tokyo Three."

"Tokyo Three? Tokyo Three. Bejasus there's more than one is there?"

A mystified Eamon snatched the papers from Chas.

"Never mind feckin' Tokyo feckin' Three, can you see what else it says? Feckin' Top Secret, feckin' Top Secret!"

Chas had seen it, but he had also seen the date on it.

"Pull your neck in. It's long past the time secrets can be kept. They're not going to send us and a kid to deal with stuff that's still serious."

He sounded like he knew what he was talking about although it was a guess. As it happened, he was technically right, thirty years was the standard release date for classified documents.

"Chas, I'll follow you to hell but before I do, I have to warn you. This is a can of snakes, not worms."

The taxi man shook his head.

"Saints preserve us. How often recently have secrets papers been left somewhere they're not supposed to be? – Three to four times on trains alone. The evil eejits, it's always happening."

Over the top was where Eamon tended on issues like this. He was usually wrong but not every time.

C6

"Bless me, we know each other, don't we?"

On names he wasn't so good, but Eamon was good on faces.

"Do we? I don't think so"

The question was to Billy, but it was Ashley replying and she had started to close the door.

"No, not you, her."

The voice and the accent were familiar to Billy. Initially, she wasn't sure and then she was. This was a retired teacher from her workplace who had left under a storm cloud.

"Ah you were at the school when I arrived there," Billy said.

"All I could do in the end was batten down the hatches. If you're sticking it out there, lass, you're special."

She loved the job. Chas stepped forward to speak to Ashley.

"But you do know me."

Ashley looked.

"Ah, it's the local hero. Also, one time candidate for Lord Mayor of London, I've learnt."

So she had been checking him out. Chas continued,

"Ah, never mind. I've been pouring over this old box of papers,"

At first it had been curiosity and then he was driven. Anything connected with atomic bombs he took seriously.

"I went to the library to get some help searching on the net. I don't have the skills – I'm low-falutin when it comes to it."

He had checked the history and tried to understand some of the technical detail and diagrams in the papers. He could see they concerned a mission to Tokyo at the time of Hiroshima and Nagasaki. The last few pages had thick black lines through them and the documents finished abruptly. He wondered if it was purely a paper exercise and never happened. The librarian helping him could find no historical references. It was as though the plane and the purported bomb it carried disappeared. It had crossed his mind that it could simply have been a dummy like the one his father spoke of. Even that was a serious business.

"You're a journalist and you wrote up my tale a treat. Is there a story here? If there is it could be a big 'un." If there was anything to it, Chas wanted it exposed.

Ashley was tired and this wasn't the sort of thing she had anticipated. She paused, woke up a little and thanked him for the box. She would look into it. Chas was delighted.

"Nuclear bombs are a bit of a thing with me. Could I come back and check how it's going? Any leg work to be done, we'll do it."

Eamon's face suggested he wasn't up for it, but Chas was sure he could bring him round.

"Best not. This'll be a job for professionals. But let me know of any developments from your end."

Billy offered the two old fellows tea, but they thought it proper they should leave the youngsters to themselves.

Closing the front door of the flat behind them Eamon had kept a sheet from the old box. On it was a photo of Mount Fuji with the words Tokyo Three along with a few more beneath it. They meant nothing to him, but the image struck him. He folded it into his back pocket.

On the way back to Eamon's Chas commented,

"You were quiet."

"That's the feckin' noise I make when I'm seething."

Eamon frequently seethed. He had tagged along, not realising what Chas was up to. He berated his friend. One of them, poor girl was a teacher and must have enough to contend with. If Tokyo Three was nonsense the young couple had far better things to do. Then again should there be anything to it, it shouldn't be allowed anywhere near the poor innocent creatures.

"I'm disappointed in you Chas, you've either left them with a waste of time or something truly God awful."

Chas wasn't abashed, Eamon often spoke out at

being disappointed with all sorts. Minutes later he would have his arms around you. He had run up against his melodramas often enough over the decades. The man wouldn't hold it as a grudge, not for long. What's more his fears could concern little more than phantoms - although not always.

Back in her flat Billy, who liked old folk, was asking,

"They were nice, weren't they. Are you really going to take on the dusty old box, then? Is it worthwhile?"

A quick glance through the box' contents had Ashley's head spinning.

"I'm really not sure. Maybe, but I doubt it's genuine news – not anything I could put to use, anyway. Effort might be better spent elsewhere."

Her new post was full-on and Ash' was being worked off her feet.

"Anyway, I've been taught you have to go out and hunt for scoops, they rarely land on your doorstep."

For different reasons they both wanted her career to take off and Tokyo Three was probably little more than a distraction. Yet Billy could tell Ash' wasn't entirely happy to let it go.

"What about you and your editor's instincts for a story then?"

It would take a lot of research and there was no rush. For Billy, however, there was a rush. No more than a year and she wanted a baby – sooner if things worked out.

"My hobby is history. I could poke around the file a bit."

"Where would you get the time?"

What's more Ash knew she was often home alone. Her new post was making that worse.

"Google'll keep me company…I might surprise you."

She was ribbing Ash' a little. Her partner smiled. Of course, delve away, if she wanted – who knew what she'd come up with? Perhaps the old boy was the gem she hoped. There was a training day at Billy's work. That would be less hectic than a normal day. Then and during her scant leisure hours she would take a scatter gun to it.

C7

"What's up with the front door? You're not ill, are you? Are you in bed, came home early to sleep? Did you lock up by accident?"
Ash' replied to Billy,

"What…no, no definitely not. I'm at work. Is anybody in the upstairs flats?"
They weren't, no lights were on.

"The yale key turned and the mortice but the bolts top and bottom seem to be on and the curtains are closed."

"Don't do anything. Stay where you are. There maybe someone in there. I'm coming."

Ash' was tall and broad, a bit of an athlete and had the confidence to go with it. Billy liked big and chunky bright girls and she trusted this one's judgment. Ash' kept the call going. She had warned, hadn't she, there were dangers in their area? There was no point in ringing the police. Chances were they would be two days, dust for fingerprints, go through other rigmarole and yet there was feint chance they would catch anyone or recover anything. Burglaries had become like that - and that was pretty definitely what this was. The second the call ended Billy nevertheless rang the police. Ash' shouldn't have to deal with this alone.

When Ashley got there, she had brought with her a small length of scaffold pole abandoned near her workplace. She would use it to poleaxe anyone who came for her. Billy giggled. She couldn't be serious.

"The alarm would have gone off, darling."
It should have, Ashley knew that, but the closed curtains and bolting the door so burglars couldn't be surprised was standard stuff. Theirs was a cheap battery system inherited with the flat. She had seen it more than once where burglars club-hammered the devices and the alarm ceased, with neighbours being relieved to know it was merely a blip. The local paper she worked for had reported on several similar crimes.

The old next door neighbours arrived home. They liked Billy as a 'thoughtful girl' and were happy to let her partner through to their garden. Billy was wishing she had never alerted Ashley. She begged her to wait for the police, but Ash' went through to the back, parting her way through a flimsy fence. The wooden frame of the sash window was broken along with the glass where it had been jemmied open. Her phone rang, Billy wanting to know,

"Is it safe? Are you ok?"

Ash' muted the phone in order to concentrate. Billy went to try and peer through the front curtains. Meanwhile Ashley scanned through the broken window. Light never got down the side of the long back addition to this Victorian flat, so it was dark and difficult to tell whether or not there was anyone in there. Her phone battery struggled. Its torch was poor.

She could hear Billy shouting through the letter box, asking if she was alright. Ash' wished she hadn't. If the burglars were in there, she wanted to be the one giving them the surprise. She pulled herself through the broken window, a trickle of blood running down her leg when she caught her thigh. The internal floor was lower than the outside area, so dropping down onto it led to her twisting her ankle.

A light flashed and there was movement. She struggled to get upright and had to use the scaffold pole to lever herself up. Car headlights entered the room and shadows moved. Various strewn belongings nearly toppled over on her as she limped defensively into a corner. Edging her way along the wall of the room made the odd cracking noise when she trod on items. She was heading for the electric light. Relieved to find it, she depressed the switch and nothing happened. The mains had been switched off. There was silence from Billy, she had stopped shouting. Ashley moved forward holding herself up by leaning on the wall. She was aiming to make it to the front door when something dashed towards her. Any moment an axe or a machete could comc down on her.

She lurched and found the mains switch. On came the lights. She breathed out as next doors' dog which had come through the broken window was propositioning her leg. Ashley realised the light she saw was stray beams reflecting off the tv in the room. It was a smart tv. If this hadn't been taken it was an unusual burglary. She breathed out again and made for the front door, but a hand snatched at her arm.

Back went Ashley's scaffold pole to smash it down onto the assailant's skull. It was on its way with force.

"It's me, it's me sweetheart,"
Billy said leaping to one side. She might not be brave enough to confront any burglars herself, but she couldn't leave her partner facing them alone. She had also come through the broken window. They went into the kitchen and the bathroom where a tearful Billy insisted on dressing the cut on Ashley's thigh.

Any vigilance drained from them in the last room checked. In the bedroom, they fell back on the divan, embraced, giggled, laughed and then roared. These burglars had to have been useless, more frightened than them. Billy recalled kids from her school had been caught in various houses where they had gone more out of curiosity and dare than criminality.

There was a crash out in the hallway.

"Wait there,"
Ash' told her girlfriend limping into the hallway, but Billy forced her way alongside her. It was the dog. It had finished off a vase that had been nudged to the edge of a cupboard earlier. It was a favourite of Billy's, but she leaned down, stroked the startled dog and picked it up. She delayed a little, while she gave it some treats she kept specially. After that she cuddled it back to the old pair of neighbours who by then were standing on her doorstep to offer help.

When Billy came back Ash' told her,

"It's weird. Everything was left upside down, but no laptop was stolen and the jewellery was untouched. Never seen a burglary like it and I've seen a lot."

"Ash' we'll clear this up later. C'mon down the pub, now. We need to chill."

While the police arrived to find no one in, the pair were arm in arm strolling along chatting. Ashley asked,

"How are you getting on with that old cardboard box?"

The papers in it were now in some kind of order. There were dates, locations and routes, diagrams, blueprints and some other technical detail although at least one page was missing and there was a lot of redaction in the two final pages. Some of it was very difficult to follow and was of no interest to Billy at all. That apart, if it didn't seem like fiction, it all seemed very serious. There were written orders, official looking military stamps on virtually every page and the phrase official secret all over it. When she wasn't talking and when Billy paused, Ashley was constantly,

"Hmm…hmm…hmming.

"So, as a layperson, what do you think?"

"I've been trying to find out whether or not there is really anything to this. There are no references to Tokyo Three anywhere online."

In the box was what appeared to be an address by the U.S. president of the time to men on a bombing raid. Ash' hmmed again.

In response Billy enthused that she was going to go back online for as long as it took. In reality not only was she tiring of it, but oncoming events would mean she felt driven to abandon it.

Ashley on the contrary didn't.

C8

Billy's research wasn't going well. She guessed she was one of the first to be looking in generations. The contents of the box were ancient, exotic. It was intended for specialists and there was a lot of it. At the beginning she was delicate, like brushing dust from a fossil bone but beyond initial discoveries this yielded little. If there was a mission which did take place neither it nor its actors appeared to be recorded anywhere. Billy asked herself if her efforts were worthwhile. Furthermore, books to be marked and report writing amongst other things were stacking up. Patience running out, she gave up on finesse and hammered away with basic requests all over the internet. Once and no more did she uncover what could have been useful but within seconds it disappeared from the screen and no amount of going over precisely the same ground would bring it back. Tiring though she was, she carried on when she could. Should she take a rest from it, let it lie, it kept coming back at her, disturbing her sleep. A frequent dream was of defusing a huge file- come-bomb that looked like a hold luggage case – with labels in Japanese script on it. It usually exploded in her face.

Ash' was trying to build her career and they were seeing less than ever of each other. Weekends, however, were spent together. During an evening meal Ash' asked,

"How's my Tokyo Three project going?"

"Yours? You can have it back anytime. There's so much general info and nothing specific. It's grinding me down."

She would stick with it but not for much longer.

"Tokyo Three,"

Ash' said trying to lighten things,

"it could be from the same school as the Seven Samurai. Now that really was a story."

Then again that was fiction.

Matters eased a little at school and the after-hours club Billy ran finished with half term. She devoted her laptop to searching for Tokyo Three but it was fruitless. She went back to more general research for more context, with the war in the Pacific, Truman's administration and the nature of Japan's defiance. The results were the exact opposite of her other searches, more information than she could handle. What this background knowledge did do was make her believe that the dropping of a third bomb was plausible. The school holiday ended, so she was forced to slack off from her research.

Come Halloween Ashley had left for work. Working she would sit in the caged area at the back of a police van with a stab proof vest, her camera, shorthand pad and pen. They were after a violent gang and whilst she was no coward, the police were adamant she stayed safe. One old sergeant, Bill, "Old Bill" she liked to think of him, in particular wanted her under his wing.

Drawing up by a house, to Ash' it was pretty much becoming routine. Two o'clock in the morning and the single thing that moved was a curtain opposite twitching. The entrance was smashed in before anybody could get down the stairs, let alone out the back door. A mother screamed and two toddlers, one in a nappy, cried. A woman police officer escorted them outside while tv style checking of each room with torches and laser sights trained took place. Two uniformed men shouted instructions, followed by others pinning the male occupants to the floor without resistance and reading them their rights. The cuffed culprits were locked in the cell at the back of a police van with Ashley now on a rear seat the other side of the bars. She started interviews there and then.

Billy was alone and despite being generally spooked by Halloween she was expecting trick or treat callers and couldn't settle to preparation for school. She casually piped up Tokyo Three on the dark web – Ash's suggestion. She was rocked once her searches were underway. Instantly she started to get warnings.

"You arc being tracked' was hardly ever off the

screen. Some warnings were from online security companies she had never heard of. Multiple images from them parked themselves on a third of her screen and try as she did, she couldn't get rid of them.

Billy's laptop had been becoming difficult to work with. Now it was nigh on impossible. Rebooting, every time she switched the machine on the screen told her her IP address was showing. The machine constantly froze, deleted apps, closed other items she was working on and opened others. She re-booted non-stop and tried a whole variety of search engines. She paid for and downloaded an anti-virus software to clear the problems but within minutes they were all back. Knowing she needed the machine to function for work the following day she was panicking.

Completely absorbed she leapt up when the bell rang. Opening the front door, she found no one was there until a pair in skeleton suits jumped out from the side. She spilt the box of treats she had on to the doorstep where they would remain for the rest of the night. Looking once more at the screen there was more to unnerve her. The pictures on her screen were of men and women working in a huge office at desks festooned with images of eagle profiles perched on two rifles. Underneath were the letters IFL. It wasn't unlike the CIA logo she had come across. There were multiple displays on screens everywhere. Some of those in the office wore uniforms, some carried firearms. On the wall at the back of the room was a banner which read, 'International Infrastructure Logistics'. The operatives there didn't seem to be aware she could see them and indeed hear them, although not distinctly.

Billy rubbed her eyes, yawned and then choked on an intake of breath. An image of her on her laptop was vividly on one of the IFL screens. Two operatives were staring straight at it whilst busy on keyboards. The image changed to one of them virtually giving her eyeball to eyeball contact. The second they became aware they switched their camera off. Moments earlier one had pointed his finger straight at her and mouthed what looked like her full name. The sound was poor but as she replayed the moment in her memory she could read his lips. He was definitely saying her name. She snapped her laptop closed so quickly it fell to the floor. It wouldn't be used anymore if she could help it. She was exhausted by it. Despite this she stayed up for Ash' to come in so she could relay this to her. While waiting she tried to stay awake by taking up her phone. She couldn't stop herself checking who IFL were. It emerged they were a private intelligence company who worked closely with the CIA.

"That's it,"

she told herself,

"I'm out of there."

Coming in too late for Billy to be awake Ash' used the convertible.

Abandoning her laptop didn't bring Billy respite. In a series of other occasions on her phone her twitter and Facebook accounts behaved weirdly. Random faces and comments would appear there. Images of her as a school child and as a teenager also appeared. Odd things also occurred with her Alexa. She began to get texts, emails and mobile calls, telling her she had won prizes and had been specially selected. All demanded verification details of this or that account. She could tell the volume of bogus stuff simply was unprecedented. One time particularly struck Billy. She was included in a call that wasn't to her and had already begun. In it there was clearly talk around information about herself. It wasn't the place and date of birth kind, it was where she had last holidayed and a recent cinema trip. She blocked all calls from the number involved.

Subsequently she blocked another number after she was rung and spoken to by name. She was told she had strayed into illegal activity and that it was believed this was unintended. The woman wanted to meet. It wasn't just the internet now but a real person hounding her. She knew better than to agree to a meeting. During this period she hardly saw her partner, Ashley being sent on a week's course. Billy was dazed by it all and at times questioned her own senses. Was this a product of nightmares and a troubled mind? Was she vastly getting things out of proportion? She persuaded her doctor to prescribe sleeping pills.

Several good nights' sleep and Billy decided her life was too full to carry on with an extracurricular activity that had become so toxic. It wasn't solely the work hours she and Ashley kept that were causing a cooling in their relationship. It was the way Tokyo Three had gorged on her time and her energy. She would get a new laptop but use it cautiously. She had obviously strayed on far too many questionable sites in her late-night wanderings on the dark web. It was dark indeed, too dark for her to find her way in. But for others she had lit paths straight to herself. That had to be it. She would shun the issue altogether. In her mind she visualised dumping the issue of Tokyo Three in an incinerator.

Despite that the box remained not simply in her dreams but by her bedside.

C9

Interlaced with events in the U.K. a conversation took place across the Atlantic. The first was within weeks of Chas and Eamon having set off to Cheltenham. It was between officers of a different generation but who were working alongside each other with only the ocean separating them. They weren't old enough to have been active in 1945 but had been around sufficient years to have a record of carrying out orders in the decades since then, no matter what. The American had hair with black roots but which went from dark to light. It should have been an Afro but it stood straight up from his scalp, looking as though a hurricane had sprayed it with lacquer. Like Don King he looked like someone's uncle and harmless. He sat wheelchair high behind a desk that had a photograph of his family – each brandishing one style of gun or another. The older man, Coetzee, was housed in one of those small offices immediately alongside the main GCHQ building. His head was oddly elongated, the result of a bad forceps delivery. Coetzee sought shelter in the U.K. having fled South Africa shortly after the murder of Chris Hani. In a profession that was a mix of expedience, mendacity and the unthinkable the two shared an affinity. For them the fight for the 'free world' had become a reflex.

"Langley to the Doughnut…"

It was a stab at humour, but the Coetzee didn't get it.

"Wanna shoot the breeze?"

"I don't know what shoot the breeze means."

It sounded more like 'shooot' when the Boer said it.

"Brass tacks, eh. Well, let's hope some shooting is avoidable. I've been given a free hand and the regular blindfold to go with it. I know little and understand less, except this is serious. We've made the request. For the moment it's in the good hands of ol' Grand Britannia. You guys need to shut it down."

"'Shut it down'? It's not been opened up. We don't even know what it is. Five Eyes are supposed to share intel.

You've shared nothing."

"You, the Aussies, the Canadians and the Kiwis aren't up to speed on it, because it's nothing to do with you."

"Yet you want us to work on it."

"It's happening on your patch…look this goes way back - to the war in the Pacific. It's old – too old for the current White House."

"Come on."

"I'm serious you've got to go way back beyond Clinton for this to be in living memories".

"So, no White House but you say you have authority?"

"It's a lift on my pension to facilitate it. All I can say is it's a big-league secret."

"Tokyo 1945…anyone involved must be retired, senile or decomposing. You need grave diggers not intelligence officers. It's too old for me - and you too."

"They've given it to me, because at my age I'll get some of it. I'm trusted and I know you can be relied on."

"It's fucking kak, almost everything from those days is declassified. Anyway, I thought you people stopped sharing nuclear secrets."

"So, you do know what it concerns then."

"Drivel about an antiquated plane and obsolete bomb that failed to kill a few thousand nips and should be in the scrapyard."

Coetzee was irritated but blocked the knowledge he was a kaffer, appreciating this American was his senior. He would never cross him.

"There's a handful of mean and I'm talking real mean citizens taking your end of this personally. To begin with it was two of your senior citizen guys…"

"Yeh one a skeef tax driver and the other an Irish retard with republican links."

There was an audible cough from the U.S side of the call, followed by,

"Now some youngsters have marched right into the

epicentre of where they're not welcome."

"I hear you. It's days since you raised it and we will be dealing with it. But we don't get it, the whole business is nothing. These people are little more than slugs and your response is enormous."

"Asymmetric, that's what it's called these days. C'mon I hear you used to be all ends justifies the means, no prisoners taken."

"Rest assured it will be dealt with - despite not knowing what it is."

"Good. Should you not shut it down, we might have to."

"Alright if it comes to it, it'll be no questions asked, it'll be done, whatever it takes."

"Great to deal with our oldest ally."

Coetzee wasn't the greatest fan of the 'special relationship' but revered rank. He nearly saluted the screen, stopping himself solely because he thought it would be disapproved of. He was chosen because of his attitudes, loyalty and a disregard for anything digitised, cyber or virtual. Across the Atlantic there were two concerns. One was to preclude discovery of information online. The other was that something direct and in the flesh might be needed. Coetzee had a record for that.

Coetzee spat into an ornate ivory cuspidor by his foot. What was involved was obscure. To get anywhere with it, he would have to tell any team the request came straight from Langley. He would transform the lack of information into an advantage, using it to stress how vitally secret this was. Nevertheless, he wasn't convinced. They were supposed to be partners and this was all a bit one-sided. He poured a double from a bottle of vodka into cold tea – his third of the day. It would happen no matter what it took. It couldn't always be flag waving and medals. That said he saw no need for a hurry. The Yanks often got hot under the collar over next to nothing. For the time being he would put juniors on it.

After a further series of events another call was made from across the Atlantic. Coetzee tutted at the interruption. His mind was on other things. He was sat in front of a screen leering over a young woman of colour, Samantha, who worked at GCHQ. At the bottom of the screen was a translation of a maxim on a plaque she had on her desk. Among the words on it were,

'Order 1: non-interference with other cultures and civilisations.'

He stared, shook his head and muttered,

"Shame, she has great tets."

The American insisted on his attention.

"The two old guys have been shaken up, grilled. And we agree with your assessment, they could have some potential to be a problem. It may well be minor, but the issue outweighs all that. It makes everything crucial."

"I'm not sure they have any idea of what they're involved in, but they are involved and that is tough luck."

"I'm afraid that's right. The taxi driver's put 'Palomares' on the side of his cab, for Christ's sake."

Coetzee would go through the motions but too much energy spent on details with the old men wasn't justified. They didn't have long to go in this life, so if it came to it, he would give nature a nudge.

"The Aussies have been put on dealing with the girls – they're a pair of foking letties you know."

The American knew they were lesbians, of course he did. Coetzee continued,

"We think there's at least one more character we have to deal with but they're elusive. That's the trouble with all this online b.s. There seem to be problems with the file."

"That could merely mean they know what they're doing. Surely you guys are up to that. We already have some people with you, more expertise can be supplied."

"No, I accept it is my patch. We're not all thick as pig shit thick here, some of our troopers are clever too. They'll get to the bottom of it. We won't give it too long."

Coetzee kept it to himself that other agencies in the U.K. were likely to poke their noses in and make matters complicated. He hadn't realised that was anticipated in Langley which was why they had chosen him. If needed he would bypass the lot of them. Obstacles, delays; he would go for the throat.

C10

It was the day prior to the second trans-Atlantic call. Eamon wistfully told himself he wasn't getting any younger. In the gathering murk and mist inside his skull he believed he was running out of time – to do anything he needed to. One instance was long overdue. He didn't tell Chas where he was going because he didn't want to involve him in something where he could get hurt. He didn't tell his wife on the specific day either because she would have told Chas.

"I've left it too long. I'm feckin' duty bound," he announced marching down the road. On the piece of paper Eamon held was an address he should know. It was in the catchment area of the school he had worked at and in which he continued to live.

He knocked softly on a door in the way people do when they hope no one answers. He knocked louder and then through the obscured glass he made out a huge figure coming to the door. The lad was big for his age. So, of course, would his dad and brothers be – and his uncles too, should they be there.

A woman answered the door looking him up and down silently, forcing him to state his business. He had come to see her and her husband concerning an incident at school with their youngest boy. It was a bad thing, he had left it too long and he had come to explain and to take what was coming to him. For the life of him Eamon couldn't recall the lad's name. He had taught thousands, the first few years all of whom he remembered pretty well. As for the rest it was all a sea of faces in which names had sunk to the ocean floor. The woman obviously didn't understand what he was there for. She said something in a brogue so strong he didn't get one bit of it in spite of being steeped in the accent and the language. She went to get a better, more anglicised speaker. He waited. Idling, he checked his piece of paper hoping that what he needed might be somewhere there. He cursed himself by name and in so doing remembered – the name he was trying to remember was the same as his.

"Eamon…it's Eamon. I've called about Eamon."

A figure approached almost filling the space between the walls of the passageway it came down, its breadth complemented by a belly sagging over a belt. The man was followed by two much younger men who were without the belly but had the same shoulders. And behind them was the lad he had come to see, who appeared to have put on six inches since they last met.

Eamon got his words out quickly, stressing his accent in the hope it would extenuate his offence. He wanted to use the lad's name, but panic meant it had gone already.

"I know, I know, I swear to God and cross me heart, I am truly sorry."

He sought out the lad's eyes and projected towards him,

"It was my fault, my fault entirely. I'm to blame. My responsibility. They should never have expelled you."

The father's bicep suddenly peaked beneath its tattoos and fat as it bent at the elbow.

"You should know, they sacked me, so I lost out too."

It wasn't quite true, but if it prevented upset and bloodshed – his own - well it was justified. The father's arm reached Eamon, grabbed his hand and shook it. This man kept a closer eye on his son's schooling than the former teacher thought.

"Bless me, he wasn't expelled, we decided he was best off at another school…The boy told me you were one of the few decent teachers in the shebang."

"Really?"

"You paid for his school trip."

It was to the Imperial War Museum and Eamon had paid for this lad amongst others.

"He was full of it. He's at college now."

Eamon looked at the lad who in an unforgiveable, moment he had wrestled to the classroom floor. The boy looked back at him, astonished a teacher would come to his family home. He nodded in a way that was the equal of offering a handshake. Eamon had assumed the boy was expelled. He was pleased they had both been shielded. He himself had been allowed to 'retire'.

Eamon was invited into the living room and obliged to sit down. There was no refusing the whiskey. After several glasses the lad, himself a little tipsy whispered in his direction,

"Tread softly because you tread on my dreams…D'you remember?"
The rest in the room didn't seem to register the Yeats that Eamon had coached the lad in when forcing him to sit by his desk in a classroom. It was meant to convey that they shared a culture. His old student was in his initial year of teacher training. Visibly the entire family brimmed with pride in him. Maybe it was the whiskey, but Eamon offered his help if he would have him. The lad thanked him and said he would think about it.

Eamon left the house in a state he didn't want to be, not that early in the day. He staggered out, going yards in the wrong direction. He should be happy, more than happy with the way matters had gone. Wandering along he tried to prevent a smile from becoming a cheek splitting grin. He had gone quite a way when he realised he wasn't heading to his own home at all. Not directly but nevertheless definitely he was working his way to Chas' house where his friend had gone to attempt a trial reconciliation with his wife – he couldn't stay at Eamon's forever.

Arriving there, a short while before Eamon were two men. Chas' wife Anne had let them in because she believed she had no choice. Of the two men one spoke English like a fifties newsreader, wore tweed and had a terrific mop of swept back locks. He was slim and six foot with the superstructure of an athlete but no longer the muscle. He would have been a good looking young man.

"Not so bad now, either,"

Anne thought eyeing him up and down. The other was American. Through his suit, she could tell that to go with broad shoulders he had good pecs and bulging biceps. They had flashed credentials.

"Good morning, madam…"

the Englishman said,

"…is Charles at home?"

"Who's that?"

It was Chas' voice coming from the living room, so they went straight in there. He got up and greeted them with a smile and an outheld hand. Both went unrequited but they did tell him,

"We're here to take statements, sir."

The "sir" was recognisably police polite. Rather than courtesy it implied menace. They wanted the OSS box he had taken charge of. He told them he hadn't a clue what they meant and was busy. From then on it began to feel like an interrogation. His response to this was to tell them they had no right to come barging into his house and that he would call the police if they weren't careful. The Englishman flashed a credential again which Chas couldn't quite read.

"Tokyo Three,"

said the American,

"You took possession of the papers."

Chas insisted he never took charge of anything. The American spoke of the cab journey from Cheltenham and the box that was left with the taxi driver.

"That was a private fare. Just wait there."

They assumed he was going to fetch the box. It was going to be easier than they thought. He reappeared with his taxi driving licence, expecting them to be satisfied it was all legit' and then leave. All the while he and Anne remained standing. He made a point of staring at the time on his watch. He had been told to dispose of the box, they said. Oh no, no he wasn't told, he was asked to. He had never wanted it to begin with. He had taken it as a favour.

The men told him and his wife to sit down.

"If you haven't got it, who did you give it to?"
Chas picked up his landline phone and feigned dialling nine-nine-nine. They told him having broken anti-terrorist laws he could be arrested. He put the phone down thinking maybe he genuinely could be in trouble. He supposed telling them he had taken the box to a young reporter would be no good for him or the youngster. He told them he had used it to start a barbecue. Anne stared at her husband. For a long time, too long a time she had been familiar with every inch of him. She knew he was lying, was scared and began to cry. He put his arm around her, assuring her he could carry this off. The box had gone up in smoke.

"So, you're saying that's what happened. That's your recall is it, sir? You want to stick to that story?"
Certainly his memory was good enough to remember that he told them.

"Are you actually saying you didn't have those papers in front of you when you were on the internet in your local library?"
They knew about that – that was a bit worrying.

"You're right, I've got a good memory."

"Why did you go there?"
It was a library. What was the problem with that?
It could have been his intention to avoid being identified.
With that they thought they had him but Chas was annoyed. Who were they to come into his home. He had the right, no one could stop him using a library. He had half a mind to tell them to do their worst or take a walk.

Anne went from weeping to sobbing. With each question both men got physically closer to Chas. Moisture in their breath brushed his face. He was rattled but took a tissue to make a show of wiping the likes of spittle from his face.

There was a noise, Eamon was outside the house trying to open the front door. He fumbled dropping the keys - he and Chas sharing keys to each others' houses. Picking them up was a struggle because he was carrying an extra large paper cup of boiling coffee. In addition to the keys he had dropped the old black and white photo he had kept of Mount Fuji but failed to notice it. He walked down the hall, heard the sound of weeping and unfamiliar voices and kicked the door open. He had been wearing the smile of someone who knew they would be welcomed. Now he glowered. Chas and Anne stared at the cup – their friend didn't drink coffee, didn't like it.

Straight away Eamon saw the situation for what it was. He had met the sort of men who were in this living room in his life – more than once. His friend and wife were seated with the two men standing over them. It was unmistakeable. They were operatives, military of one kind or another. He recognised the small bulges in their jackets. These two men were carrying guns. There was nothing else to consider, no encumbrances, no other thoughts. For him the evil rising from them was a vapour more palpable than any from his steaming coffee.

"Who the feck are you two feckin' spivs and why have you brought guns into this house?"
he demanded. One of them yet again showed his credentials.

"Give me a second more and I'll shove that up your jacksie sonny."
The other repeated what he had told Chas regarding anti-terrorism and the laws.

"Don't insult me with your feckin' 'sirs'. Terrorism laws? What's it to be electrodes on me testicles. It'll be the most action they've seen for a while,"
he said thrusting his pelvis forward. They were stunned and they hesitated.

"Experiencing a high level of calls are yous?"
The intelligence agents looked to each other for a clue as to what was going on.

"Ya pair of gobshites, special rendition is it?"
The two men looked at each other afresh. They hadn't said anything like this and they were baffled as to how this point

had arrived.

"I'll feckin' rendition you two, ya feckin' cunts." This wasn't how things were supposed to work. The men looked at each other again. It was the Irishman, his friend and his wife who were supposed to be intimidated. People were meant to be cooperative once the seriousness was established and threats implied. The reaction was out of all proportion. Was the late-comer mentally ill, a madman, a paranoid schizophrenic? A glance over at him revealed he was weighing up a heavy brass ornament with his free hand. There was no telling what he would do, or when or to whom. When they met the threat of violence with violence it could be portrayed as an unprovoked attack. That wasn't in their remit. What they had there was near zero chance of anything useful and some chance of being injured themselves.

"Who the feck sent you?"

Silence. They were supposed to be the ones asking questions.

"Ah non-disclosure agreement, is it? Ya lick-arses?"

The intel men looked around the room. These people were white haired and any violence would reflect badly on them in a review. The likelihood of these pensioners being involved in a security issue was roughly nil, if not a minus. This wasn't how it was supposed to be.

Anne whispered to her husband,

"This is frightening, he's winding them up."

Chas had seen Eamon like this quite a few times. The two operatives wouldn't have the balls for what he had in mind next.

"Winding them up? No, he's reeling them in."

The two operatives standing there had never come across anything like it. Take risks, maybe but there was no point in this.

"Go on feck off, the ugly pair of yous, or you'll get this in your face."

A snarling Eamon stepped towards them, bending his elbow back, tilting the cup and ignoring the blistering of his index finger when drops fell over it. He was going to scald the villains with it.

C11

The two agents who entered Chas' house prided themselves on an ability to make quick decisions and act upon them. They judged the insane old Irishman was set to injure at least one of them. He was unhinged, didn't remotely respect let alone fear them. He had edged forward, with a crazy look on his face. It wasn't possible to calculate risk with madmen, they weren't like normal people, too many variables. This one was out of control. Who knew what he would follow this up with. Was he about to throw boiling coffee in their faces or swing an ornament against their skulls? Maybe bite them? This wasn't covered in their briefing or the training they had had. They weren't authorised to disable a mentally ill old man, especially with two senior citizens as witnesses. Had he been younger, they would have feared he was on amphetamines or hallucinogens, but he didn't need anything like that, he was clearly off the wall already. In unison they stepped backwards and edged their way around the room towards the exit. One went left, the other right which stalled Eamon and gave them time. When he exited the room one operative shouted,

"If you're lying, there'll be consequences."

Eamon made to give chase with the cup of coffee in his hand although he wasn't serious. On the doorstep the other agent bent and snatched up the photo Eamon had dropped. In the debriefing it would be rated significant. There it would be decided that whatever his mental state Eamon should be of at least as much interest as Chas.

When they left Eamon slammed the cup down on the nearest surface, shouted "Jasus" and stuck his burnt finger in his mouth to cool it. Chas beamed saying,

"So you do in reality feel pain, then. Do you feel fear, you beautiful mad man?"

"Bless me, yes, but in me youth I came across bastards like that more than once. You can't pay it any attention when your confronting 'em."

"They're the sort that did for that doctor, Dr David somebody or the other,"
Chas' wife said. Surprising himself, Eamon supplied the surname,

"Kelly."
Chas doubted the answer, his friend generally thought anyone of historical significance was Irish. Eamon blethered on about it. Chas didn't believe that sort of thing truly happened, so he told him

"Come on you won't find a shred of evidence for that."
But his friend was adamant.

"Exactly, feckin' exactly. What more proof do you want? Clear as day."
Ah well, Chas told himself, it was like visions of the sightless, voices heard by the deaf. For him this wasn't open to reason, so he didn't attempt it.

Anne kissed her husband's old friend for his bravery, but not so fervently as Chas hugged him. He loved the bones of the man. Chas took the unsipped cup of coffee and swigged a mouthful that burnt his throat. It felt right.

"We've got something better for you,"
he said, fetching a bottle of Jamesons.

"Ah I've had enough. It's not for me anymore – it plays with me head. Tea'll do."

"We're celebrating our hero, a brave man,"
said Anne.

"You need to know what you're doing to be called a brave man."
So saying Eamon crumpled down into an armchair and ceased to be substantial. It was like a magician had swished away a cloth resting on a bulky object to reveal it was no longer there. Husband and wife attempted to keep the conversation going. Eamon recognised it and tried to join in, his voice sometimes trailing away, sometimes fading out altogether.

After a brief eternity of this Chas offered to walk

home with his friend. Eamon rose, forgot to acknowledge Anne and walked out of the front door, followed by Chas who said,

"They were a pair of mavericks, weren't they?"

"Mavericks? No. They were standard stuff."

"Anne reckons your performance there was like the man you used to be."

It was meant as a compliment but didn't quite sound like it.

"I don't feckin' recall being the man I used to be. Y'know, I can't tell if I ever was."

C12

Billy brought home a hefty computer from school to write reports, her own having become virtually a source of torment. It worked fine at the beginning but after a few emails it started going rogue.

Several times on her journeys home from school she thought she was being followed. If she was, they were dipping out of sight whenever she looked round. On each occasion, as far as she could tell, the person was the same height and gait, although differently dressed on different days. When she crossed the road and crossed back again the person following did the same. When she slowed or speeded up, they did the same. When she took different routes, went in a full circle or walked up a road only to reverse, so did the character tailing her. Should it be a stalker, he was simply more able and less obvious than she imagined the regular sort could be.

Crime continued rising in the area and Ashley was having more rides in the back of police vans bouncing all over the place as speed bumps were ignored. She and Billy were seeing still less of each other. Being shadowed was getting worse, as far as Billy could tell. This was confirmed one evening when she left work at six fifteen. It was unusually cold and cloud made it especially dark. The figure following her was closer than normal and at one point the wind sent his visible breath dipping over her shoulder. It was one step from being touched. She shone her phone torch behind herself, hoping it made whoever was there wary. She raised Ash' on her mobile. Loudly she called out about the shadow behind her, giving exact details of where she was. Whoever was behind Billy wouldn't have been able to tell that it went straight to voice mail. She rattled off a short text, even though texts between them had often failed to arrive in recent times. The footsteps behind Billy were regular heavy stamps.

This time Ashley did get the text. She was in a marked police car, following a van transferring prisoners from a station cell to a prison. The jogging up and down didn't help but there was little story in this evening job, so she could focus. The reply said Billy should dip into her nearest coffee bar and wait there.

In the course of Ash' arriving Billy spotted her stalker was across the street, eyes hidden deep behind a hood gazing unfalteringly towards her. Ashley shot outside. Billy shouted out across to her to stop. She wanted to be walked home not become the cause of blows. She rushed out to join her. Ashley poked the hooded man hard on the shoulder and demanded,

"What do you think you're doing? This is criminal." At first there was no reaction. Then the figure slowly rotated, almost creaking when it did. Eyes retreating further inside the hood stared. Tufts of white hair poked out from the side of a skull lacking much flesh. The figure steadied itself on a road sign and gazed. A feebleness bordering on frailty became obvious. He was hard of hearing and hadn't fully caught what she asked. His daughter was late he explained and he was waiting to be picked up by her.

In a restaurant the teacher and the journalist were embarrassed by the event. Clearly Billy had got it wrong. Ashley thought she might be getting things out of proportion. Saying that would wasn't likely to calm her down, far from it.

"Maybe you should carry pepper spray."
She said it reaching out for the hand that would wield the weapon she would shortly obtain for her. Her hope was the thought of it would quell any fears.

During the meal and glasses of wine they talked of the cyber problems Billy encountered over Tokyo Three.

"They were right to call it a web, I reckon."

Events of the evening didn't mean she wasn't being followed. Billy still believed she was. Ashley didn't challenge this, but having reacted wrongly once she wasn't convinced. Besides they had gone over it enough, too much, in recent months and she wanted a lighter mood. She believed the offer of the spray would do the trick, but it had had the opposite effect, Billy going over the burglary, suspicious internet problems and being followed. The rest of the meal was awkward.

Billy urged Ash' to use her police connections to delve a little. She opened another bottle and poured a third glass for each of them. This was one of those occasions, however, when alcohol deepened a mood and made talking an effort. It wasn't how they envisaged it and the evening ended early. The walk home wasn't what they hoped for either. Billy kept glancing behind and jumped when a figure emerged from a side street. Ash' stifled a 'tutt'. She was tired of it, yet not too tired to be alert to the shadows by their doorstep when they arrived there. Whoever it was had been waiting. She and Billy prepared for fight or flight.

"Ah, great, you're in."

It was the local hero and his side kick. Chas had Eamon for company. Billy invited them in for cup of tea. Eamon had had to be coaxed, he didn't want to be there, thought it was all wrong. He glanced a 'sorry' to Ashley.

"We have a bit of a story for you" Ashley's pen and notebook were at the ready. Might the old bruiser have something. The four of them sat around the kitchen table. Before long a half bottle of whisky was out, Ashley was pouring and Eamon didn't abstain.

Chas gave them a blow by blow account of the encounter with the two intelligence operatives and then some. At the end of it Eamon rushed to tell the young couple that not a word had been said regarding passing the box over to them. To him it was important.

"You were kept in the blessed clear, left out entirely."

Ashley was struck, telling them,

"They may already know – at least about Billy."

"I knew it, I feckin' knew it. These people are devils. Keep clear, don't touch it."

Ashley would never let this go. Chas' local story was a real story and this could well be another and much bigger. Fleet Street was beckoning. Details written down, commitments to meet again made, Chas and Eamon left and the doubts in Billy and Ash's relationship abated. Ash' spoke of an impending step up and the possibility of a baby.

The young couple made a decision which suited them both: Billy would drop Tokyo Three definitively and Ash' would take it on as a matter of work – professionally. The young teacher would be distanced from it. For her it would subside. That didn't stop Eamon's warning to keep clear from resonating, but she knew Ash' couldn't be deterred. The young hack would use her skills to dig out a nugget and hopefully get paid for it while escaping the problems Billy and Chas and Eamon came up against. Journalists, after all, had protection under the law.

C13

"I feel bad, we shouldn't have feckin' done that. Left them in it like that."

"We're not leaving anyone in it, Eamon. I'll be back down the library tomorrow and I'll be the target."
He didn't actually believe targets of that sort were involved but hoped this would placate his friend. Ashley had humoured the old fellow saying he could Google to his heart's content in the library. She would crack on, using the resources of the paper and her own knowhow.

While Ashley toiled, Billy was called to her Head Teacher's office. It was unusual because it was in the middle of a lesson. She worried if it concerned her giving a difficult student time on a laptop notebook. It was to motivate him, but some complained she was too lenient and rewarded bad behaviour.

That wasn't the issue. The Head introduced her to a someone who was clearly to be taken seriously. The man had a coiffured hair and was dressed in a grey suit which could have been from Saville Row. With a respect for the Head Teacher bordering on awe Billy presented the records of her work she had been instructed to bring. Within a short while she could tell that on the screen of the guest's laptop was an account of her work and details not from her entire career alone but beginning with when she was at secondary school. She had no idea information on her going back that far was accessible.

Billy surmised the stranger was an Ofsted inspector. In an east coast American accent, the person, who neither introduced himself nor so much as 'helloed', asked questions regarding her teaching. Billy loved her work. The records she passed over were more comprehensive than most in the school. She gave prompt complete responses to the American. As the session developed, she realised her questioner knew nothing about teaching. He wasn't an inspector.

"May I ask who you might be?"

It was polite and formal to show anticipation of a professional relationship. There was no response. She looked to the Head and got no support there. She was at a loss and did what she would have done when she was a child - gazed out of the window. Concentrating hard might mean she wouldn't need to dab at her eyes with a tissue as she was more closely questioned. They were scrutinising the data on the screen and she was left to stew in the silence.

The breaktime buzzer went and they were all still there. Billy looked for a sign from the pair of them.

"May I…"

she asked rising to go. The signal was she must sit back down. What had become two interrogators discussed her as though she wasn't there. They considered clubs she was a member of in her sixth form and societies with peculiar names she joined when she went to college. Asked about them she faltered with embarrassment, ending with a giggle. It didn't go down well.

The midday break buzzer went. Billy ventured that it was dinner time to no response. Her head teacher and the American conferred with each other, notes being typed on the latter's laptop. The questions were resumed, becoming ever more biographical, slowly turning to Billy's current life, home and partner. She had been rattled but became indignant: whatever it was, Ash' had no part in this. She was set to protest but a look from her head teacher meant she should contain herself. That didn't last long.

"This isn't professional, it's not educational. Please may I go back to my class?"

They weren't speaking to her as such, it must be over. She rose expecting a 'Yes'

"Stay exactly where you are,"

snapped the American which was followed by the Head saying,

"Wilhelmina you are not free to leave. Questions have to be faced…it wouldn't look good for your career were you to be let go."

Billy slumped in the chair. Now she needed her pack of tissues. Children and teaching were huge things in her life. Working in a school was always her goal. Everyone who had come across her knew it. The Head's tone was a shock. The young teacher thought of her as a good people manager, far from being a martinet.

Billy was pressed on her use of the dark web. To begin with she simply stared back at them stunned. How could they possibly know that? It had been no more than a few times, having found her way there chasing material on Tokyo Three. She had promised herself she would never be drawn into that subject again. Unable to think of a sensible response, she blurted out the obvious answer.

"It was for porn."

Billy went red-faced but the American dismissed the comment saying she didn't need the dark web for that. He added,

"We know your partner has also been there to buy pepper spray."

Another hour and the interview finished. The American closed his laptop and was ready to go. He cautioned Billy,

"Tokyo Three is a matter of national security."

It was the first time he had mentioned it and Billy finally began to understand where all this was coming from.

Billy was instructed to avoid any dark web activity. She would have to be scrupulous in her phone use. The American stood. Billy looked away, refusing to acknowledge him. The Head warned,

"Wilhelmina, it's been made clear to me and the chair of governors we are all under scrutiny."

"But…but…

"Understand it or not – and I don't – official secrets are involved. Put it behind you. Concentrate on teaching our students and…"

It was rare for the Head to struggle to finish a sentence but unable to think of anything civilised she stopped there.

Billy gazed unblinking at polystyrene tiles on the ceiling.

"Wilhelmina, Wilhelmina…"

the Head called her attention so the American could conclude,

"You talk to no one about it. You lay off web activity, media activity outside the regular."

Saying that he strode out.

The young teacher's fists went from resting on her quads to pressing down so hard they bruised. She felt preyed on as well as alarmed. There was so much, official secrets, threats to her job and threats to Ashley. She thought cyber mayhem and stalkers had been more than enough but now the threat was bigger, huge. Underpinning it all was the Tokyo Three business. More than ever she determined to go nowhere near it from then on. She would implore Ashley not to.

Billy was a dedicated professional and the Head Teacher appreciated that. She told her,

"Don't worry, we can get beyond this Wilhelmina."

Billy wasn't impressed by the use of the word "we".

The Head put an arm round her, which made her shiver.

"There's nothing I can do with this. That disgusting man is some sort of spook. He spoke of terrorism. It's beyond us. We need to be wary, maybe frightened. It's not you alone under threat, Wilhelmina."

She added that there was half an hour left in the day, but she should go home and unwind. Billy accepted the offer, mumbling a thanks she didn't mean. Her whole future had been threatened.

Walking home in a downpour Billy shivered once more and thought she might be coming down with an illness. Tokyo Three was bad for your health.

C14

Billy told Ashley of the incident. Ash' was sympathetic but rather than deterred she was spurred on. It was a sign there was something real there. Something was going to come out of this. On Herald headed paper she fired freedom of information requests to the Secretary of State for Defence, the Permanent Under Secretary and the military Chief of Staff. That was for starters. She followed this with emails to the Washington Post, the Chicago Tribune and the New York Times. That was followed with a flurry of enquiries to bodies known for investigative journalism at home and in the States. Next came communications to the Japanese embassy and the Japanese foreign minister, the minister who had the brief for Hiroshima remembrance.

Before long she was beckoned into her editor's office. It was all leather furniture and oak bookshelves. There should have been gaslight. The sole concession to the twenty first century was an overweight computer on the desk.

"What have you been up to, young lady?"

The questioner was ruddy cheeked and had a nose streaked with deltas of dark purple veins. Arthritic bunions led to him wearing slippers at work. Ashley liked him a lot. He wrote well, had been a top hack and was usually prepared to take a risk for a story. Most winning of all, he rated her highly.

"They've threatened to D notice our esteemed old rag."

The paper had been implicated. Ashley wasn't sure of her ground here, so she told a part truth.

"Nothing, same old same old for the most part."

The old editor smiled knowingly.

"There has to be more to it than that to get those despots interested. They're trying to scare us off. Sit down,"

he coaxed. His striped waistcoat settled in folds as he seated himself.

"Cogitate for one minute. What you've done, no matter what it is, can be traced to here."
Ashley replied cautiously,

"I'm not sure, you'll have to explain it a bit more to me, C.B,"
which was what he was called by all the staff.

"I know I should know this but what have you written up lately?"

"There was the raid on a cannabis farm in a flat, lots of other raids, some hooliganism in a shopping mall and before that a pensioner riding to the rescue of a woman being beaten."

"Think on. It has to be something. Have you dealt with anybody who's done something left field as you young chislers have it?"
Left field? Ashley hesitated. C.B. didn't want to put her on the spot but these things could get serious,

"You're partner, do you share your laptop?"

"Sometimes. Is that a problem?"

"Depends what she used it for."

"She works in a school and that's her life."
She felt awkward, hacks protected their sources but she had great faith in C.B.

"Hmm, we're missing something. Revert to me the instant you're ready to talk."
Ashley was set to return to her desk, but instead said,

"I am ready to talk C.B. It's a source you suggested would come in handy."
Ashley filled him in on the recent visit by Chas. It sounded more slip-up than secret service.

Then the editor thought anew.

"Hmm, hold on. I'm not suggesting you drop your story, but this could be dangerous. I travailed once alongside Chapman Pincher, heaven forbid. These are merciless people. You don't mess with 'em. There has to be more. Sit down, let's get to the bottom of this."
Talented though Ashley was, she was inexperienced. C.B.

gauged she needed help.

"Tokyo Three sounds unlikely, doesn't it? Fetch your laptop – I'm not interrogating you I'm trying to preclude trouble. We're all vulnerable, you know."

Ashley's original computer had become largely inoperable, so she was told to fetch the one she was currently working on. The old editor looked at both, hmmed again repeatedly and knew he was looking at logos for the OSS and the CIA. He raised his bifocals.

"That's suspicious."

Ashley looked over at him.

"Nothing about MI5. Our lot will be there but they're far sneakier."

"You think this is a real story?"

"No doubt. I think you've poked a nuclear hornet's nest young lady,"

he laughed.

"One laptop is ruined and the other one is on its way – and they're threatening to shut us down. Well done, congrats."

He meant it. The editor's experience was the hotter the reaction, the more of a story there was.

"There's definitely something here but you haven't got to the nub of it yet. They don't like you looking at nuclear facts and figures, of course they don't. They don't like you looking at their bombers either, not even obsolete ones."

"But that's all there is in that dusty heap of papers."

"No, no. You've got something there to get the intelligence services frothing. Give those two laptops to tech and get them cleaned up and dig."

The editor would talk to the chairman and the firm's solicitors. There were no grounds for D notices, not a single article – not so much as a draft - yet. The issue the young reporter was looking at was more than double the years needed for information to be released. There were exceptions, but they were serious matters indeed.

The editor did something unusual for him; he insisted that although working on her own, she must constantly consult with him. Whatever emerged would be far too big for the Herald, but the owners wouldn't tolerate her selling it elsewhere. It would all have to be confidential and she should use a pseudonym when it was first published. Ashley listened carefully to a man who knew the business. If he thought there was a story there, there was.

C.B. enabled the use of professional researchers he knew who he had paid for from the newspaper's accounts. The old editor advised Ashley she wouldn't get much worth having from freedom of information requests, but to send them anyway and in the name of the Herald just to worry them.

"Officials, reveal very little, that's their primary responsibility. Look for the people too unimportant to be sworn to secrecy and look for spots the big boys don't think matter."

Ashley guessed she already had two of them in Chas and Eamon. C.B. also joined Ashley in using the resources of several institutions, all military, mostly museums. One ancient curator emailed him he had had papers on an abortive Tokyo bomb drop. He had read and re-read them and was convinced they were true. Within days C.B. was there to get copies but they had been removed, never to be seen of again. The old curator's recall was poor, except for one thing. He was certain the date involved was 1945 August Eighth. Using that date in several chosen venues C.B. found when he arrived he was being refused access. This response confirmed the gravity of the story that must be there. Sooner or later more would be revealed and of course he would be threatened. He accepted that, it was all part of the job when it was done well. He hoped he took the flak and not his young reporter.

Ashley set to searching archives for the old newspaper coverage of the time, a lot of it on microfiche. There was nothing in the national press either side of the

Atlantic. It all seemed forlorn. Flagging she came across a Daily Express scoop on Hiroshima, entitled, “The Atomic Plague…a warning to the world”. She read and re-read it and came back to her research with more energy.

After what seemed endless humdrum days, turning into dull grey weeks she uncovered evidence of sorts. In a transcript from a U.S. armed forces radio service there was a reference to men in the U.S Twentieth Air force who failed to come back from a raid on Japan. It was for the precise date she was working on. Days later she came across a piece in the Stars and Stripes magazine. Next to a picture of a young Marilyn Monroe, it lamented the loss of a brother along with an entire crew which was based on an island in the western Pacific. This was weeks prior to the Japanese surrender. Written in the form of a poem with tears and flowery anguish it had escaped the censors. The island could well have been Tinian.

Buoyed, Ashley had to switch from this success to doing what she was paid for. There was no opportunity to go home. She was on another raid that would go on long after Billy had gone to bed, so she texted her a simple “Goodnight. x.” The raid was a pretty routine affair with her in the van and two houses in the same street to be hit. There were additional forces involved and police whose faces she didn’t recognise. She looked for Old Bill who usually looked out for her, but he had been sent on leave. She wasn’t on this occasion issued a stab vest. Having given undertakings to Billy she requested one. Evidently there weren’t any - spare at least - because nobody returned with one. It wasn’t a worry to her personally since she merely got up close when the action was over.

Doors were simultaneously smashed in. There was almighty noise and unusually there was a shot fired. Once gang members were subdued, she was allowed to get out to perch her camera on the van bonnet. She crouched, the camera dangling from her arm whilst she strived to get as much detail down in shorthand as she could. Mostly dazed villains were brought out, cuffed and hemmed in by officers. They stood in two groups opposite the car while she continued crouching behind it. One huge man, arms behind his back felled a policeman with a headbutt on the bridge of the nose. Blood flew everywhere as he charged at another. One taser didn't work and a second merely caused a pause. Multiple truncheons and two more tasers brought him down.

Ashley snapped dozens and dozens of pictures at different angles, different exposures and with different lenses. Other lights were flashing from all directions. Figures were alternately lit, then in shadow. Once cuffed bodies were splayed out flat on the ground, she stood to take more snaps. Her notepad in one hand and camera in the other she stepped further out and further forward. Additional officers wearing balaclavas arrived. The big man who had been tasered managed to get to his feet and leap forwards in her direction, yards from her. She faced him and adjusted her position one way and then the other to select the best angles.

While the man was again pinned down her phone buzzed with a text from Billy, her sleep disturbed by a dream. It asked Ashley if she was getting the story and photos she wanted and what time she thought she would be home. The young journalist had a moment to gaze at the text and smile. It was good to have someone who cared for you even if they worried too much about the job she did. However, Ashley wouldn't be writing up the most sensational story she had ever been a part of. Her photographs would accompany a different headline to the one she intended. Her shorthand book would indeed be evidence in a court case, although it was unreadable. She wouldn't be coming home to Billy. She dropped to her knees when a bullet smashed through the back of her skull. Exiting the other side it took half her face with it, fragments of bone and flesh falling on blood drenched shorthand notes which became illegible. A nine millimetre shell case lay a short distance away.

C15

In Benhall, three miles plus from where Chas and Eamon had recovered the Tokyo Three Box a tall, broad young Australian was joshing a woman of like proportions. It was a relatively warm winter's day, shortly after Ashley was killed.

"Beam me up mate…Are you shitting me? You're a regular bloke,"
which, of course, Samantha wasn't. The Australian was handing back a device with a games app on it the young GCHQ worker had created.

"Don't tell the bosses. They'll go gonzo and ask where you get the time."
Sam got the time because she didn't mix much.

"Sharing a secret like this, now that's what I call Five Eyes."
Ned was a fan of the way the five English speaking nations worked together on intelligence. He had been partnered with American intelligence for a year and by this point he was involved in an exchange of operatives with the U.K meant to strengthen ties. He was shared between different British intelligence agencies with two days a week in Cheltenham and three in Millbank. He was ridiculously good looking, apparently not aware of it, had a self-deprecating charm and, it was said, had bedded or been rebuffed by pretty well all the women at GCHQ. It was more myth than legend. With his long variegated blond hair, dark blue eyes and flip flops he looked like a posterboard surfer. Originally, he hoped to bed Sam. He was unique in this.

Making their way Sam loped along little awkwardly, much like she always did. She couldn't have been more out of fashion – without being in fashion. She wore generous straight trousers, a baggy white cotton blouse and used a minimum of makeup. Her hair was dense and uneven in helix shaped curls. She didn't carry a handbag, merely a laptop in a large zebra stripped ruck sack. Usually with earphones on it was difficult to engage her in chat – which was the intention. The nearest she got to being sociable was in her membership of dozens of web game sites. After initial forays Ned understood she wasn't a fan of boys or men. She didn't like him at first, but once he accepted he couldn't bed her they became mates, especially when she volunteered to dog-sit his little mutt. After that he said they were "besties" but since he also called his dog that, she wasn't impressed. He knew any number of filthy jokes that made Sam laugh a lot which was a plus for both of them. Additionally, they were both Trekkies. He had a collection of Enterprise models back home and she had learnt Klingon. In one quarter of GCHQ there were doubts about her allegiances. This is not to say that amongst most colleagues her abilities were not rated. It was accepted also that she was a hesitant slightly troubled personality. Her sole friend, Ned, on the other hand had a mind untroubled by doubt, or nuance. Some of her colleagues were surprised by the relationship, believing it showed she was capable of treading the beaten path more than they had thought.

Sam and Ned had met at lunchtime on the huge GCHQ internal walkway, 'The Street', but left for one of their regular strolls. Ned was full of every acronym in the intel lexicon. That had grated initially, but he had a certain scholarship in it and knew a lot and was relaxed when it came to sharing it with Sam. His loud love of country also grated at first, but his sheer uncomplicatedness and being so laid back made him easy company.

The Australian was a big meat eater, but he was taking her to a vegetarian restaurant that would suit her taste.

"They allow me in with Dishlicker."

He meant the tiny dog he carried in a shoulder bag he wore. She stroked its little head and touched something metallic and heavy by its side. She thought she recognised the shape.

"That's never stopped you. How or why they let Dishlicker into the Doughnut, I'll never know."

"You can't abandon your bestie."

He used to smuggle it in by tucking it down in the bag. It

helped that he was friendly with the door security woman who simply used to wink at him. Sam thought she was also one of his 'besties.'

"Why did you choose a place so far away?"

"This resto's too far out for our colleagues.

"So we won't be listened to or observed?"

"Fat chance, I know. Wherever you are security's as tight as a nun's proverbial. Zero is undetected these days. Have a phone they've got you, a smart bog roll dispenser'll do it."

"Hopefully we can unwind."

If Ned unwound anymore, he would flop to the floor. He decided on going the distance they did because he had something to reveal to her.

On their walk Ned would have preferred to go past the telephone box where the old Banksy 'spy booth' mural had been. For him it was a place of pilgrimage. It had been his favourite piece of art, in fact the only piece that interested him. Unfortunately, the spot was heavily trafficked and he knew Sam didn't get on well with the fumes, so he led in a different direction.

As they strolled side by side, a senior operative came by. She smiled at him and reached into his rucksack to stroke the mutt and 'aaaahed'. Continuing the walk Sam asked,

"You haven't?"

He screwed up his face and ignored the question. Of course he had.

"Do you do it to make friends, to influence people."

"Oh no, I 've had to do other stuff to get influence…but I like to make friends"

Ned high-fived the proprietor of the 'resto' – he seemed to know people everywhere - and got mates' rates. They squeezed into a faux leather booth which he reckoned was a pale shade of Viagra blue. Sam slipped, plonking herself down heavily. She usually kept her games consul out but paid her companion the compliment of putting it back in her rucksack. Ned was opposite and placed Dishlicker beside him on the bench. When his shoulder bag squeezed against the seat back, a shape other than a dog's stood out. Sam did a double take looking at him and the bag, back at him and then the bag once more. The outline she saw there was clear. It was a gun barrel.

"Tell me that isn't what I think it is,"
she said quietly looking all around. Ned shook his head. He'd had these discussions before and they went nowhere. It was part of the job they had chosen to do.

"You're no wombat but how did you ever get a job in intel?"
She was head hunted whilst in college. He moved on quickly. Across a rough wooden table, he held out his phone with a picture of a young women on it. It was meant, he said, as an early Christmas present.

"It's a black bag oppo. I've got mates in the field on this one. I'll be there soon, myself. Langley wants us on it."
Sam rolled her eyes and then let them steadily focus. Her Aussie friend swiped the screen again and again, displaying shot after shot of a young woman wearing different outfits, clearly going over days and weeks in her life. There were videos too. He stopped at one picture spreading the image with his fingers on the screen. Sam grabbed the phone, pressing the end button.

"Other people in here can see."
Ned laughed,

"This sort of thing's all part of the case. Plenty more where that came from, mate."

"And this is what you're working on?"

"No, not yet. And I didn't take the pics, not my style. It's all there; where she shops, eats, drink, everything, work, leisure. What's more she's not into blokes"

"This is plain wrong."

"Hold on, you meta-data grabbers are working on this too. You make all this possible."

"It's seedy, smutty, worse. Lingering over her like

that."

"Not all of us. Not me, she's not my sort. All some of us are trying to do is our job mate, no more. We love our country too."

Ned explained he had been told that the woman under surveillance was involved in something that could turn out to be weighty. She probably wasn't aware of the extent of it, but he confessed neither was he. She was a young teacher in an inner-city borough. Serious, people were worried about what she might be up to. She had to be investigated and the whole affair closed down. Sam stared at one picture in particular of the young teacher. She looked like a teacher. Teachers had been good to her, she admired them and the profession.

"Don't you think people like her have got enough to contend with, without the details of their life being pawed at?"

"You're in the wrong job if that's how you think…" He more or less knew that was how she thought.

"I hear she's a bit academic and a bit lonely. Her love life ended recently."

Saying this Ned swivelled to stare Sam knowingly in the face. He knew someone else who was lonely.

Gone from the screen, they might be, but the images would stay with Sam. One video in particular was re-run many times in her head. It was of the young woman with her head cast down and to the side, wearing a cloak with a hood. For Sam she could have been a Renaissance pieta. She wasn't simply beautiful she was radiant. Yet she was being explored, examined and then she was being passed around by people she and Ned worked with.

"I don't like, I don't like it. Truly I can't stand it. Aren't we supposed to be a force for good? How is this in the national interest?"

"Come on mate, there are baddos out there. That they look innocent is why our job is needed. We identify the problems and fix them."

"But when mistakes are made, do you go along with it? Please don't tell me how you fix them."

Ned passed the menu to Sam and changed the subject.

"Mate, didn't you get a Phd in cryptology two years early? You must have intellectual stretch marks. You should know Veganese, decode this for me."

"Do you never have doubts?"

Ned shook his head but qualified it with,

"Sometimes I think we should build a massive henhouse for chickens to come home to roost."

The fact was thinking like that got you nowhere. Sam squinted through thick lenses at all six foot two of him.

"It's not what I signed up for – and don't say it's there in the small print."

"I won't, it was in the large print…Look all I know is she is a chalky, but deliberately or not she's involved herself in something dangerous."

"What is it about her?...I'd like to know…about her."

With the last two words her voice trailed away. Ned craned his neck around again to look at Sam. To her it felt like she had made a confession and it did to him as well. He liked her, she was different, she had scruples. He could tell she was interested.

"You worry too much. She's not going to be an angel, none of them are. Anyway, our mates across the pond are interested, so that's that."

"Why, what for? Concerning what?"

"Listen, mine's not to question – advance Australia fair and all that but I heard it's something that goes way back."

"The CIA should take a long surveillance off a short pier…Perverts."

"We're besties, if you feel that strongly…I'm sorry. There's nothing I can do to stop it."

Ned could read the mixture of emotions. The chalkie did

look vulnerable and for some that would be compounded by her beauty.

Whilst the Australian went to the toilet Sam picked up his phone and depressed a few of its buttons. She fumbled to put it back down when he returned, looking to the floor and feigning a cough whilst looking for her inhaler. He pretended not to notice. She looked at Ned's feet in flip flops and thick socks and sighed. He was as straight forward as you could get, without sides to him, without subterfuge. He was generous, rarely with a bad word to say concerning anyone. In spite of jokes about him, she believed that his biggest organ was his heart. She said they could walk back, knowing he liked to.

"Nah,"

he said booking an Uber. He had experienced it before - once she started coughing, walking became difficult. His aim, in part, was to get himself out of her bad books.

"C'mon we're in the 007 business. It's how we get anywhere."

"I suppose they'll be compiling minute detail of her daily private life, everything."

Ned believed he was unerring in romance, believed he could be an agony aunt, so he took a chance.

"Ok, ok. You're obvs totally struck, mate. Don't carry on like a pork chop, there's opportunities for you here."

Sam hmphed. To her this wasn't the issue.

Entering the Doughnut, Ned had to say something.

"Look back in Straya I was told there are no rules. So, there are positives."

"How do you make that out?"

"We know her partner's been taken out of the picture. You've got a free run. Go straight to the poolroom while you can. Christ the beaut's lonely. Use what we know. You could..."

Her look made him shut up. At times it seemed like Ned came from much further than half a world distant. They went their separate ways on "The Street'.

Sam sat on a gas lift chair at her desk in front of a screen, doing little but musing. If things weren't like they were, if she wasn't in Gloucestershire and the young teacher in London and her own job wasn't what it was and Ned wasn't all over it and the world was a better place maybe, just maybe, she could have given the London teacher some of the help she needed. She could at least warn her. In subsequent days this thought came to her every time she picked up her phone. On it was an image of the young teacher she had forwarded from Ned's phone when he was in the restaurant toilet.

Another day and Sam was due to take care of Ned's little dog because he had been called to a meeting. A promotion had come through. She wondered what he had done and was doing for this promotion. It was his second and in a short time for someone who hadn't been in the country that long. His patriotic zeal and what he was prepared to do in pursuit of it worried her. It didn't fit with the rest of the character, she knew. She believed people who were kind to animals were kind in general. Some at GCHQ bragged he was a public utility for the lonely. They said he slept around but insofar as she could tell he never abused anyone. Above all there was never a hint of violence about him. Far from it.

Sitting at her workstation Sam's keyboard was idling whilst she brooded on the intrusions into the life of the young teacher. Surveillance sounded clinical, forensic but this peeking and gaping was squalid. She felt herself tainted by her job and her workplace. Lowering her chair, she reached into her case for her inhaler. The pause made her screen go blank. Sitting back up there she stabbed at the keys and an image appeared. It was the same picture of the beautiful young teacher that she had on her phone. She had no recollection of having put it there, no idea of having strayed into that area and that file. Her immediate reaction should have been 'delete' but she gazed at it instead. At that moment Ned approached her, looking one hundred and eighty degrees around himself. Stepping quickly towards her he shook his head and drew his finger across his throat. The meaning was clear: what she was doing there was dangerous. He slowed, raised an eyebrow, grimaced and mouthed the words,

"Not here, not now."

When she cleared her screen, he leant over and whispered,

"I knew you were struck. You're intel. While my mates are on it there's a window which may not be there much longer. Use what you know, set it up and pay her a visit. Do the deed. I'll make sure they cover for you."

Sam simply glared and he moved off. That couldn't be further from her mind. That wasn't the nature of her interest. Wilhelmina, Sam had discovered the young teacher's full name, deserved better. She was being abused. That Ned's mates were involved was no comfort. She needed someone to look over her and protect her.

C16

Sam was quirky, an 'odd ball' some called her but at GCHQ, that wasn't unusual. It was inherent in recruitment there. Being so solitary was notable but not seen by most to be a matter for concern. She was increasingly appreciated in the Doughnut for her skills which led to her being given a lead in manipulating online communication. Her limitations were seen, however, when she was asked to demonstrate to teams. After she pre-recorded her whole talk and sat virtually unavailable at the back of a conference room she wasn't asked again. Nevertheless, she received more recognition afresh and more responsibility when she adapted items from hackers and trolls for GCHQ's software tool kit. She was deep but she was deep and intel savvy. That there was no talk of advancement disappointed her.

Ned was treated differently, liaising between services and being weapons sanctioned. He was in Cheltenham less. Sam was seeing more of Dishlicker and less of him. When he was at the Doughnut she had no idea of when they would bump into each other. On an occasion Ned was in he surprised her by leaping out on her in 'The Street' and saying,

"You've been drooling over that pic you stole from me. Come on, you know where she lives, but there's been no dash, no pash, no deed done yet?"

She had guessed he knew she had the picture but not that she looked at it frequently and had traced the schoolteacher's address. If it was anybody else, it would be alarming.

"Better go sooner or not at all. There's lots my mates are not being told. I gather things on this op' are hotting up. Some extreme things have happened already. Give me advance notice – I'll make sure the guys are looking elsewhere."

The implication was the people he was in contact with team and had growing scope. That didn't explain how he was familiar with so much of her own activity. How was that legitimate?

Misgivings or not Sam moved on from gazing at pictures to dipping more and more into the intel on Billy. Then she plunged. Billy lived in a small flat in London's east end. Sam went over the catalogue of images of the interior of the flat checking for cameras and microphones although she knew these were no longer used regularly. A mobile phone and Billy's other devices were adequate to observe her. She noted the locks on windows and doors, fire exit signs, security lights and alarm systems in the building. She made herself familiar with everything from the facade of the three storey building where her flat was to when refuse was collected. Without forethought she was piecing a way through the minutiae of Billy's life. Out of character, there was little that was systematic or deliberate in what Sam was doing. She would throw herself into it when time and scrutiny allowed and sometimes when it didn't when the mood struck her. Engaged in this she glimpsed from time to time some of the security concerns about the young teacher. Uncovering the connection to the Tokyo Three file she looked into it and decided whatever it was it had had its day. The whole intel interest had to be a passing aberration.

Sam bought the biggest screen tv she could afford and played every minute of footage she could on Billy. When there was no new footage she binge watched each episode, from the beginning over and over. Using pause at times she dwelt on an image. In the course of this she couldn't but notice that Billy usually wore dark clothing and accessories. Ned had said her partner was out of the picture. Sam wondered if she had taken the parting badly. Was Billy suffering a form of bereavement over the loss of the relationship? Sam had caught scenes where she seemed doleful and downcast and some in which she was tearful. It didn't need much viewing to see the poor woman was forlorn. She was hurting and vulnerable, yet intel voyeurs were pawing at her in every aspect of her life. Sam's thoughts were dominated by the idea that Billy was defenceless with no one to safeguard her.

In spite of being preoccupied Sam continued to excel at work. She mastered the recovery of deleted twitter accounts. She made solid progress when she was asked to find a way of undoing the end-to-end encryption of WhatsApp. It was inevitable she would be noticed.

The call to report came when she was in the small museum in GCHQ. It housed a note from its predecessor with "keen" written underneath Tolkien's name. It invariably made her laugh. For her it was a guide on how to pronounce his name, no more. What always grabbed her interest was the original Enigma machine on display. That was the sort of intel work that impressed her. It should have been her station manager who called her in to discuss her future. But she wasn't asked to go to one of the screen festooned stations or a desk behind the partly boarded island in the middle of the desks. She had to go to a spot where filming had not been authorised when prime minister Cameron allowed cameras into the building. Someone else altogether took the role of dealing with her, someone she was told to be wary of.

Entering the office, she used too much force to close the door. It clanged loudly and the frame shook as she went in. There was a seat there but the man behind the desk, Coetzee, let her stand. He blew cigar smoke at her. Given his reputation she didn't want to antagonise him, so she ignored it. That meant she had to stifle a cough

"I fancy you think you're too good for the grade you've been stuck on. You will get no further, not while I have got a say in it"

Twiddling with the small games console she was holding, Sam had no idea how to respond.

"You think you're untouchable – but there's more to this game than techie stuff. It can all be got round: CCTV, easy, put on a hoodie. It's the same with all of it."

It was an example he loved to use. She wasn't expecting this.

"We've got plenty of weirdos, wackos and freaks

here besides you. But you're not a team player. You go around all the time, with earphones on. Sometimes you mutter like you're on the phone when you're not."
Was this what some people called tough love?

"It's, it's, it's how I, I, I think things through."

"That alien script on your desk…"
He meant the Klingon she had on a little plaque

"…I've had it translated. The last thing we need is some anti-colonialist bullshit here."
She would have expected someone where he was from to approve.

"When you're spoken to – you're doing it now – you're always fiddling with that little games machine. It's self-abuse. Teenagers wank less. Put it away. You never look anyone in the eye. Agh, look at me now, will you!"
She managed it but for just a moment.

"Your spectacles and those bottle bottom lenses - no one wears those, especially that thick."
She noticed his eyes were not on her glasses but on her breasts and wished she had put her coat on.

He continued,

"You should consider whether this is the place for you."
Others at GCHQ gave her to understand more and more people were depending on her and yet he was virtually inviting her to resign.

"You're being watched. You're a brak, a mongrel. Being a clever-dick won't help you, we've plenty of those."
He nodded towards the door. Turning to go she made a point of being on her games consul. Leaving, the remark from behind the desk to her was,

"The single person you associate with, the Aussie bucket shop Casanova, thinks he's a player. He is out for himself. He isn't your chommie."
Referring to Ned like that was, in some ways, reassuring. If someone disliked him, they could dislike anyone.
She slammed the door. He re-opened it while she was

making her way back to shout after her,

"Furthermore apply some topiary to your head. Haven't you heard of a hairbrush?"
It was for general consumption.

The reality was Sam had never felt she was the same as the people around her, not when she was a child, as a teenager, not in school, not in work, not anywhere. She had never minded. She preferred it. At times she could even have done without Ned's company. This session however had put her in a different place and she had to ring him. Apart from warning her against using her phone to ring him he wasn't particularly worried.

"Yeh, not exactly H.R. is he? He's an arse wipe, been bitter ever since they took him out of the field. Heard he was called the 'binman' back in South Africa. That's what they call people who enjoy the dirty work."

At the end of a consoling conversation he asked her if she wouldn't mind looking after Dishlicker again while he was absent. He also expressed surprise she hadn't "done the deed" yet. It was perplexing that he could know that. Could it be part of the scrutiny she seemed to be under, she wondered. Ever greater care was going to be needed if she was to find a way to help Billy. Sam made sure she was seen to be working well in her job. Her spare time she devoted to keeping an eye on the monitoring of the young teacher. In the footage once in a while she caught sight of Ned near Billy's home and workplace. With his mates there it was to be expected but still it was disconcerting.

Dipping in and out of the file each new image agitated Sam more. She and Billy shared something – they were both under scrutiny. Although it was on a different scale for the young teacher, with operatives crawling all over her intimate life. But for Sam there was another, much greater, difference; she could protect herself, Billy couldn't. The amount of information was constantly growing. Day after day, hour upon hour she endured seeing an isolated Billy preyed on with no buffer between herself and the systematic gaping at her. Two items in particular got her attention. The minor one was a shot of Billy on the till behind the counter of a charity shop. She knew she would be kind. The second item was speculation on Billy's monthly period based on her purchase of tampons. That was too hard to take. She deleted the entire section.

Ned contacted Sam. It was on a number she did not recognise but from the opening word she knew it was him.

"Mate did you…"

Was he set to harangue her about not doing the deed? She didn't want to listen to more of that nonsense. He completed the sentence,

"…delete items from the teachers file? They don't know it's you, but it's been spotted."

Sam had to tell him she had. They discussed it and he convinced her it might lead back to her. She understood it but that wasn't necessarily going to stop her. She would simply cover her tracks better. Ned also told her about ringing him directly. He would get safe phones for her to use but in the meantime, she shouldn't.

What she was being told confirmed implicitly she was under scrutiny within GCHQ and she had to restrict interventions on Billy's behalf. She was to be left to the mercy of cold hearts and abusers. What she did next wasn't considered or calculated. She didn't reason it through, consider the options and reflect - she was convulsed into action. Her response would have surprised anyone who knew her. She was going to go to her, her street and see directly what her situation was. Ned had encouraged her to go to her and she would. Maybe she would simply stand there and observe without a screen or a cyber gulf in the way. Going direct in lots of ways wasn't as risky as phoning, texting or emailing her. She told herself it was to make a first-hand assessment. And then to do what? She could only judge that once she was there. Hopefully it might reveal a way to warn Billy. Intel operatives reckoned that in-person encounters yielded the best knowledge. Ned was in the field thereabouts which might help. He had warned against using her phone to ring him so she would see him there.

The weekend was coming, she would go there, she would do it.

C17

Sam scuffed her way into the carriage of an early train to Paddington. She sat in the first seat she saw and played on her games console. Opposite a young couple poured over honeymoon brochures. It was obvious to everyone except her they were intent on their own company. Once they began kissing, she did however move. She sat in a priority seat where she would have stayed but for a pensioner pointing out that sort of seat was meant for the likes of him. The last half-hour of the journey was spent standing.

Not familiar with the tube or London buses Sam had adapted the games consul for a map app and if signal was bad, she had brought physical maps. Arriving where she wanted by eight o'clock, she wasn't aware she looked like a comic book spy. She was wearing a hood and her new prescription sunglasses on a cloudy day. Beneath the hood was an off-center pick comb which managed to make more sense of her hair. Having listened to Ned she knew to avoid all CCTV cameras where possible.

Entering Billy's road she made notes on her consul about the physical make-up of the spot. Note making was a habit which could sometimes come in handy. From two hundred metres the young woman whose outline she didn't need face recognition software to spot appeared. She was walking directly towards her. When she neared her, Sam stalled putting her head down, twiddling knobs on her consul. While Billy headed to her flat with a carton of milk, Sam was having to steady herself, having just heavily barged into a man who was simply standing there. She hadn't counted on coinciding with her in the road. She had rehearsed a doorstep chat, in which she introduced herself and the issue that meant so much. Getting any reception, let alone being welcome, had always seemed a bit far-fetched, but now it felt impossible. How on earth would she get listened to? Most likely she would have the door slammed in her face by someone who thought she was, at best, odd.

Worse she could be seen to be a threat.

Sam had come all that way. A lot of sleep had been lost going over how she would approach Billy. She had been both urged to get physically close and to do it quickly because intel was getting more intense. She agonised over how artless she could be, but she was duty bound to help Billy, at least warn her. That said she knew that done badly it might frighten her. It started to rain and she was wearing a light top. She shoved the games consul in her rucksack and readied herself. Her phone ringing sounded far louder than it usually did and she jumped. Off came the sunglasses and rain drops splashed into her eyes. She peered at the screen, not recognising the number.

"Move. Now, Sam. That was an intel agent you sent flying. No, the other way. Shoot down the road on the left fifty yards ahead."

It was Ned on another number she didn't recognise. She got the urgency and race-walked away, holding the phone.

"This isn't the way to do it, yah gallah. Can't you see there's another feller across the road who's also intel. Put your hood up and keep going…I said ring me when you were coming."

"How, how? You said not to use my phone. You said you had mates there."

"Soz, you're right but they're not there every day. Look things are developing. The area's swarming with intel. Some of it is old school. My fellers don't recognise a single one of 'em."

"It sounds bad. What's happening?"

"I'm not sure, but it's something. I need to talk to people."

"So, I'm to go back to Cheltenham - and what?"

"Well to start with use your skills, check you weren't identified and you're not being connected to your chalkie. If there's the slightest hint get rid of it. Carefully!"

Walking off, Sam's emotions were mixed. It felt like she was fleeing a preposterous encounter with Billy as much as avoiding intel. What she experienced was relief rather than disappointment, although that wouldn't be long in coming. She asked herself what she might have attempted had she stayed there and what it could possibly have achieved. Spontaneity simply wasn't her strength.

A couple of roads, a left and a right and Ned rang her again.

"I'm sorting out the phone prob."

A dejected Sam asked herself, exactly what difference that would make anyway.

As though he had read the thought Ned said,

"Look, the whole idea is the path is cleared and it's not. I did say, mate when you deleted that intelligence it was noticed. It might be people have begun looking at you. Defo they suspect an unidentified threat of some sort is involved. They'll be looking to neutralise it."

"I, I know that… you are right."

"They've not stopped looking at her."

"What can I do?"

"Look I'm being moved out of GCHQ altogether. I've officially been put in charge of surveillance on this case, so I'll have a better grasp. Hopefully you will get a free run but don't be a fuckwit. I'll give you the nod."

They agreed to meet three hours from then in a pub half a mile from Billy's. In the meantime, she went to a coffee bar where after three coffees she had to go for a walk to calm the caffeine waves in her head. Walking along she came to a halt, a smile startling her. It was merely the politeness that occurs when strangers' eyes meet. Sam stood rigid doing her best to smile back. Billy strode past on her way to shop for her ageing neighbours. Sam got out her phone and the image of Billy lit up. Lingering there she examined the nose, ears, eyes, hair and forehead. She had wondered if the photo she had was an enhancement or if it was taken on one of those special days where every aspect of a person appears at its best. But no, on an ordinary day that was indeed how she looked. Quite wonderful. It wasn't an exaggeration. Sam wouldn't give up. Her visit had been all hope and no plan. Next time would be different.

With the effect of seeing Billy still telling, she headed for the pub she was to meet Ned in. She would have to sit there longer and hope alcohol would dilute the caffeine. The pint didn't calm her or make better sense of the day she had embarked on. The bar tender delivered an egg and cress baguette she had ordered and brought another, unasked for, pint. He meant well. She waited. Ned had said he was working on something. That must mean a way for her to reach out to Billy, but doubts chipped away at her confidence in him. She had heard third hand of covert police operations, where outrages against vulnerable women were committed by undercover agents.

The pub she was in was an internet pub. With nothing better to do she started on a machine sipping her second pint. A few seconds in and she was reading accounts going back more than a decade. Clandestine officers had insinuated themselves into women's lives. From joining the same clubs and organisations, to being in the same workplace, from giving lifts home to sleeping in the same bed, the sole purpose was to gather information. One relationship produced a child. Sam held up her hand for a third pint. When the barman came over, he looked at the screen and said,

"Oh yeh he used to drink in here with his uniformed mates. They were good lads."

He meant they spent a lot and were jolly. She glared at him. He shrugged.

The undercover man Sam read of couldn't have looked less like a police officer with his long hair and beard and casual clothes. He reminded her a little bit of Ned. With that thought she gulped most of the rest of the third pint and took a risk she knew she shouldn't; she dug out the file on Billy and a file on Ned. As usual matters there were carefully worded and people, operatives in particular, were alluded to rather than named. Nevertheless, it was clear a plan was being formulated to have an agent gain Billy's complete confidence and infiltrate her life. She was to utterly depend on the affection of this agent. There were to be no barriers, or restrictions on the steps taken.

Closing the computer lid Sam was too shaken to think to shut down and wipe the searches she had done. She finished the pint of beer and the barman came over to offer her a fourth. She shook her head and could feel her senses washing around her skull. A siren sounded from the computer which had to be properly powered down. The image on the screen alarmed her when she opened it. The image was of Ned prominent on the first page of a file and it wasn't from his own file it was Billy's.

C18

Sam had been in the pub longer than she hoped and had drunk more than usual. Her phone rang and Ned was on his way. He was a friend, her sole friend, or was supposed to be. She asked herself if in his own pleasing way he might be exactly like the rest of them. She had learnt not to row in her life because slow burn though it could be her temper would finally flare up and be uncontrollable. In spite of this what was coming might be one of those times and she had no inclination to dampen it down. He would have some bland excuse, a turn of phrase and it would be difficult to dismiss. He had a way that made you want to believe him but it wouldn't happen, not this time.

Ned bowled in, exchanged greetings with the bar tender and ordered a lager, shouting across to ask what Sam wanted. She didn't respond, instead staring rigidly at one of the few remaining etched glass windows in the pub directly opposite her. While his pint was being poured, he nipped over to ask her again. For once she ignored Dishlicker's little nose poking out above the shoulder bag. She wanted to snap at him but simply whispered,

"Nothing."

"Ok. You look like a bit of a stretcher case."

He returned with his own drink and a glass of fresh orange juice for her. Had she chosen, it would have been this. He seemed more upbeat than ever. After the first mouthful from the glass he said,

"Beer's dire. Brewer should be tried in the Hague for crimes against humanity."

The orange juice hadn't diluted her anger. She had made up her mind to confront him. She would tell him that the fact was his new post involved the sleazy entrapment of Billy. What's more all his charm and good looks, all the reassurance of his relaxed Australianness would be deployed for that purpose.

Sam began,

"Seriously Ned, seriously?..."

He interrupted her,

"I've got something for you and it's a big-ee."

She wasn't going to be deflected but she would let him get his nonsense out of the way. Firstly he briefly referred to her computer activity in the pub but could tell it wasn't a good time to berate her. That he knew this confirmed for her that his reach must long have been greater than she could accept.

"It's going to be better than you ever dreamt."

Ned had begun his main topic, but Sam thought he was merely attempting to lull her. She sat straight up in her chair and was ready for him.

"Between me you and the dunny door, I don't think she is involved in anything other than a coincidence. It will blow over but not yet."

"Precisely what are you proposing in the meantime?"

Her sharpness surprised him. He took her hand and was even more surprised that she snatched it back. He was set to protest that they were intel and this what they did but he paused. Looking at her reinforced what he had already surmised. For Sam this wasn't work with benefits. It wasn't work at all and it wasn't earnest lust either, she felt an empathy for Billy matched only by a fascination with her.

"I am so sorry mate, but you never said, never gave much away."

Sam didn't respond, she didn't want his sorrow. She wanted him and intel out of Billy's life.

"Look, without me and without you the surveillance will go on for a while. The less they get from her… "

That there was little or nothing to get from her would make her life more difficult in the short term.

"…the closer to her they will want one of our lot to work."

Sam knew what was coming, how he would dress it up as the least worst option, how he would be in control and mitigate what was to happen. She felt violent waiting for the appalling truth that was about to be revealed. Almost as bad

Ned was reaching out to make her complicit when his role would be unforgiveable.

"I can't get close and neither can any of the guys. We have some women operatives who might be able to although I doubt it. Anyway, they're as bad as any. You and I don't want them anywhere near it."

Sam's hands gripping the side of her chair slackened off but not entirely. She was listening so hard that her ears burned but still she was getting lost in the verbiage.

"The person who gets the job will have to be upfront and personal. I told you it wasn't all bad, didn't I? To hang on and there would be opportunities."

The nails she chewed were near to pressing into the wood of the seat again. What wasn't all bad about this? What was he on about? Opportunities? This was one of those occasions when being agitated made it hard for her to even begin to take in words, let alone make sense.

"Of what and for whom? What does all this mean to me and to Billy?"

Ned was labouring over what he was telling her, struggling with her mood. He could tell she wanted to hear something categorical, definitive. Would she welcome something that very nearly was?

"Mate, I'm working on something. I think I've pulled it off."

If he thought he was pacifying Sam he was wrong. The vagueness was stoking her anger.

He went on, being the officer in charge he could swing it, but he hadn't succeeded in quite tying up every loose end by then. 'Loose ends?' 'Swing What?' He was so steeped in intel disguise and deception.

Ned saw there was a storm gathering in her.

"Alright I need to speak plain Australian but you need to listen to what I'm saying."

She shrugged, let go of the chair sides and threw her fists in the air. She was out of patience.

"Hold for a little while."

Hadn't he been the one rushing her to go and 'do the deed'?

"Hold what? No, I've had it."

"You're not listening. We're very nearly there..." Sam sighed loudly.

"The old Boer has been quietly lacing this with poison, he's perpetually trying to kick up a shit storm. He's got it in for me and for you and he's slowed me down a bit."

Sam picked up the orange juice, emptied it and banged the glass down on the table.

"I don't get it. First it's go fast, then it's go slow, then it's ready, then its days way. What exactly are you telling me Ned?"

"Look when I egged you on, I thought we were talking a bit of pash, a harmless night of naughty." Sam's grip on the glass tightened.

"I didn't know the case well and things have moved on. People are all over this, I'm decluttering. A few days that's all. And stop making life so hard, leave the file alone...It's all but done. It's you, you'll be intel's woman on the inside."

Her life had been spent painstakingly researching, investigating and proceeding step by step. Now she was ready to hit the take-off board and leap as far as she could.

"Are you saying my role will be to move in on Billy?"

She wanted no allusions, no euphemisms. Ned's answer was one word,

"Yes!"

followed by,

"That's what I've been trying to say."

It was never a member of his team or himself he was lining up for the intimacies of the young teacher's life, it was her. She could wrap herself around Billy. Intel information would be shaped primarily by her. The instant he declared the path was ready she would be there. Sam believed she would find the backbone to go direct to Billy. She could safeguard her.

C19

There was emergency work to replace asbestos cladding in Billy's school and the staff were excluded. She arranged to go to the Herald office to collect some of Ash's belongings. Immediately she arrived she was shown into the old editor's office. She had met him previously at work do's and liked him.

C.B. met her with a condolence of a hug, using a cloth handkerchief to dab wet from his own eyes. He told her he was so very sorry, how talented Ashley was and how popular she was in the workplace. If he could do anything for Billy, she merely had to ask. His warmth was almost staggering. He ushered her into a chair he held for her. Ignoring office rules on smoking, he lit up his blackened briar pipe, inhaled and then put it down again, fetching a bottle of whisky and pouring her a treble, about which there was no question that she would drink and he wouldn't. She looked at the crystal glass and then at him.

"I was once a devotee,"

he breezed. Clearly, he had had to give it up. She noticed he was less ruddy cheeked and had lost maybe two stone. He joked his braces were overworked whilst the trouser belt had a case for constructive dismissal.

"How has it been m'dear?"

She didn't make much of her grief but it still made him dab at his eyes once more. They exchanged memories of Ashley managing to laugh at some stories. C.B. worked his way round to his immediate concern. He explained he had worked on the Tokyo Three story with Ashley.

He hid some of his thoughts from her, for her own sake. The young reporter's death pricked him constantly. It wasn't that Ashley had a love of investigative journalism – which she did. It was that there were elements in it that were more deeply criminal than others seemed to be able to see. Rather than a random ricochet or an accident – the enquiry hadn't reported by then – it was more consistent with a deliberate killing. He had spent time looking into the events surrounding Ashley's last days and gone over police reports of the tragedy. Having previously discussed with the young hack her research into Tokyo Three he was convinced that the killing had additional enormous dimensions. When he pored over his laptop he saw that Billy was in those files, not referenced in the background but current and to the fore.

"May I have the old box of Tokyo Three papers?" In asking this he was content for her to think he wanted to carry on Ash's work. He was welcome to them. She had lost all interest since the shooting, but she had bad news,

"I've looked high and low. I knew exactly where it was. I don't know how but it seems to have gone missing." What she couldn't tell him was that unbeknown to her Coetzee had it. Lifting it from her flat had been easy.

"Aha. On its travels is it? I can guess where to," the editor said, as though he'd been given evidence, not denied a vital piece of it.

"Everything else normal?"
Billy herself wondered, wondered at times about her own senses.

"I don't know what to make of it. It almost seems the fabric of the flat is getting at me."
C.B. raised an eyebrow.

"The letter box opens letters prior to them coming through, the tv goes to stations I don't want it to, my lights have a mind of their own. As for my laptops and phones, I've almost given up on them."

The former Fleet Street man was taking notes. He adjusted a bow tie that was constricting the flow in his carotid arteries. Ash' at one stage made her doubt but C.B. was giving her confidence.

"Sometimes I think I'm being followed and by more than one. I think they're outside my place all hours and then they're on keypads all the time, like they're making notes or reporting…Sometimes I think they're taking photos."

"They've never come to your door, or been inside?"

"No. Well, I don't know, I've come back after work

and I swear some of my things have been moved around."
The editor hmmed.

"The laptop screen had a pair of eyes staring at me the other day"
The old editor's head shot back and he squinted hard.

"Look Wilhelmina I don't want to worry you but it's important you know this is serious. I doubt this is stalkers, not at least, the sort you're thinking of."

Billy breathed out. This was the first chance she had had to truly air the business since being intimidated in her Head Teacher's room.

"You're giving me a hearing. I thought I was losing it."

"Losing it isn't the half of it. I saw something of this sort years ago but without the modern hi-fi technical dimension to it."

Billy went through every scrap, every twist and turn she could think of. The old editor gave her what was known at her school as 'a good listening to.' He offered her another shot of whisky but she said no. She could feel the effect of the one she'd had too strongly.

"Here's my advice, ditch all your current tech equipment, especially your phone and laptop and change email addresses and any internet accounts."
He reached behind himself to find a Herald laptop which he gifted her.

"In fact all the accounts of any sort you might have, have to go."
Ideally, she should sever connections, move job and move house, move area. There was no point, however, telling her to do things nobody would do.

"One other thing,"
she said. He put his pen and pad down and looked up.

"I could be wrong, but it seemed to have died down a bit for a while and then it's come back to at least the same degree."
He went on not being absolutely open with her,

"A pause? But really days, weeks, months are a blink of an eye in this game. A couple of years and you might be free of it. Be patient and keep away from it no matter what the temptation."

His penultimate words to her were,

"Think of it as an old, closed coal mine. There's stuff of value down there but it's too dangerous to dig it up."

She was happy to take his word for it.

The old editor didn't tell Billy his guess was that if surveillance on her had dropped temporarily it could be because some resources were being diverted to him. Having begun working on it when Ashley was alive he had carried on, confident there was an important story in it. He had less to lose than the girl and greater backing. Years back he had known some of the younger guys working out of the MI5 building in Gower Street. Those that remained in the service had become quite senior. He had made tentative soundings and had begun to get a response. He knew it could involve elements of danger, but he was also sure he had the contacts and a history that meant he could get the story out there.

C.B. had work to do and Billy had reports to write. He left his desk and as she rose put his arm around her, half enveloping her, as though he was shielding her. He guided her to the doorway, saying,

"Steer clear of it. Stay safe."

Returning, he put the bottle of whisky back in its place. He kept it there like a trophy. He had a victory over it every day. Sitting down at his desk, he re-lit his pipe, put his bifocals on and re-opened his laptop. The search in his browser was for yet more information on Tokyo Three. In due course he would go to meet an old contact at Millbank and see what he could do.

Reassured, Billy wasn't as vigilant as normal when leaving the building. She didn't notice a man standing close by peer at her breasts. Nor did she hear him under his breath say,

"A lettic. What a foking waste."

C20

"I need your help."

"No, I need your help."
was Chas' response but he didn't truly need Eamon's help. He was simply keeping him busy by asking him along to the office of the Herald – where the editor had invited him. Eamon on the other hand needed Chas's help because he had lost his shopping list. He was faffing around in his house until Siobhan brought him the list and Chas told him to,

"Get a wriggle on."

A supermarket sweep in which Eamon seemed to have trouble negotiating aisles – he'd never been much of a shopper - and they were on their way to see C.B. Chas guessed it was a follow up to the article on his heroics.

"Maybe they want me to write a column."

"Jasus you should wear a hard hat the number of brick walls you hit your head against."

Instead of firing back, Chas' attention was on a dog owner who had missed something. His dog had pooped on the pavement and he was walking away. Chas caught him up.

"Excuse me …"
It wasn't meant to be courteous. He was set to tell him exactly what he had overlooked. The man who knew why he was being approached taunted,

"Happy New Year",
and marched off with a grin. Eamon shouted,

"Feckin' clear that shite up, will you?"
Chas wished he hadn't said it. Regardless the dog owner strolled on.

Eamon rolled up his sleeve, caught the man up and pulled at his arm hissing,

"You gobshite."
The dog owner looked up and down at the old pair, shrunken shoulders, sunken chests and smirked. Chas tried a different tactic.

"Byelaws, massive fine."

He built upon this.

"He's…"

he said pointing to Eamon,

"…an environmental enforcement officer. Already got your picture on his phone."

Eamon by then had taken out a bottle of wine and was holding it like a weapon.

"Like some amateur dentistry would you?"

he offered,

"Cos I'll remove ya front teeth, if you like."

The rightful owner of the poop, looked. It was a case of 'if the left one didn't get you the right one would'. He paused and scooped up the mess in a bag.

Eamon's nose needed wiping and his wife, had given Chas a packet of tissues. Why the man couldn't be trusted to bring his own was a mystery.

"Listen local hero, if you want a newspaper column take on mutt muck. Call yourself the Turd Terminator, it'll have an audience."

After handshakes in C.B.'s office Chas immediately started in on his ideas for a column. This wasn't what the editor had asked him there for. He couldn't think of anything to say that wouldn't sound rude, so he said nothing. Chas saw the man was stumped but optimists can take stumbling blocks as stepping-stones. He used the dog mess incident as an example, spoke of the relationship he had struck up with Ashley. The old editor knew it would come as a shock and did not enjoy being blunt, but it was best got out there quickly.

"She died I'm afraid, shot in the head at a crime scene."

Chas was seated but had to put his hands on the desk to steady himself. Eamon's bag of shopping crashed to the carpet nearly smashing its wine bottle. C.B. delayed and then went on to explain he was looking into the shooting. Ashley had taken up their journey to Cheltenham and the old editor wanted to know more of it. To the best of his memory

Chas gave him details of the booking and of the box' contents, including the plane and its departure airfield. Seeing the state Eamon was in, C.B fetched him a chair and poured a whisky for him and Chas. Whilst they gulped, he called in a journalist to search the name he had been given and the woman passenger's address. He was to go the whole hog including tax records and contacts to access police records.

C.B. helped the two friends towards the door. In so doing he warned them they should expect visits from other agencies. Eamon, who had not said a word stood straight and exploded,

"This blessed eejit can't take a warning."
He pointed at Chas and went on to talk of the set-to with intelligence agents at his friend's home.' The old editor took down the house number and road and the date. Finally, he saw them out on to the pavement and went straight to the phone himself. He knew his calls must be monitored but believed he had to act.

Going, Eamon gave Chas a hard time over the shooting of the journalist, but he couldn't see it. He insisted the editor never made a connection between Ashley's death and the old box of secrets. Eamon told him,

"Bejasus it's supposed to be me who's finalising his divorce from reality…That editor knows what he's doing, he's not going to spell it out to two civilians."
Perpetually looking on the bright side could blind Chas. But in this instance he was beginning to wonder if his friend had something, albeit a little far-fetched. Eamon added,

"Old pro' or not that editor'd better watch out for himself."

Once those words were out tyres screeched and a police car pulled up in front of Chas and Eamon. They were bundled into the car. Eamon had seen it all before. The pair were told they were in the station for a disclosure and barring service check on Chas because of the renewal of his taxi licence and Eamon because his wife had enquired about part time teaching posts for him. Eamon glared at the nonsense. Chas thought it was a little over the top.

They were interviewed separately. Unlike Eamon, Chas was surprised at what came close to a grilling. His interview was recorded and taped which quite impressed him. Fingerprinting and a blood test seemed excessive, but the modern world was full of surprises. A bizarre twist came when he was asked about his abortive death in the pub fight. He dealt with it and gave it little more thought. Questions regarding trying to stand for Lord Mayor "got his goat", he later said. He had every right, he could've been Mayor, might still be. He made no mention of the money problems that occurred and the subsequent breakdown he suffered. They demanded more information on the cardboard box from Cheltenham but Chas had become wary since Eamon saw off the intelligence officers in his house. He brushed it aside by telling them it was full of dusty decrepit stuff he had got rid of. There had been no tea, no coffee, no courtesies, nothing. He'd had enough. Whether or not they were done, he declared, he was. Heading to the exit, he told them they needed to sharpen up their act; he was a Hackney carriage driver and a livery man. He meant he wasn't a man to be mucked about.

He waited a bit longer for Eamon to appear from his session and wasn't surprised his hair was tousled, jacket off and part of his shirt hanging outside his trousers.

On the bus home the former teacher spoke in a way he never did in school. He was all "feckin bastards", "lickarses" and "gobshites". His sleeves were rolled up. Chas guessed he had cut up rough. When pushed Eamon wasn't clear on all he had been asked but he remembered,

"They asked about our trip and that feckin' cardboard box of doom."

He looked at Chas whose face gave few clues.

"Some shite, Tokyo something. Tokyo Three. Blessed if I know. It's them should have a background check. And you?"

"Same sort of thing and they went into my tilt at the Mayoralty. Told 'em I'll do it should I want to. I'm a livery man, member of the club."

"Jasus. the only club you'll get is one across your cranium. Lord Mayor. You don't know what you're dealing with."

"You remember Ronnie?"

Eamon didn't have a problem with memories going back that far.

"O.U. dropout with more blackheads than a bucket of frogspawn? Obsessed with heraldry and the like?"

"He knew all about it, becoming Mayor. Said there was a door they kept hidden behind a curtain they didn't want you to know of. But it was there - the residential vote."

"Ah but they feckin' stuffed you in the end."

"Maybe."

"Look at what they're doing to us now, will you?"

"It's a check, that's all."

"Check? In God's name, for what, a Cat' A prison?"

Close to his home a spasm of recall had Eamon ask,

"Do you think the big blond lad with the gun and mutt in a bag was the same we had in the ride to GCHQ?"

Eamon had worn out neck vertebrae from a life of looking over his shoulder. Sometimes he saw real things, others he simply imagined them. Chas thought for a minute and he recalled a blond lad had popped into his interview briefly.

"You know, the one with those whatchamacallits…oh…flip flops and socks who said 'G'day when we drove back from Cheltenham."

Chas hadn't given him a thought, let alone seen any sign of a gun. He didn't want to give it any credence and summed up the occasion with,

"Well at least that's the end of that."

His friend leaned round to look him in the face with a smile suggesting lunacy, except it wasn't him who was meant to be the lunatic, it was Chas.

C21

In Cheltenham Sam was moonlighting more than ever. Having scanned for evidence of herself being in Billy's locality she made sure her activity on the computer in the pub fell into a cyber black hole.

Ostensibly she concentrated at work on WhatsApp decryption, but it was proving difficult. Throughout she pined, hearing nothing days on end from Ned but she kept to the advice that she should not ring him. With him stationed in London, the one time she saw him was at his leaving party in Cheltenham to which he insisted she came in her 'glad rags'. She pressed him on when she was going to be able to join Billy. He was relaxed with the delay telling her things were in hand. The interest in Billy was going to taper, although one or two individuals were causing problems.

She asked if one was Coetzee to which he responded,

"Why him especially?"

She thought it was obvious but then again he hadn't had the same experiences with him she had.

She dressed in the way she always did for the party where she was entirely alone until Ned asked her to dance. The rest of the evening he danced with a smartly dressed older woman. Pressed he told Sam her name was Jessica. He confessed he had,

"Turned over a new leafo…"

adding,

"I'm going in for the classics".

Any more than that he refused as completely as any intel agent might. There was something military, senior about Jessica which was almost menacing. She had been in intel from the old days and must have seen some pretty awful things. Sam wasn't so keen on her.

"Hammered", as he admitted he was, Ned gave a speech championing love of country. He finished singing at the top of his voice Advance Australia Fair, his very own God Save Our Gracious Pommes and This Land Is Your

Land. It all seemed totally sincere. Obliged to, Coetzee made the briefest appearance. While Ned laughed with friends at the bar the Boer was in a huddle with Jessica. He was nodding towards Sam and then Ned. Leaving, he walked backwards almost tripping over himself he was so deferential to the older woman. Once the party finished Ned left with her.

Sam waited and waited but was hearing nothing from Ned. During this time as much as at work her hands at home were rarely far from a keypad. More than once she caught glimpses of Ned on the street, outside Billy's flat. Worryingly there was no sign of the surveillance diminishing although he said it would.

More than a week had gone by since Ned's promise of a few days wait before Sam was inserted. She started to devise ways of protecting Billy insofar as possible from a distance. She had the time and she always believed in some extra back up. She had it in mind to produce a stock of measures centred around her, for use just in case.

At last she heard from Ned.

"I had to ditch my last phone and it was necessary. Look mate you're to be seen in places online you shouldn't be."

She was going to say she had been careful, but Ned didn't let her.

"Mate, it's no time for a brain melt. There's more interest than we hoped, especially from the Seppos."

He had said previously that the Americans were getting more involved.

"The idea was this business would be getting smaller but it's getting bigger. Each time you play around with the intelligence you make it harder to get you in there."

That much made sense and she had gauged how the intel traffic had mushroomed. But other concerns were her priority.

"You said days and all the time intel is molesting her…Shouldn't I be there right now?"

"Ok, ok. At times it's like trying to swim up a waterfall. After work meet me by my favourite telephone box. I have a few things for you that might help put your mind at rest."
Unless it was keys to Billy's front door it wouldn't work.

By the former site of the Banksy mural Ned handed Sam a bag of phones. Each had a number on by which he could be contacted. She was to use them once and then disable them.

"Stroll," he said.
On their journey he briefed her on the devices in the house which were constantly monitored, only one of which she wasn't aware of. He also told her of the peak times when Billy was being observed and when there might be lulls. He was confiding in her, so she could have faith in him. She knew that. She also knew that the lulls were mentioned because they offered some hope of her slotting in some contact if all else failed.

"It could happen sooner than you think. Who knows the pair of you might be flat out like pancakes this coming week."

Was this drawn from his usual blank calendar with no dates? Experience said he had no firm idea. She reached across, stroked Dishlicker and recoiled. Her hand had unmistakeably come in contact with the handgun that was there. Issued with a gun, swift promotion what did that tell her about Ned? It nagged away at her. Recently he had hardly reacted to that vile man Coetzee and his woman companion was clearly high caste, close to command. Balanced against that it was certain he liked Sam. There was warmth. She was convinced they were true friends. It wasn't in her to think badly of him, but some things had to be admitted. Hidden by his charm he was unreliable. He struggled with undertakings and a timetable. In the end time missed wasn't a temporary loss, things withered, they died. Rather than an aid to her efforts to help Billy he might be a brake on it. Yet he was the single support she had, so for the moment she had to wait.

Out of the blue she was summoned by Coetzee. He allowed her to be seated this time and was brief.

"You were seen in London in a pub with the Aussie."

He said nothing regarding her proximity to Billy's flat. She was stumped for what to say.

"Seeing your mate, were you? Getting it together, are you?"

There was something in it that made her bath immediately she got home. At the same time his timbre at least suggested he had revised his opinion of Ned upwards which seemed odd. With not much more than that he let her go. That she was tracked was worrying but for the moment she could detect no consequences.

Direct action wasn't Sam's strength, but reason and patience were getting nowhere fast. Any other time with any other issue caution would have restrained her. The problem was, she realised, she was capable of losing self-control.

C22

Sam waited for the few days Ned said but heard nothing. She waited for a few days more. Still nothing. The one time she tried an alternative to waiting hadn't worked, so she forced herself to bear with it. During this she caught yet more glimpses online of him on the street, outside Billy's flat. She used one of the phones he had given her to ring him.

"Look mate there are developments, some of which may suit you down to the ground. Give me a chance. Days, that's all."

Even though it was often a repeat message when they spoke it usually rekindled her confidence, but this was waning. She had been offered the keys to the treasure chest only to find it remained out of her reach. Having almost no choice she would give him a little longer, but she was tiring of this routine. In the meantime, she didn't have to be idle. Flash drives were being loaded. She was preparing blocks and traps on Billy's file. In some instances getting through them would be hard work, in others it should be near impossible.

As it developed Ned's transfer wasn't to give him the job of surveillance of Billy alone. The second surveillance he was given was of two pensioners who lived near Clerkenwell Green because of their connection to the Tokyo Three file. One had mixed with Sinn Feiners into his thirties. The other was a student radical and made an attempt at taking the Mayoralty of the City of London.

Ned did the job whilst not believing any of the parties were a threat. Nevertheless, he thought he should gen up on Tokyo Three. The electronic file had far more security than anything he had ever dealt with. The task of unearthing links from Billy and the two old east enders to Tokyo Three revealed little. All he understood of the file was that it involved aeroplanes and bombs. To him that was unremarkable, a given since Nine-Eleven except this stuff came out of the ark. He knew intel history was famously full of cases that used exaggerated claims to justify exceptional use of resources. The impression he gave was different, telling people, he was going, "flat out like a lizard drinking". In reality he would make sure he was seen to be doing a job of work but no more. That little of the master file had been revealed was fine by him.

Ned understood that Sam was at her wits end and knew she had had the ultimate prize dangled in front of her. She was his 'bestie' and he knew he needed to deliver – something.

"News,"

he said, ringing her,

"We're working together."

He didn't expect an accolade and he didn't get one, or any response at all.

"We've got two sets of quarries. The first is the two oldsters who tripped over the Tokyo Three box."

There was still no reaction.

"The second is surveillance of Billy. It's real, it's now."

"Now."

She all but screamed it.

"Oh Ned…"

It was one of those tiny unfinished sentences that convey more than any gushing. They were both pleased with him. He had used contacts and pulled some strings. This went part way to fulfilling his commitments to her. If he had managed that, then it was perfectly possible he could eventually honour the rest. It took the edge off not being able to work with Billy directly. She was free to delve into the operation around Billy and use that as a veil to put yet more effort into building fortifications for her. Being on the same cases with Ned also had the advantage that contact between them about Billy should go unquestioned.

In their different roles Sam and Ned weren't meant to join dots, but simply to observe and report. They might come to understand more of Tokyo Three or not later on.

Regardless their allotted tasks had to be carried out. Ned accepted that they could simply be instructed without an iota of justification. Sam didn't.

For Sam the two old characters had virtually nothing to offer to intel. Dust was gathering long ago on Eamon's republican connections. Of late his wife had been posting on an iPad her concerns about her husband's fragile mentality. That was sad and not for intel activity. The taxi driver's student rebel days were even longer gone. Ned did see some importance in him, especially in his shot at Lord Mayor although it had been stamped on. Sam couldn't see anything of interest there. His wife was busy on Tinder but at least they agreed that was to no threat to security. The one tangible link to Tokyo Three was the ride to Cheltenham but to both Ned and Sam that looked like no more than happenstance.

Ned was immune to boredom and could actually enjoy observing the old friends spend so much time together. Sam asked him if he thought there was more to their relationship than initially appeared. He replied,

"They're the maximum mate. They're besties, it doesn't get bigger than that."

Yet another task was given to Sam. It confirmed for her growing misgivings with her career choice. She was to follow all Ned's internet activity and report on it. He was under suspicion, he was under surveillance. She would make it look good but it would be him who was reported to and him alone whatever came up.

Days were stacking up and there was no advance in bringing her together with Billy. Her patience wouldn't be endless, but Ned deserved to be given a little longer. The work on the cabbie and his friend was numbingly tedious. She and Ned were in regular formal contact, although he had made it clear that on those occasions they were not to exchange anything outside of the official. Time was passing and she was increasingly aware the promised consent to see Billy had been brought no closer. Ned never aired it. She had one burner phone left. She could ring him and belabour the issue, but he would simply give her facile assurances. Online she watched footage of Coetzee following Billy from her visit to the Herald office. He was appearing more and more in footage on Billy. Once when leaning on a wall opposite her house while he was staring over the hand in his trouser pocket seemed very active. A day later she saw Ned there and he was in conference with Coetzee. It jarred. Ned could be relaxed with anybody. But Coetzee. Really? They looked all but arm in arm. No sooner had Ned left then Coetzee resumed gazing at Billy's home, hand in his pocket.

Counting down the seconds, Sam in a break took the remaining burner phone on which Ned's number lit up. Jabbing keys she rang Billy. There was no answer then, nor during lunch, nor in a toilet break. Neither was there when Sam was on her way home and nor was there after her meal. Finally, at ten o'clock in the evening Billy responded,

"Hello…hello."

Sam in reality was completely unprepared for a conversation with her. She wanted to warn Billy about Coetzee but all that came out was,

"Er, er er."

Just as she was finding the words the phone went dead. No light, no screen, no response, not so much as a crackle. She recharged it, opened it to examine its innards, slammed it up and down on a table. It was as useless as she had been.

C23

"Howzit?" Coetzee introduced himself. C.B. had agreed to see him over the threat of a D notice on the Herald. It was Coetzee's usual greeting but this time he didn't prolong the fake cordiality. His original intention was to have a professional chat with the editor, but he had been outside the day Billy exited the newspaper office. He immediately turned to demands to know about C.B.'s 'relationship' with the girl. He put meaning into the term which revolted the editor. Had he still been able he would have physically thrown the man out but a stroke meant those days were gone. Two employees were called to escort Coetzee from the premises. He wasn't remotely put out. His parting shot at the editor was to look at the bottle on the shelf and tell him,

"Pour yourself a drop man…You're gonna need it."
The South African knew the editor was an alcoholic. It would have been close to mission accomplished to have tipped him off the wagon. C.B. understood Coetzee's game which made it easy to rule drink out for that day, at least.

C.B. knew a story when he saw it, but once in a while got it wrong. That could happen to the best but after he had spoken with Billy he was more confident. Once Coetzee was escorted from the premises he was certain. He rang one old contact in particular but had to leave a message with the basic facts. He came back to him within the hour.

A meal first, at a men's club? That would be discrete, so he agreed. He'd had some fun times with this contact years back. When they met he was surprised at how fit he looked. He was probably still a rower.

"So tell me all you know, Phillip."
The old editor's request was met with an index finger to the lips and,

"Best not here."
C.B looked around, the place wasn't busy and nobody was within hearing shot. He put up with it.

Whilst they ate what wasn't much more than a

snack, he pressed Phillip again. The whispered response came after a glance around the club.

"All I can say here is that intelligence is all over it, Claude. This is a hot Maris Piper. The yanks are prioritising it."

"Why? It is ancient history after all."

"Oh no. The relationship with Japan is very much current. Don't forget there's fifty thousand plus U.S. troops there. Key ally – and we want them to forget all about Article Nine, especially why it was put there to begin with."

C.B. hadn't thought much on this and now he did. He knew pretty well the rest of what he was being told. It explained little.

"Why is an obsolete bomb that never hit the target, so important, now?"

The man opposite him stood, called for the tab and hissed,

"Not here. I know just the place where there's no ears and eyes. Follow me."

C.B. trekked after his source and was convinced he was getting somewhere. The first piece of real information came as they strolled towards the embankment.

"After that appalling box of secrets got into the wrong hands…"

He was talking about the Tokyo Three box.

"There was a mission, all hush, hush…"

He didn't need to tell C.B. this was top secret – no journalist in the world, let alone newspaper had had a hint of it.

"…Once the box came to light a sub, divers and a bathyscaphe, kit and caboodle were sent to find the wreck. Special cameras, geiger counters, advanced detectors."

The newspaper man was scribbling down shorthand notes.

"And?"

To his surprise information was coming freely and easily. Normally when not paid for it had to be heavily plied from a source.

"Not a sausage, not a fly peck. The bomb was

definitely not on the plane."

"Which means it must have been dropped."

"Exactly."

Old wireless communications from the plane had been re-examined. Weather reports, especially on wind direction for the day were poured over. The topography in a sixty mile diameter around Mount Fuji was being looked at in 3d imaging at that moment. The bomb was definitely in Japan somewhere, waiting to be discovered.

Phillip shifted his focus.

"So fill me in on this harridan reporter of yours and her girlfriend."

"What?

"I've given you something. Now I need something in return."

The description of Ashley could hardly be more wrong. The information the MI5 man wanted was of someone C.B. liked and was driven to protect. He was having none of it. Instead, he asked,

"Tell me about Ashley's shooting, then."

Maybe he would, maybe he wouldn't. If it wasn't to be stalemate C.B. had to give a little.

"You won't budge on that? At least let me look at your notes."

Agreeing wasn't difficult, the MI5 man wouldn't be able to read the shorthand.

On a damp night they were by the granite walls on the north bank of the Thames. Descending down to the river itself, Philip laughed, unzipped and urinated. With his free hand he waved the shorthand notes beckoning their owner down to collect them. C.B. stopped a few feet short but he coaxed him closer down towards the Thames' edge. The old editor wasn't the most mobile and slipped, stopping with a bang on the mossy steps. He sat down winded. He had got what he needed, so soon he could be off.

"Some fortification."

It wasn't a question. Phillip produced a huge whisky flask

from his coat inner pocket.

"Ah, I think you know better - that's not for me. I'll settle for my notes back, thanks."

The MI5 man crumpled them into his own pocket.

"You never made life easy for yourself, did you?" He lurched behind him, cupped the back of C.B.'s head in his hand and rammed the metal flask against his mouth. As his lip split and bled, C.B. was shocked at how strong this agent was.

C24

“What are we, the blessed blunder brothers? I’m supposed to be the problem, not you.”

This was Eamon in answer to being told,

“I’ve got to report what’s going on to the police. I’ll try my M.P. At least have a stab at it.”

Chas had been thinking about events since the trip to Cheltenham. He didn’t want to put two and two together and come up with twenty two but if something was going on it was best to get to the bottom of it.

“What is fucking wrong with you? The writing on the wall is huge, in upper case, in bold and lit up. It’s fucking poison. Fucking leave it.”

Eamon used the full f word solely when he was boiling over with something. Chas would let contacting the authorities drop for a while.

In a coffee bar the talk, led by Chas, was of their glory days. It rarely failed. It mellowed Eamon who revealed some of a conversation he had with his son. His son was plainclothes CID, having moved on from uniformed police. Eamon was eventually prepared to overlook their differences, his son took longer. To the lad his father’s past was worse than embarrassing and his views were infuriating. The son’s anger with his father had spontaneously tempered when he hit his forties. They both strived for a truce, but it was often awkward. It didn’t go too badly if they avoided certain subjects. It was stilted but allowed love some expression. A recent phone conversation between them, however, hadn’t gone too well. To fill the spaces that riddled their phone calls, the son told his father,

“I’m up for promotion. The meet’s at end of the month...”

There was a silence in which Eamon battled for words.

“It’s my second shot at it but there’s no reason I shouldn’t be ok.”

Eamon was still struggling, genuinely wanting to show an interest.

"That's uhm…that's good…er good luck."
This was followed by a silence until the son eased matters with,

"It's alright you can put mum on now."

Chas knew the relationship between this father and son was nothing like his with his dad. It had long agitated Eamon, so he tried to move the chat on, but it simply went back to a worse spot.

"We're too fucking' old to take up arms. It's always been knuckles versus tanks anyway."
For Chas you were never too old.

"M.P.s, police, Chas? There's liaison between higher ups in all these organisations. They cover each other's backs better than any overcoat could. Don't go poking a fucking MI5…"

Chas assumed it was emotion making Eamon struggle for a phrase. He suggested,

"Hornets' nest?"
Eamon nodded. Chas told him the little people had to make a stand.

"From the mouths of babes and halfwits. Will you fucking listen to yerself? 'The little people'. Those at the bottom of your garden, I suppose?"
On it went.

It had at least dawned on Chas that the box of papers they brought back from Cheltenham wasn't benign. Pressed, he declared he would not to go to the police. It was a promise to his best friend, so he would keep it. As he saw it that needn't stop him from writing to a minister or two or going to his MP's surgery. There must be support there.

His friend pacified, Chas's attention was grabbed by a newspaper front page on a shelf by the table they were sitting at. It was the Herald and he recognised the man in the large photo there. He asked Eamon to get another coffee in whilst he held the paper back to front so his friend wouldn't see it when he returned. His finger followed the headline and then all but poked through it. He never looked for bad news, never put the worst twist on events. Good people were teeming in a world which was crammed with good deeds, but Eamon would know what to make of this. Chas wouldn't. Bit by bit and in spite of himself he might draw closer to it. Then again he always wanted to believe in the best.

C25

While the two old friends were drinking coffee, Billy was in her school staffroom making cups of it for all. She switched the urn on and arranged the cups and saucers. The loss of Ash' wasn't sitting so heavily with her on this day. She had steered clear of anything that caused problems on her laptop and phone. She hadn't noticed figures gazing from across the road, although she was looking a lot less. Her relationship with the Head Teacher had begun to mend – largely because the Head went out of her way to make it happen. Being put in charge of a training weekend was mooted, in spite of teachers more senior being available.

From coffee making she went to water the pot plants over by a window. Water from the little plastic watering can dripped on to a copy of the Herald the pots stood on. It was the same edition that Chas hid from Eamon. As Billy glanced at its headline, the can tilted and water poured down her smock and over her jeans. The can dropped to the floor. She grabbed the windowsill and then clung to it. Others in the staff room stared and then rushed to support her. What was wrong? Was she ill?

Helped to a seat she was lowered on to its sagging cushion. None of those helping knew C.B. personally. The front page of the Herald was sad without impact for them. Much needed tissues were given to Billy. The headline she saw was,

"Herald Editor Drowns in Thames."

The following lines told her he had slipped down steps and hit his head before plunging into the river. The autopsy showed there was half a litre of whisky in his stomach. Despite the headwound the police weren't treating it as suspicious nor were they looking for anyone else in connection with the incident.

The Head Teacher saw the state Billy was in, knew she wouldn't be able to teach and sent her home. Billy was allowed the following day off and, later, to attend C.B.'s funeral. A doctor's appointment led to a week's diazepam prescription. Billy’s grief was real and far greater than any thought for herself. Nevertheless, with the loss of C.B. on top of the loss of Ashley she felt without support in the world. Intelligence surveillance, agents, stalkers, hackers: she had to face them alone.

C26

Billy wasn't the sole person to cry. Eamon was also fearing isolation and also wept. Lent began the following day and would be enforced in their household. His wife had sent him to the shops for lemon juice for pancakes, but it had slipped his mind. He was not only asking himself why he was there but where he was at all. He knew it should be familiar and he knew he should know his way home but when he looked around he didn't have a clue which way to head. What he used to know now mocked him. Did he have his phone? He did. On it was a picture of him and Chas side by side.

The last number he rang, in fact the single one for some time, was Chas'. Who else would it be? He pressed the button and waited and waited. It went to voice mail. Thank goodness the greeting was Chas' but leaving a message for who knew how long wasn't what he needed. He had been dwelling on images of when his own mammy went doolally. The early signs were familiar. When it started for him, he had been struggling with names, then he struggled with nouns. Now it was any word. The little he still knew couldn't be brought to mind without prolonged effort, if at all. Birthdays, festive days, even his anniversary had all been forgotten. He had been hiding it not simply to avoid embarrassment but because he feared what would happen were it to be detected. Having suffered, his mammy had been interred in one of those tragic foul-smelling places. He would top himself rather than that. He said that long ago.

Starting to sob his phone rang. It was Chas. Eamon brightened up, got control of himself and told his friend he was lost, didn't know where he was, although he knew he should.

"Lost? We've all been there mate. That's why there's a name for it, a 'senior moment.'"

He laughed and continued,

"The other day I was driving and suddenly realised I hadn't a scooby where I was going. Had to pull over. So, pull over yourself and I'll be there in a trice."

He got Eamon to describe a local shop and was on his way.

"Alright, shorten that long face of yours,"
he said arriving. Eamon told him of his woes.

"Most of that's run of the mill old pal. We all fail to remember things. And you've struggled since you left your job, but you'll get over that."

"Mother of God, you don't understand Chas. I couldn't remember your name when we met the other day."

"At times I can't summon up names immediately. Google's become my memory, Thesaurus dot com my working vocabulary. Look you can't run and jump like you used to, or for that matter do anything like you used to but it's not sinister."

"Sometimes kindness can be a torment. You're the only one I can talk to about it, Chas. Will you take it seriously."

"Ok suppose for one minute you're right, there's so many new drugs out to help. It's not like it was for your mum."

Eamon wanted to believe it but wasn't sure. He was sure, however, when told,

"I'll never leave you in it, Eamon. Better or worse, sickness 'n' health, you know that."
That he could believe. Chas would stand by him.

"Will you feckin' cherish me, darling?"
he laughed.

"You're the toughest man I know."
It was a compliment and Eamon knew it, he wanted to be tough. No more weeping then.

Walking off, it might be smiles all round but that didn't stop Eamon from whispering,

"Death solves a lot of problems you know."
Chas didn't want to hear that, let alone answer it.

C27

"Same old phone box 8 o'clock sharp."
The note was in a folder placed on Sam's desk by an older lady in a grey suit whom she recognised. She had seen her with Ned at his party. For sure she wasn't employed at GCHQ, although she must have clearance. Jessica gave her no eye contact when she passed by.

At eight o'clock Sam was in the phone box feigning its use, enduring its odours. Ned arrived a quarter of an hour later. She would tell him she had been given the task of tracking him online, that he should realise he was under physical surveillance as well. Opening the door of the red booth Ned saw someone agitated.

"Set phasers to stun mate, no need for more…"
It was a Star Trek reference he knew would appeal. It meant she should go easy on him.

"The wait could be over. But that's not why we're here. You're phone call…"
Sam sighed a quick interruption,

"You have to know, I've really got to tell you…"
She wanted to get her responsibility for tracking him out of the way before anything else.

"That you're tracking me, that I'm under surveillance."
Sam was dazed.

"I'm supposed to be tracking you too mate. That's intel. No wuccas."
He was relaxed about it, neither of them would do anything to harm the other. It had been launched by Coetzee and discovering this led Ned to a re-assessment.

"He's not softened on you, it's a ruse. He's got it in for both of us and he's under a lot of pressure from Langley. That and your antics've got him busier than a one-toothed man with corn on the cob."

"That stops him being dangerous?"

"Webster…"
It was a nickname. He was reminding her of her skill set,

"… carry on doing your thing, suffocate him with facts and figures and I'll do what I do. He's not up to it, tech's beyond him. He'll struggle to cope."

"Is this why you're here?"

"Partly, I know you worry, mate. I'm taking care of it. He's not the only one with contacts in Langley and Millbank."

"Is one of them Jessica? She passed me the note. Who is she?"

He wasn't going to answer that.

"'Hello…hello'. Your phone call to Billy, mate. It was heard. Any contact on her phone is a bad, bad move."

Sam wasn't in the mood to be admonished.

"Yes, yes, I did. Times up. I'm dying with Tokyo Three and as for tracking the two pensioners…I want to be close to Billy. I was supposed to be there by now."

It was obvious she was beside herself.

"Ok I'm almost there. I can cover this. You're being moved into the field on this one. Be packed and ready to hop on the Cannon Ball Express as soon as mate."

"What do you think of the scrutiny we've both come under?"

"The source of that is being handled. He tried to ban Dishlicker, no one messes with Dishlicker. Be ready to take leave tomorrow. One or two things need checking. Pack your rucksack but wait for the call from me, wait."

Where had she heard that before? Not weeks, not days, now he was talking a day. The record said she shouldn't get excited. She didn't say it and was glad she didn't when Ned reminded her she would be working alongside him. They would be in it together. Things could be a lot easier. Maybe things truly were imminent.

She recalled her last foray to Billy's and her look spoke of nervousness more than excitement.

"I'm local for a night or two. If you like I'll coach you, go with you when it comes to it,"

the Australian offered. She shook her head vigorously, that

wasn't happening.

"Ok, I might be your first mate..."
he laughed,

"but I'm never coming on your maiden voyage."

"It won't be my maiden voyage..."
she lied,

"...so thanks, but no thanks. Don't take offence, please. I could doggy sit for you tonight."
Offence wasn't taken and as it happened that would be handy.

"No worries, it's not like you've abused my barbie. Look work out what you're going to say. Your last trip was bad. The phone call was hopeless. Do that any more and you'll get Buckleys. Just be you as you are – systematic, be pre-prepared."

With that he passed her another bag of phones. She said she could get her own. He retorted they wouldn't have the one-time numbers he put on them.

Walking away cuddling Dishlicker, she was nervous at the prospect of meeting Billy. She was also uneasy that Ned knew of her phone call to Billy. In that instant it hit her. The phone she rang Billy on that went dead was one he foisted on her and insisted was to be used with one number alone. He had somehow stopped the call. Then again what could she have said to Billy - that she was part of a surveillance team and had spied on her for months, that she wanted to get close to her to protect her from what she herself had been doing. Ned was right, she should prepare herself if she was to meet her. Maybe she did need coaching.

Failing that she would be completely stumped for words and what to do. Rather than Billy seeing she was there to protect her, she could believe she was playing a lead in violating her.

C28

Sam rushed from her telephone box meeting with Ned and called in at a late-night clothing shop. Although it wasn't yet Spring she didn't need anything too heavy because the temperature was exceptionally mild. She went home to pack immediately after and hung up a new outfit. Refusing colours and flowers she had opted for a black and white outfit which in fashion terms was reasonably benign. It had a hood and was chosen because it looked like something Billy wore. Sleeping that night was difficult.

When the media was full of Foreign Office advice that travel to Wuhan was advised against it didn't register with Sam. Along with the vast majority she knew nothing of the first thirteen pandemic cases. Readying to see Billy she had no idea that for weeks Coronavirus droplets had been wind surfing the breaths of humanity unhindered. Nor could she have guessed the impact it would eventually have on her.

Ned's call came and she was ready to travel.

"All bets are off, mate."

Interest in Tokyo Three was ballooning, not abating as he thought it would. He told her one of the two oldsters was a marksman when it came to shooting himself in the foot. The photograph from the Tokyo Three box which Eamon lost on Chas' doorstep had been spotted by intel agents. The pair had been to the newspaper office where Billy's partner had worked. A police interview had been unsatisfactory and MI5 were to have a fresh crack at them. It was going to be the real thing with truly heavy operatives. What's more Billy remained a suspect.

"If we start moving you in now, if you're not careful – and you're not always – it'll help nobody. Mark time and I'll get you in the second it calms a little."

Another delay was hard to take.

"Come on, I must be able to do something on it. I thought I was being put in the field with Billy."

"That's a problem. Coetzee cracked the shits over it. He's been talking to his buddies once more. I know I've got you right - this isn't a one off, you're in it for the long term. We have to be cautious."

"You said that vile man wasn't going to be a problem."

"I'm on it, mate. but he has real connections. It's taking longer than I thought…it might need something more extreme."

It was pointless asking but she did,

"How long, how long is this going on for?"

He heard her voice break a little with this.

"I get it. Believe it or not I do know what love is. You will get what you want but don't blow it now."

For a change he didn't put a time limit on it. It made it sound more credible. On the one hand Sam had to ask herself if he was up to it. The commitments he made could be beyond him. The steps he would need to take might involve a level of influence and standing he didn't have. On the other hand, if he was right then her being placed by Billy's side at that stage would endanger her and that was the opposite of what she wanted.

"Take my word for it, you'll get a crack at it."

Taking Ned's word at face value had become difficult. Dates had been made and none of them kept. Compounding the doubt was a feeling, somehow, that she had been jilted. Totally illogical, she couldn't shake it, yet she had to find a way to contend with it. The nearest she could get to that was the uphill path she generally took which was by working harder and longer and with ever greater concentration.

She had begun work earlier on dual tasks whilst ensuring she was seen to excel in her day job. Now she had to step it up. The aim was to make two people disappear. The first would be Coetzee which would be tricky and would take some time. Replacing Billy with a character she created from an old missing person's list should be easier. The preliminary work had been underway for a while when she was suddenly summoned to Coetzee' office. She put on her puffer jacket and did up to the top so he couldn't scrutinise her cleavage.

All she had been doing was done as preparation offline, no actual moves had been committed. She was confident there was nothing he could pick her up on. Rather than worried she was curious as she entered the room. He glared, snapping down the lid of his desktop computer.

"Close the door - gently for once. What great progress has there been?"

It was rhetorical. He didn't wait for an answer.

"A magnificent zilch! It's gone nowhere fast. Using a fishing line to raise the Titanic would be quicker. I hear you work hard…I don't know what at."

"I, I…"

She was set to protest, listing a number of completed tasks which should compare favourably to the rest of her section. She stopped. Why waste her breath? Instead, she followed his eyes which were attempting to make out her breasts beneath her jacket.

"I'm referring to the file on the bomb in Nippon and that shiftless young teacher."

Sam had come across opinions like this many times: teachers had short days, long holidays and produced illiterate louts. People like him deserved little more than expletives.

"You're off Tojo Three …"

His use of, 'Tojo', was not a mistake.

"…How you were ever designated in the field?...Well I suspect I know where that came from."

He looked her up and down. It was akin to being pawed.

"Get in touch with job agencies. They'll have equal opportunities and diversity programs for people like you. Don't ask for a reference – telling you that is me doing you a favour."

He was enjoying this, but he wouldn't had he known that she wasn't worried about leaving GCHQ. She wanted to leave. She was simply there to protect Billy. However long she had left there would be spent perfecting a shield. She wanted Coetzee to see insolence in her manner. Not waiting to be told she could leave, she knocked papers from his desk to the floor, swung round and headed to the door. Coetzee hadn't remotely anticipated that, so he rushed to the door shouting out for her fellow workers to appreciate,

"There's no hope in your Aussie boyfriend, the smart Alec's not as clever as he thinks he is."

She sprinted off hoping to put herself out of hearing distance.

Coetzee's audience with her was outstandingly unsuccessful. Sam wasn't intimidated by being threatened with the sack and when he damned Ned it renewed her confidence in him. She also decided that if, as a colleague in GCHQ, she could be threatened by prejudice, then with an intended quarry like Billy intel would be absolutely ruthless. She had to intensify her work there. It was unclear how much longer she would have easy access to the workings of GCHQ. At home, locked away behind a curtain in a recessed tall oak cupboard were flash drives, pre-loaded and a bank of zombie computers - a mix of P.C.s and laptops. She had collected dozens and renovated them for a bit of a hobby. All of them had been readied with disabled cameras and disabled locator software and with hidden IP addresses. Some were already crammed with bogus accounts covering everything from Twitter to Amazon and hybrids of those. They would lead to a manifold of false trails. It was all gentle compared what Coetzee's coming fate.

With half an hour to go before Sam was due to finish for the day she sat comfortably at her workstation when a note on headed paper was handed to her. It was from Coetzee and signed 'yours truly' which could have caused her to guffaw. The note read,

"Oh, did I say? You're off the two decrepit krimpies…I'm handling them…"

She felt sorry for Eamon and Chas.

"…and your work is to be forensically examined."

C29

"Really, so it's threats, is it? Get on with it," was the reply to a warning about national security Eamon had been given. It made him more alert than usual. His would-be tormentors looked at each other, beginning to believe what they had been told regarding this man. The notes they had were unusual and included medical records. It was possible he was unhinged but the suspicion was he was simply a hard nut to crack. Whichever, they had the tools for it.

Eamon had been taken down sets of stairs and walked along passageways. It was far enough for him to no longer be in the same building he had been brought to with Chas. He was sat in a beech spindle back chair at a rough wooden table where a couple of LED lights flashed to show a recording machine was powered up. The former stockroom was largely bare, making the only focus anyone seated there. Diagonally across the room a camera peered at Eamon and across the table were two antagonists. One was an athletic looking woman who wasn't MI5. When she questioned him, she loudly laboured over getting the words out. It was done in the belief he might be deaf and a bit simple. He was having none of it.

"Can't get your words out, eh? Dental anaesthetic not worn off yet?"
he shouted back. The second antagonist had a fringe combed forward six inches from crown to forehead. He was a naturally big man.

These intel officers gave Eamon hard stares long enough to unnerve an ordinary man. What they got back was a reflection of their stare. They attempted to add to any tension with a warning regarding the Anti-terrorism Crime and Security act. Eamon drummed his fingers on the table, gazed and then slumped. They wore no black caps for passing sentence, but the agents tried to convey that without cooperation the penalty would be severe. Their voices were harsh. He feared what was coming would be unpleasant but believed the best response was his own version of 'no comment'.

Eamon had been coaxed there, then manhandled by escorts in uniforms he didn't quite recognise. Forced down into a chair he chided them while they were leaving,

"So what are yous, recycled plastic policemen?"

Those in the room weren't new to nonsense being talked during interrogations. One switched on the recording device, the other reached up to adjust the angle of the camera and they went through a catechism to confirm basic biography. Their subject went off into long tales with colour and expletives. The woman rapped the table and rapidly questioned him on the Tokyo Three papers.

"Feckin' slow down will yous? You're talking faster than the TsnCs lady in adverts…Have you considered a speed awareness course?"

That and a southern U.S. way of running words into each other made it difficult for him to follow. He was repeatedly asked about Tokyo Three. His ears were ringing with it. Whilst the more muscular interrogator rolled up his sleeves the woman repeated the perils of breaking official secrets law. He replied,

"Bless me, secret? The single one I've ever come across is Victoria's secret and I'm still working on that one."

It was an old line he used. He then started taunting the woman as 'Birdie', telling her to stay on her perch. It was a lure. She asked why he called her 'Birdie' and he came back at her,

"Because the likes of you drop shit wherever you go."

Whilst she recomposed herself, he asked,

"Want to give me a piece of your feckin' mind do yous? I doubt you've enough to spare for that."

The way Eamon swayed, nodded and glanced around suggested he wasn't entirely with it. After a few more exchanges like that his interrogators ramped things up. They produced what they claimed was a printed record of texts on his phone relating to the whereabouts of the Tokyo Three box. They were casting a rod where there were virtually no fish. Eamon brushed his fingers through his scant brilliantined hair and it stood on end. He knew what he looked like.

They told him they wanted the truth, a crime had been committed and someone had to be to blame.

"The truth?"

he swayed as he said it, looking literally unbalanced. The woman nodded pointing at him. What they wanted was a confession.

"The truth of the feckin' finger of blame is it should be stuck up its owner's arsehole."

Was a breathalyser needed?

Eamon was grilled next on details of the taxi ride to Oakley. He asked for his phone as though to search for the information. Holding it sideways on and then upright, he then looked at its back and its front, finally dabbing a few keys. The mobile with its pitted case could be a conundrum for him. While the two interrogators were agog, he twirled the phone around examining it as though he had never seen it, ever. The bald man in denial snatched it from him, Eamon shouting,

"Feckin' give that back or your colon'll have its own ring tone, 'cos that's where I'll be shoving it."

In point of fact, he didn't care much for the thing but told himself you couldn't let people take liberties.

A breathalyser was sent for. Eamon's thoughts drifted to familiar scenes. He was a veteran and it wouldn't be a problem. Once it came the operatives opposite him suspected he hadn't blown into it correctly, so a sample bottle was called for.

"Good feckin' luck there. You might find a dry sample on me cacks. Best chance'd be to wring out me balls."

Eamon sighed and relented telling them he would need a drink before he could produce. After water drunk from a discoloured plastic cup, he told them there would be a wait.

They checked their records on him. A few minutes more, after insisting they turned their backs, he was ready to pee. It wasn't much but a result was conceivable, so they had it whisked away. Questions resumed and responses were given which were short on facts and long on rhetoric, with the odd line of poetry thrown in. Metal cuffs were placed on the table. Eamon hadn't seen a pair of those in years. Depending on who put them on you it could hurt.

"Ah, good timing", he said, "those things would've made peeing in a bottle a mite difficult. Unless, that is, one of yous was going to hold it for me."

The interrogators started from the beginning again, asking Eamon details of his life once he had reached England. He was dizzy with it. He answered with an anatomy: he had developed housemaid's knee, tennis elbow, frozen shoulder, hammer toe, fallen arches, bishops finger and a slipped disc, most of which he didn't have. He finished with,

"You can't do me as much damage as the years have, sonny."

The interrogators were losing hope of a resolution but they had instructions so they carried on. The big man resumed.

"You are obliged to reveal what you did with the Tokyo Three papers, who you shared them with. Understand this, you could lose your freedom here and that would be the least."

The woman added,

"If we inter you, it won't be pleasant."

Being interned is what Eamon heard and he knew of that in detail and hated them for the threat.

"We can make you take this seriously," the woman warned.

"I'll see your ultimatum and raise you two."

Eamon spat it out making a display of closing the fist on either hand. Each of the experienced intel interrogators looked at the other and there was a pause which became a long one.

“Ah derailed your train of thought, have I?” Eamon mocked. The comment was too reasoned for them to believe he didn’t know what he was doing. Should they have to break him, they would.

The cuffs were opened and banged leaving dents in the table. Two more operatives arrived to remain standing. They placed a metal box on the table and took out a syringe from it. They meant business one way or the other. Eamon told them,

“Thanks but no, I’ve had me flu jab.”

It wasn’t true, he hated injections and avoided them. Because of this, they managed to get some sense from him, although there was little real detail in it. When they pressed him, he knocked the cuffs off the table, shouting

“Suffering Jasus, what’s this got to do with anything?”

The woman operative alone was seated at this point. Eamon managed to recall elements of the return from Cheltenham leaving out any mention of Chas. He followed this with blethering of this, that and the other with obscenities a plenty. The retrieved cuffs were banged on the table louder this time and the signal was given for the two men who had entered the room to get closer to him.

“Why are you feckin’ asking me all this Tokyo Three bunk?”

In a flash he saw it clearly.

“You don’t understand it either do you? I’d plead ignorance if I were you. Anybody’d believe that.”

The four operatives in the room simultaneously pounced on him forced his hands behind his back and snapped on the cuffs. Eamon managed to see that also in the metal box was a small dark bottle, cotton wool and sharp looking scissors. He smelt iodine of the sort used to sterilise. This was going beyond what he expected. He went rigid when they took out a syringe. Putting his legs against the table side, he threw himself back to the floor and rolled around all over the place. The needle was aimed at him, but the first one was broken. Next an operative got an inch of the remaining one driven into his forearm. Free of being grappled for a moment, Eamon twisted up and headed for a corner. Were they going to cut him? The other thing on the loose in his head was the tune of the Celtic Tiger. He went wildly into flat dancing which became legs kicking out all over the place.

"Heard of mixed martial arts, have ya? Well, the Irish have feckin' Mick's martial arts"

Eamon came round. With the only eye he could open he saw blood daubed cotton wool on the table in front of him together with the scissors used to cut a plaster for his wounded eyebrow. He spat out blood and murmured to himself,

"Bless me, back to the feckin'old days, is it?"

He hummed a verse of the Black Velvet Band and then feeling exhausted gave in, nodding to signal he would tell all. The woman snarled that wasn't what was needed, not at all. They'd had that. They wanted relevance and they wanted it there and then. He appeared to understand and spoke of taxi journeys and boxes of papers. In reality all he produced was a re-mix of the words they had given him, letting them fall in any order. It gave him some respite but in a short while they spotted this and two operatives moved to either side of Eamon's shoulders.

A different line was tried with questions concerning a bomb. He told them about the one he had taken students to see and then set to talking over the 'Troubles'. The big intel agent told him to,

"Shut the fuck up,"

which he did. With the woman interrogator pacing the room yet another line was begun with respect to a young journalist and her schoolteacher partner who lived not far from him. Eamon ad-libbed some interesting 'facts' regarding the latter, drawing upon his own teaching experience at the school she taught in. They soon understood there was nothing in this. There was finger pointing and digs in the back during questions regarding aeroplanes, atomic weapons and Japan. It was gobbledygook to him. He couldn't help himself.

"Ah it's the Inquisition, is it? and I thought you were all protestants."

There were other methods, other tools they could use to get at the truth. In a huddle all four operatives went through his notes and considered again his mental state. Eamon started mumbling over and over "Tokyo" and "Three", trying to fathom the occasion himself. He wanted out. Dribble dropped from a split lip as he hit on an old tactic. His interrogators had come to the obvious conclusion. He might have a background and been deemed an element in the case. He might have been thought of as easy pickings. Yet beyond elements of history from an expired century there wasn't anything there to be had. If anyone else thought there was more, they should go for it.

They conferred over the report they had to make. A weary Eamon leant back, his head sinking into his shoulders and his chin pressing down on his chest. His throat concertinaed into a series of tight folds. He was crimson and dark veins pulsated in his forehead. His breathing was deep but sporadic. One side of his body strained away from his seat. With the effort he wheezed a loud low groan. Buckling he gasped. Two operatives grabbed his shoulders, not to maul him but to stop him crumpling over sideways.

C30

Sam's station manager had said nothing to her about her work being forensically examined, so it had to be Coetzee's decision. She had been careful but the meeting with Coetzee made her step that up, going over everything she had done. She had taken her part in the research on Tokyo Three down plausible blind alleys. Those clever enough to spot it should conclude either this was other perpetrators or at worst that she had made mistakes. Hopefully there was no one smarter than that looking.

The biggest problem she had was physical not virtual - with the myriad computers and flash drives she had in her own place, if it was included in any search. Should she attempt to take them to a storage facility, she would be easily spotted. Ned agreed.

"Bloody oath, I'll look into this. Just don't let anyone in in the meantime."

Sam locked her doors and clicked the light off. There was loud knocking at her door. She stood there in the dark but her phone rang. She jabbed it onto silent and waited motionless. There was more knocking but it finally abated. Peeping through her door spyhole she saw a figure moving off who could have been anyone. Ned made his second attempt at a call.

"I've spoken to people. The investigation's been postponed. Coetzee's been told to look into something kicking off in China."

It was the next best thing to sending him there.

"Who made that happen? Was it Jessica?"

It was, Jessica.

"Two things Webo: stay flat out with all the safety measures I'm sure you've been working on..."

Sam wondered how he could possibly know of that. Although he knew her better than most, she doubted he grasped what he was giving her leave to do.

The investigation postponed Sam powered up her computers. Before long she would plunge a series of enter buttons in rapid succession. She was feeling a yogic calm yet when her phone rang, she jumped. It was Ned again. He would talk of delays and bright prospects somewhere down the line.

"Hold what you're doing. Need to see you now."

"Is it bad news?"

That he didn't respond directly was ominous.

"See you in our vegan resto. I won't keep you waiting."

He was already there.

When Ned showed Sam to her seat she clearly saw the outline of a gun in the material of his shoulder bag. It was obvious what she was staring at. Ned wanted it out of the way as quickly as possible.

"They carry guns too you know and knives and nerve poisons. You can't face them down with an app. Weapons have their place just like keyboards."

She was going to ask if he had used it.

"Don't ask, mate. I told you it's not allowed."

The best he could offer was that it was small calibre, nine millimetres – implying it was somehow not so lethal a weapon.

"I can't put up with this business anymore, Ned."

"Don't get cranky mate you're stronger than you think you are. You wouldn't have got where you are and stayed there with all your funny ways unless you were."

Sam looked at him and liked him more than ever. The compliment might have been back handed but sometimes that was the best stroke to play.

"It's getting hotter, Sam. That includes for you and me. Coetzee has been all over it. And when he's not his mates are. Safety first."

She said nothing while Ned studied her and did what he was good at – read the emotions in a face. She was committed. It would be no good telling her simply to quit on Billy.

"Like I said mate, carry on what you're doing, but

for both your sakes you have to forget about seeing her – for now."

Although this was delivered by a trusted someone who looked to soften blows it would not do, it was not enough.

"I've had it with this Ned. It's not in me anymore. The signs are I won't be able to continue much longer."

"You can carry on because you have to. I know you, you'll have made all sorts of preparations. You think those will protect us all, but they won't, not yet, not until I'm done. Cyber security is only what it says it is. I'm learning the hard way that people can operate outside of it. That's what'll happen until I'm done."

She shook her head.

"Give me time, it'll be apples. Think of the delay as being hit by an airbag. It hurts but the alternative is far worse."

Sam half swallowed a breath, coughed and reached for her inhaler. They sat in silence for minutes. She gave him no commitment and he was aware of that. Ned looked to the ceiling.

"I might not be able to see her, but I've got to make sure they won't be able to leer. No intel operative will be able to lay a filthy finger on her. Failing that everything will go up in smoke."

Ned knew she had a little bit of a temper and noted the doubt and anxiety had gone from her face. He nodded and his flat hands went up and down patting an invisible cushion. He hoped it would work better than words to get her to go softly and slowly.

"I know mate, knew you'd have everything in place. What I would say is wait and be careful, be careful."

All Sam could think was that she wasn't getting to see Billy when shortly before she was told it was going to be her paid job.

Ned broke more bad news to her.

"When you sanitise Billy…"

So, he had worked out that, that was what she was preparing,

"… there is a definite consequence you won't like." Whatever it was it couldn't compare to the blow she had already received.

"If you take Billy out of the line up, then the two oldsters will become the exclusive focus. Resources and personnel will be drawn down on them. You might make concerns over Billy disappear but neither of us can do that with Tokyo Three."

"But the whole thing is preposterous, above all the idea they can threaten national security."

"Your people don't like these two old fellers, so they'll invest in them."

"Why, why?"

"To start with and crazily they're both linked to Tokyo Three, of which they'll understand even less than us. 'Once information rings a bell, the bell cannot be unrung'." It was a piece of classic intel gibberish.

"Secondly there's bad initials here: IRA and CND connections. What's more this last one had a stab at Lord Mayor...of the Corporation of London – that's serious business. They don't take chances when there's that much at stake"

"Of what? They're clever enough over in Langley, surely. They'll spot these two are beside the point."

"Look another oldster found himself in the firing line – truly. It didn't turn out well for him."

"What did you do?"

"Not me, never. I liked the old feller… but there was no stopping it."

"Don't tell me, I don't want to hear. And I still don't get it, the Irishman was Sinn Fein, not IRA."

"Work it out, mate. Should somehow the Seppos decide to back off, for the Brits it's the precious City of London we're talking here. One of the oldsters threatened to take it over and mates of mates of the other one bombed the financial district a few decades back."
That was thirty years ago. Sam shook her head.

"It might not be as far in the past as Tokyo Three but it should be pensioned off. I can't see the threat."

"Mate it doesn't matter if it's got cataracts and a zimmer frame when it's a threat."

Didn't she ever think how weird it was that the City was a local authority and a private company at the same time? The old man's aim to be Lord Mayor couldn't be taken lightly. The city's defences had been holed before back in its 2017 elections.

"To add to that Coetzee's leading on it. He'll want to know what team is behind the oldsters. When they can't find it, they'll dig and dig."

"Into the flesh of the old men, I suppose."

Sam wanted to be told 'no' but Ned couldn't oblige.

"The oldsters are due some grief no matter what we do, it's happening…Lot's isn't under our control yet. So concentrate on Billy, help her all you want."

To which he added his mantra,

"Wait, wait and careful."

Sam's focus had to be Billy. If there was room left, she would track the two pensioners and do her best to soften their fate. She didn't like to think too much about what might happen with them.

In her home Sam's entire bank of computers remained on. She powered them down one by one until she got to the last two. If she had revealed all of her thinking to Ned, he would have vetoed it. She went to the unlocked cupboard and went through the flash drives carefully choosing one. Putting it into the port of one computer she uploaded its contents and then checked each component of it. When it came to it this would be devastating. It would have to wait but not forever. If Sam clicked there would be a whirr and file contents racing up and down. Coetzee would be awarded a promotion so big nobody would want to spurn. He was going to be very busy and very, very far away. He wouldn't so much be history as geography.

Sam sat back, satisfied with what she had planned.

Turning to the second computer she casually browsed recent weeks' footage of Billy. Had the screen shattered and sent shards into her flesh she couldn't have been more wounded. What she witnessed was Billy trembling and sobbing. In shaking hands Billy had the stained copy of the herald from her staffroom and was reading over and over of C.B.'s death. While a rapt Sam stared, Billy let it fall to the floor and clasped her head in her hands.

For Sam that was it. Delay was no longer an option. She jabbed the key on her computer and Coetzee was on his way – far away. Billy had been at the front of the waiting list long enough. She was going to her.

C31

It was almost a simple day out in London. Chas loved the Guildhall and that Eamon was invited was surprising but a plus. Chas had made a fresh enquiry concerning qualification to stand for Lord Mayor. He worried when Eamon was led off the minute they arrived at the Guildhall. He had no idea of what his friend was about to undergo. Chas himself had been shown into the City of London police headquarters there.

His interrogation wasn't anywhere near as intense as the one Eamon was having but it shook him, nevertheless. He was sat in a comfortable chair and there was never a physical threat. He was asked about his student days and demonstrations like the big one in Grosvenor Square. His response was open and honest, he believed in peace.

"Patriotism, loyalty what of those?"

A little bemused he was still able to tell them of course that was ok. The officers weren't sure where to go with that but asked him if he had an allegiance to another country. He knew they meant was he a traitor and he told them they were peeing up the wrong tree. After a mug of coffee another officer came into the room. He was senior but Chas thought he had a kind face. He demanded to know of his activity in CND.

"That was years ago. You probably know more about them than I do. Blimey I don't even know where their head office is today or who the big cheese is there."

"You can cut all your cockney bonhomie. It won't wash. Espionage is serious, you're facing prison."

The kindness had gone from the face.

Chas reasoned this man had to put on a show for those around him, so he decided he would play the game.

"A trial first might be an idea, wouldn't it? Time for a phone call to my silk."

No such person existed.

"Look sir, you're out of your depth. Under section 21 we can hold you for fourteen days and schedule 7 means you'll wait a long time for your phone call."

Chas had been trumped and knew it. Yet this was England and he had rights, on the other hand it was all so beyond him that maybe prison was a possibility.

"Is this connected with that Tokyo Three business?". He went on about his father, Palomares and his life in general. Twenty minutes of it and the recording was paused and then re-started. Questions moved on to his attempt at becoming Lord Mayor.

As it continued he was essentially being asked who or what was behind it.

"I live in Farringdon."

It meant nothing to his questioner.

"It's one of the ancient wards – qualifies me."

"That's it?"

"I'm a livery man – Worshipful Company of Hackney Carriage drivers."

This got no response.

"I'm qualified twice over. Should've been alderman, sheriff, Mayor in that order."

There was still no response. Chas went for it, giving him chapter and verse on the arcane set up.

A further twenty minutes passed and the recording was stopped permanently.

"You think that qualifies you?"

The smile was there again and so was the look of kindness.

"That and charity work. I had it all set up. I had a team of canvassers. Plenty of city workers' votes to be had, as well as residents."

Chas blethered on yet again. He said he knew the old school tie could be used to strangle someone like him but there were gaps in the set-up he could have squeezed through.

"Sir, you simply don't get it do you? What stopped you?"

"They thought I was bankrupt. Took me years to show it wasn't true."

The senior officer grasped what had been done to Chas. He wasn't going to continue much longer. He looked at his notes and sighed at what he had been obliged to ask Chas.

Tea was sent for. When it was finished a landline call was taken. It was involved. Once the receiver was put down Chas was asked.

"You say your friend is ill?"

"He's struggling."

Grimacing the senior officer forced himself to issue warnings that made sense to neither of them, about classified information. He also advised him,

"If I were you, sir, I'd keep a low profile from now on."

Chas knew he well meant. He ended with,

"Your friend needs you."

The tone was unmistakeable – it was urgent.

Chas rushed out following the brief directions he had been given. He went down sets of stairs and along corridors that were hard to follow. Eamon appeared limping down a corridor, a trickle of blood congealing under his nose and one eye covered with discoloured flesh. He was wearing different pants to those he came in. Chas rushed to support him.

"What on earth happened, Eamon, what happened? The police can't do this."

"They can too but this wasn't the police."

"Did you go to hospital?"

Eamon shook his battered head, he'd had enough of institutions and uniforms.

"I let 'em think I'm the feckin' lead. I'd never put you in it."

Chas knew that would be the case.

Boarding the tube Eamon said,

"Got to stick clear of Tokyo, Tokyo feckin' Three."

On this sort of thing Eamon had a sixth sense – maybe the only one surviving. Perhaps with the ride to and from

GCHQ his friend had a point right all along, although that didn't explain the City of London business. There had to be a complaint made about his treatment. At the very least someone had to be brought to book.

"Where'd your own trousers go?"

"Shat meself – works every time when the cops've got you…"

His interrogators had more or less made their minds up to release him.

"They wanted rid of me and the shit made their gobshite minds up for them."

It was after that they phoned the senior officer dealing with Chas.

"They got me some pants and I shot off before they changed their minds."

On a crowded underground train Eamon's interrogation echoed in his bruised ears. He repeatedly asked of no one,

"Bejasus is there three…three…three of 'em, Tokyos, three Tokyos? How many are there? Tokyo. Tokyo. Tokyo."

Chas didn't try to quieten Eamon. He knew it would be pointless. For the first time he seriously wondered if rather than aimless since losing his career, his friend had begun to lose his mind.

On Eamon went,

"Tokyo Three, Tokyo, Tokyo, Tokyo."

It didn't stop at his doorstep where his wife, dabbing his wounds with tissues, turned her glare to Chas. Her look meant,

"What have you done to him?"

Wasn't he supposed to look after him and he hadn't. He would steer the pair of them clear of Tokyo Three in future.

C32

"I can see what you've been up to. Careful, careful."

It was a text from Ned. Sam ignored it much the same as she intended to do with his phone calls. He couldn't prevent her doing what she was set on.

On her laptop while she journeyed she caught references to what the two old men were subjected to. Given time she might blunt some of it. The train she was on was drawing into Paddington.

A few miles from there Billy was taking stock. If grief loomed large in her life, so too did the need for caution. All the way home from school she was casting around looking for stalkers. After dropping off groceries to her old neighbours she scooted inside her own flat and checked not simply rooms but bigger cupboards. She wiped the history from her laptop and phone and rebooted every device she could. After an evening meal she made sure there was no one with their phone out opposite her flat gazing across at her front door. There might have been. She had to look out for herself. Going to her shed, she used her phone torch to scan the garden for intruders. That done she heaved out Ashley's blue and red cricket bag. She thought of chucking it after her partner's death but couldn't bring herself to. Dragging a cricket bat from the bag she stood it on guard by the radiator in her hallway. It could be snatched it up whenever she went to open the front door.

That evening a trembling finger was poised above the buzzer on Billy's front door. It could have been tethered to a parachute it descended so slowly on to the button. Clutched in the other hand of the woman standing there wasn't the usual games console but, a script and flowers. To herself Sam was muttering over and over the speech she had prepared. A newly fitted security light in the porch created a silhouette which seemed familiar to Billy. It was like that of a man who regularly stood opposite her flat with his hood up. Being on the doorstep represented a new level of threat.

Billy turned off the passage light. She was hardly visible while the character in the porch could be seen in total relief.

"One minute, one minute. Wait."

To Sam it sounded angry. Billy came wielding the cricket bat. This wasn't going to be a drive, a pull, a hook or a sweep. It would be uncoached but, if she could bring herself, someone was going to be knocked for six. Completely inexpert there was no telling where it might land, head, shoulder, neck, arm. Wherever it was, the blow would be heavy enough to disable. Second and third blows would follow. Billy's anger meant she would ring for the police and not rush to call for an ambulance.

Sam had moved back from the porch light, so she couldn't be made out so clearly.

"Step forward, I can't quite see you."

Back lit she looked the height of the door frame. Billy released a bolt and turned the key in the mortice lock. She kept the chain on and opened the door a few inches, but she couldn't make out the towering figure. Common sense should have meant she kept the door secure, but she had been hounded for long enough. She took the chain off.

Once the door opened the bat was drawn back shoulder height but the person on her doorstep wasn't what Billy anticipated at all. Her bat clunked to the floor, as she used both hands to push the door closed. When she slowly re-opened it halfway to peer, peering back at her was a woman. The bouquet bought in a nearby garage that Sam had been holding out was now compressed against a chest obscuring a lanyard there. The papers she had had mostly been dropped.

The silence there felt big enough to fill the vacuum between galaxies. For Sam it was vastly beyond awkward. Nothing happening wasn't anything like she prepared for. There was the extraordinary caution, the bat obviously meant as a weapon and then the person she had come to see appeared to be nowhere near as helpless as she had thought. For Billy the gender of the person on the doorstep was unexpected. She didn't resemble her intel stalkers and she was obviously wrong footed and dumbstruck. Artless, she looked no more threat than a trussed lamb. The papers she held had fallen to the floor and were being blown in different directions while she scrabbled to pick them up. Billy stifled a laugh and kicked the prostrate cricket bat over towards the radiator explaining,

"My partner's, she opened for the local ladies team." She looked at the flowers crushed on the woman's chest. Her giggles couldn't be stopped.

Sam had rehearsed responses to a variety of receptions, but she wasn't ready for what was taking place. She checked the notes she had managed to pick up. With new glasses on it dawned on her she might have to hold the lines up and read them out. Billy started to feel for this acutely awkward woman. She opened the door widely and asked,

"Are you delivering those for me?"

The flowers were thrust forward. There was no card with them.

"Oh, they're beautiful,"

she lied.

"Who are they from?"

Billy's best guess was that standing on her doorstep was an inept courier. A red-faced Sam replied,

"Uhmmm…they…they…they are for you,"

passing her a small box that looked like it could contain jewellery. The flowers were Ned's suggestion from a while back, the box was Sam's idea. She faltered over an explanation that it could detect any intel devices in the flat. Billy suspected she had misheard. Things like that surely weren't delivered especially by a courier like this one. She was fascinated, although with some misgivings.

Relieved of the flowers Sam held up her GCHQ lanyard. Only glancing at it Billy didn't quite make it out. Sam saw this, fiddled around with her notes and selected sections from them to read out. Billy's jaw had almost became fixed with all her grinning.

"I've, I've come to help you…You have been harassed…You have been spied on."
Billy was no longer grinning. Her cheeks drew in, her lips and forehead wrinkled. Any anticipation had gone, apprehension instead overwhelming Sam. She forced herself to hold the lanyard out closer to Billy's face and more in the light whilst fumbling with the other hand to get her inhaler. A coughing fit threatened. She lowered her voice and allowed her eyes to go where they were always more comfortable – gazing at the ground.

"I work at GCHQ…I, I…"
She came to a halt and searched through her notes.

"…I am an intel operative. Intelligence agents have been monitoring you in your home, at work, at leisure. It all comes down to a file called Tokyo Three."

To Billy Sam sounded and looked nothing like any spy she could conceive of. The woman there had a large kind face, skin as dark as a southern European's, a pick comb plunged into black hair, almost black irises surrounded by huge whites to her eyes, a white hooded top, black skirt and a black and white rucksack. She was more panda than predator. There was surely no threat here. Nevertheless, what this woman was saying was serious. Sam was referring to elements from a very dark period in her life that was still far from over. Billy tried to help her by prompting,

"So it is this Tokyo Three riddle?... All the horrible prying and spying."
Sam nodded.

"Do you say you're involved?"
Sam ceased staring at the floor, closed her eyes and nodded again. It was hopeless.

"I, I know it's very wrong. I, I have only ever wanted to help…Should I leave?"

When Sam readied to go Billy examined all six foot of someone she struggled to believe was a serious secret intelligence agent. Yet this woman was revealing things an agent alone could know. On the other hand, by doing that she wasn't being secret, she was being the exact opposite.

Billy beckoned Sam forward so she could look at her fully in the porch light. Sam nearly tripped and had to use the door to steady herself. Doing so she came within six tantalising inches of the young teacher. Involuntarily leaning in to put a hand on the doorframe the GCHQ worker's breath warmed an ear on the side of Billy's head and trickled down her neck.

"I, I am based in GCHQ, others are in MI5."

"You mean spies, don't you. I've been spied on."

"You've been treated badly. I, I, I want to help you… you have to believe me."

Sam said it knowing she didn't have to believe her at all. Even less did she have any reason to trust her.

"I'm, I'm on your side."

Billy stared. Sam turned towards an empty street, preparing to go, forlornly muttering,

"At least I want to be."

During this time Sam had never given Billy eye contact.

"Look me in the face, please and tell me honestly. Are you a spy?"

She gazed into Billy's eyes. It was a half-formed thought. She was struggling for words but some forced themselves out albeit in a whisper,

"Be careful with those eyes."

It was meant to be to herself, but Billy clearly caught it.

Sam despaired. It was a stupid aside when what she needed was to explain. The trouble was paragraphs of persuasion were needed, not scrambled lines from what was left of her notes. What idiocy had made her think this might work? Tumbling back from the threshold to go, there was a tug. She had done it many times, snagged her sleeve on the door handle.

C33

Sam was wrong, she hadn't snagged her sleeve. Billy was intrigued by the cold caller on her doorstep and had grabbed her arm.

"You can't leave yet, please. You owe me more than that. First of all, what's your name? I have to know all you know."

"Samantha."

Sam stalled, grimaced and fingered her lanyard while staring over Billy's shoulder and saying,

"I am pretty well aware of everything that has been done to you."

"Have you been involved in the stalking? Have you been in my flat poking around?"

"No, never. Since I, I saw what was going on I've done my best to stop it."

"Do you know what happened to the old editor and Ashley?"

"Not right now but I can find out."

It would be a long time before she delved into what truly happened to either of them. She drew out the laptop from her rucksack and held it up.

"Most of my work is on this. I've used it and worn out others to block every intrusion into your private life that I can."

She passed the machine to Billy as though it was proof of her efforts.

"I work at GCHQ", she repeated,

"and I've been trying to help. You must have noticed your phone and laptop have stopped misbehaving so much. Also there's been less leering from across the road, although I, I had help with that."

Billy paused to think this over while Sam shifted from foot to foot. As far as she could tell this was mostly accurate – she was never quite sure about who was and was not a stalker. If Sam had done this for her, how had she managed it when she was immersed in it herself and surrounded by agents?

"You must be clever, very, to have got away with it."

Sam liked to be thought clever – it was the only positive thing about herself she had ever heard. That said she wasn't sure how to respond to this.

"So have you got away with it, then?"

In that moment Sam knew she believed her. She thought she also detected some concern for herself.

"There is still the odd issue. th…things crop up. th..things will need to be done."

Saying this she nodded towards a phone Billy had out. When it was passed to her, her thumbs were a blur as digits, letters and a variety of characters flashed up in long combinations. In the process, information and images Billy thought were deleted appeared and left the screen.

A drizzle began. She indicated Sam should wait a few feet further into the building whilst she fetched her own laptop with which Sam got the same results. Billy was appalled because she had very recently bought new devices.

"Now…it's, it's safe, you're safer up to a degree."

Their fingertips touched lightly when the laptop was passed back.

"So, they don't remain safe, regardless of what I do now."

"They tend not to."

"Will they need to be fixed constantly?" Sam nodded.

"I'm, I'm afraid they're best replaced regularly."

"On a teacher's wage?"

"Use this phone until I say otherwise," Sam said, passing Billy one she had prepared herself.

"I'll load up all you need. If, if I had time I could change the hard drive on your laptop,"

she added rummaging in her rucksack, checking for possible candidates.

By this stage the pair were standing deep in the

passageway of Billy's home.

"I believe you, I think. It all makes sense insofar as anything in that Tokyo Three business does. I hardly understand it at all."

Billy trained her eyes on the lanyard which was easier to see in the passage light. She asked to see additional identification. There was more rummaging in the rucksack, followed by Sam spilling a wadge consisting of bank cards, a driving licence, some GCHQ headed papers and her phone. She reddened. Gagged and bound by that moment she couldn't manage a word.

"Oh Samantha,"

Billy giggled once more and that eased Sam. Billy bent to pick the papers up in the instant Sam was attempting to do the same. Their eyes met once more across a few inches. Sam went an even deeper crimson and Billy laughed loudly. She went through a pretence of scrutinising the bits and pieces that were picked up. She was close to making her mind up about this woman. Sam passed her her own phone giving her the code so she could scroll through everything. Immediately she regretted it. Lit up on screen was the picture of Billy that had been there from when she initially became aware of her.

"I, I, I'm, I'm so sorry, that's from earlier. That apart I have made sure that everything that can be deleted has been."

Of course, that didn't explain it and they both knew it. Billy looked Sam up and down and was certain she wasn't the stuff threats were made of. In fact she had done her best to put a stop to the internet assault on her.

Throughout the conversation Billy had been edging towards her lounge. Sam was obliged to follow in order for it to continue. Billy passed back the various items she had picked up. As the phone was parted with, their fingers touched a second time. Hers curled closing on Sam's hand as though an electric current was running through it.

"So, you're a sort of cyberbnaut, my cybernaut."

"I, I can try to be, yes."

"But you're in Cheltenham and the stalkers are here. You say they'll come back."

"I'm, we're trying to prevent that. I have a friend"

"No guarantees, though?"

Both women were startled when a figure came straight through the open door. The man stepped back to rat-a-tat on the door knocker. Billy laughed yet once more, took a couple of pounds from her pocket for a tip and swapped them for a Fiorentina pizza.

"It's getting late. This is too big for one person. Hungry?"

It had meat in, but Sam ate a slice and shared a full bottle of wine with Billy. The table talk was of investigations, surveillance and Tokyo Three. Sam stood. She had made contact and it had gone far better than things like this normally did. It was late and she would miss the last train if she didn't hurry.

"Do you have time to change that hard drive on my laptop now?"

She could see Sam was considering it. She would do it and then work out how to get back to Cheltenham afterwards.

"Couldn't you stay until tomorrow? There's a convertible my partner used to sleep on from time to time."

When she was nervous Sam didn't catch everything clearly. She knew she had been spoken to but wasn't sure what was said. She fondled the games console in her rucksack fighting off the urge to look downwards and mumble to herself. It occurred to her it would be easy to get online and grant herself annual leave. There was little danger.

"It is possible I could station myself locally for the now. Would that help?"

Billy thought the response was odd, but this woman was out of the ordinary.

"I would love that. Please, please do it."

And then Sam was stranded, she didn't know the area and

anyway it was past the time when people could normally book into hotels. She spoke into her phone, asking for a room locally. Billy forced the phone down.

"Did you not see me pointing, silly. Did you not hear me?"

She pointed again – at the convertible in the lounge. Sam thought for a minute and did understand what she had said. It had gone in, gone deeper and was now surfacing.

"My partner often slept there. Would you do this for me?"

Sam liked the idea it was a place for her partner.

The two young women briefly breakfasted beside each other. One left for work while the other went in search of a suitable hard drive, having found she had none which could be used. Before she left, Billy pleaded with Sam to stay until the evening so she could go over the adapted laptop with her. Stepping out of a store where she bought the hard drive Sam's phone rang. It was Ned on a Face Time call.

"You got my text didn't you, I know you did. Mate you blanked me."

So he was indeed somehow tracking her - still. She thought she had made that impossible.

"I see you did the deed mate. Straight to the pool room, eh?"

Her whole purpose was to protect Billy from smutty intrusions. Being allowed to stay that night was for precaution, not romance.

"Don't you have someone you need to do the deed with yourself, rather than pestering me about it?

His look said he did. She meant the older woman she had seen him with. It was a guess. She made herself clear.

"Jessica, isn't it? You have, haven't you?"

"It's not like that. She's a mature lady…"

Sam couldn't resist coming straight out with a question regarding the older woman's diplomatic status.

"Yep, can park her car anywhere. Never mind

that…Look my text concerned Coetzee."

"You saw where I sent him?"

"He was never gonna be left exposed in South Africa. He's dangerous, he knows people."

"Where is he then?"

"Not in the U.K. but to be honest we're not sure."
So, she had been partly successful, no more.

"Whichever Outback he's in my instinct is it won't work for long and he'll come back double. …Anyway, I'm ringing with good news."
After an uncomfortable night Sam's estimation of the significance of sleeping on the convertible had dipped. She could do with good news.

"You jumped the gun, but I don't blame you."
That was just as well.

"With Coetzee on his travels I'm doing a uey. You've got the all-clear. Alright I'm a little tardy but I've withdrawn opos from the site, so you can make hey-ho. I'll keep an eye out."
Great news though it was she was nettled by his keeping an eye on her.

"Why haven't you stopped scrutinising Billy's flat?"

"It's never over until it's over. The Seppos haven't given up on this. I've filed reports claiming all devices are down."
He was covering for her, there could be no denying that. He had helped make things possible. She beamed thanks at him.

"Look mate we're besties. That's everything. Nothing trumps that."

He couldn't control everything, that she understood. He was generally belated and made a lot of promises, she had worked that out. But she could trust him, always.

C34

Time had gone by, it was the beginning of March and Sam was still sleeping on the convertible. Billy appeared content with that and her guest didn't know what scope she had there, other than to ward off intel threats. It irked that she was available whilst Billy was preoccupied with work. She couldn't think of a way of raising the subject of them being together. How she took that further, she really didn't know. Two weekends had been taken up first by in-service training and then team building. Sam told herself if she could confront Billy on her doorstep then she must have it within herself to make her feelings plain. Wherever that was though, she struggled to find it.

On the Monday after the teambuilding Ned was adamant Sam met him in the internet pub they had used previously. Her work online during this time had intel bamboozled but apparently not entirely. There had been rumblings at the Doughnut although Ned had managed to keep her out of the picture at Millbank. When Coetzee was able to get back to deal with his favoured concerns, him and her, it might be different, Sam was told. She knew what was coming next. The pattern was clear. Back off and leave it alone. But she wasn't having it.

"Look at times mate, there's little else other than me between you and consequences. Dead set…there's a tenacity with Tokyo Three I don't get. It's up and down like a dunny seat."

Alright it was his usual style but how could he speak so lightly when he knew how she felt? Bumbling though she knew she was with relationships she had imagined she was going somehow to progress from the convertible to the bedroom. It was going far more slowly than she hoped but she still expected it to happen. A no-no from him, caution about intel monitoring, any delay wasn't acceptable. She had had it with the whole abject intel business. She didn't care about Coetzee. Should he fail to force her out, she could well go anyway. It wouldn't stop her from protecting Billy.

Ned's phone was nagging away during the entire time. It had started before he entered the pub. From his manner it was clear he already had a grasp of what was being relayed. He flicked to answer phone. Texts kept buzzing and he kept glancing at them. There couldn't have been more buzzing if the phone was dripping with nectar. She watched him constantly checking messages and was becoming irritated. She would leave the second he began with his,

"Time's up for the moment,"

and counselling caution. And then it began.

"Maybe we have to wipe the sleep from our eyes."

He would offer soft words and some vague pie in the sky. Quite simply, she wouldn't have it.

Another call came in which he had to take. At the end of that call he stood up and took others, pacing up and down. It wasn't the usual Ned. He constantly looked over at her then away, then skyward. He was shaking his head, waving his arms.

"Fuck me dead, fuck me dead. Any time I'm told? Orders…Ok, whatever."

That call finished, he immediately started another, but in a gentler tone,

"What are we going to do? You're tough, but you are defo vulnerable. This is dangerous, deadly…Ok, ok ring me back, promise."

Sam was sure she could hear an older woman's voice and knew it must be Jessica. No longer on the phone, Ned mused aloud.

"Orders and protocol. She'll insist on being seen to follow them. No giving this a swerve." Ned's head was in his hands, so it had to be grave. It sounded like any manoeuvring needed to stop. Sam went to him to ask if he was alright, but he strode quickly off with another call.

"That big? It's high noon then. fuck me dead, fuck me dead."

It was difficult for him to take in the reports he was getting. He accelerated back and forth as he read texts non-stop. He walked past Sam one way and then the other repeatedly. He began drumming his fingers on his phone keys, reading the immediate responses he got back. He walked off outside shouting, mostly for clarification and for the speaker to be louder. After far too long for Sam, he came back ending the calls and placing the phone to one side where it continued to buzz. He breathed in and then out and then he looked at her inscrutably. She waited but he said nothing.

"Bad news?"

He took up his phone, glanced at the screen and put the phone on silent.

"All the same message,"

he explained. She repeated,

"Bad news?"

"For who mate?"

It sounded harsh. He carried on,

"Bad for pretty well everybody. It was a slow mo' catastrophe and now it's gone into overdrive. It's been brewing longer than a bottle of Snake Venom. People are dying…A total shit show's happening."

He had her attention.

"You heard of Hubee?"

which was how he pronounced it. She shook her head.

"It's 'our doorstep' for Aussies, the far east to pommes."
He sounded exhausted. Normally she enjoyed riddles but was worried about him as well as about what he was going to impart.

"It's a province in the PRC, China. Strewth, I know some won't, but you've got to feel for sorry for them."

"Please talk sense, Ned. What does it mean to Billy?"

"Intel is rammed with it, has been for a couple of weeks. It's here, been here for a while. Now they're admitting it."

"Ned, please, what are you saying?"

"It's going off like a frog in a sock. Haven't you spotted any of it online?"
She hadn't caught one tiny bit. She went to implore him to tell her what was going on, but up went Ned's flat palm, whilst he took a call. When that finished, he checked messages.

"It's ballooning. For intel there'll be little else barring terrorists on the streets with automatics."

No matter what it was, she wasn't going to give upon Billy.

"Look think Sars on a skateboard, think Spanish Flu gone hypersonic, fuckin' hell think of the black death, mate."

"The virus? But I heard it's thousands of miles away."

"Nothing's thousands of miles away today. It's been here for a while. They were warned, they were fucking warned… I'm getting a drink."

Ned brought back double shots for the pair of them, breathed in and said,

"It's a pandemic and it's here."
She looked at his shoulder bag. His raised voice, the

striding up and down, his entire manner, Dishlicker had ducked down cowering.

"So, it's not just me. Now you have someone to worry for too?"

She meant Jessica. He didn't deny it. They sipped their drinks to the end. Next Sam brought back more double shots. Conversation lapsed until Ned said,

"They'll announce it soon. It'll be like white crosses on doors and hand bells ringing 'bring out your dead'."

He smiled.

"Yet everybody else's shit is your fertiliser. Nobody'll be looking at you and your Dorothy."

There would be little intel resources spent on Billy, let alone Sam.

"You're free to sort out whatever you want to. Nobody'll be watching you. Talk is of working from home."

With a computer that could mean anywhere.

"I'm being recalled to Straya. It's all hands on deck in the lucky country. Only time you'll see me is on your mobile. A few days and I'll be gone – which leaves me with some big probs."

He thought Dishlicker wouldn't cope with quarantine. Sam volunteered to take her. There was nothing to be gained by Ned saying his and Jessica's parting wasn't resolvable. Going would mean leaving her behind and she was more susceptible than most.

Sam looked at him straight on and held her gaze. It wasn't the carefree unflappable Antipodean she knew. His face screwed up and he looked to the side. He turned back with a hard fought for smile. He had been helping her, yet all the while he had concerns of his own - which had become enormous.

"For once…"
she was going to say,

"it will be me helping you. I absolutely promise,"
but her voice broke. Ned smiled.

"C'mon it's alright to give me a hug princess. Let's go get blind."
He was drinking a farewell. But she didn't believe she was.

That night Billy came in late after another evening meeting at school. It had been a long day and Sam had fallen asleep on the convertible. Billy had no more than enough energy to brush her teeth and flop on her bed. Sam remained sleeping on the settee a couple of weeks later when thousands were dead and the scale of the pandemic had become known.

C35

During the first lockdown Eamon and Chas thwarted the rules to walk together by pretending to shop. Siobhan insisted it was necessary to save her husband's life because she would kill him otherwise. It wasn't the walks, nevertheless, that led an exposed Eamon to breath in at the wrong time in the wrong place. This came in early summer after the lockdown ended. It was at a clinic where he was being assessed.

Eamon's assessment wasn't asked for by himself or by his wife or by his best friend. It came from someone who wasn't a relative and not medical. The person who commissioned this wasn't concerned for his wellbeing. Rather he was checking that interrogators hadn't gone too easy on him and that he wasn't masquerading as a cretin.

At the clinic there was none of the queuing or waiting that might normally be expected. Without notice Eamon was collected in what looked like a hospital vehicle. He and his wife were told there was an important appointment he had to keep. There was a pandemic and it was continuing and special measures were being taken everywhere. Siobhan assumed it had been arranged by their G.P. and Eamon had forgotten to mention it. Eamon also wondered. She wasn't allowed to accompany him but was at least told where it was.

He was whisked off to a clinic in the Bayswater Road. It should have had a commemorative plaque but if it had he would have refused to enter the building. It was on the spot or thereabouts of a former annexe of the Imperial Order of Daughters of the Empire, a Great War military hospital. He was brought there to see a specially commissioned geriatric neurologist. The consultant leaned forward breathing out at the very second Eamon was breathing in. He cringed, the breath was bad, but it was more toxic than he could have imagined.

Normally Eamon would have played the fool in a session he might see as an impertinence. Instead, he took it seriously, neither dressing up or down his condition. He insisted on the verdict. He wanted to know. Initially the assessment was his cognitive function was definitely damaged. The consultant was finished and wanted his patient to exit.

Eamon instead plagued him with what degree of damage was involved and what the cause was. The answer was all technical ifs and buts which Eamon had no time for. To him it was mealy mouthed evasion. Pushed the consultant drew out a small box with a hypodermic and attempted to humour Eamon with a blood test. Then Eamon did begin to play the fool with the man:

"Have you got a scalpel there? D'yous want me feckin' blood? I'll slash me wrist and bleed out right now." If there was a scalpel there, the last thing the consultant would do was put it in this patient's hands. Eamon grabbed his notes, saw the military symbol at the top and threw them to the tiled floor.

The performance led to a revised assessment that Eamon's condition was worse than the intelligence service's report suggested. Despite this the consultant covered himself by echoing others' remarks that this did not necessarily mean he couldn't be a source of information when handled correctly.

Eamon was convinced the evasion he detected from the consultant mean the worst. He rang Chas who didn't complain at the 'schlep' to west London. Being greeted fondly by his wife and best friend lifted him. Their company even outshone the pleasure he got from having tormented the neurologist.

Thirty-six hours after what Eamon termed his 'release', the consultant tested positive for Covid.

The same senior intel operative who ordered Eamon's assessment also sanctioned a raid. There were those who had followed the case and believed attention on the pair of pensioners was a waste of time and resources. That could have been the end of it. However, Coetzee believed differently. Whether abroad or in the U.K. he wouldn't let this one go. He saw no reason to make allowances for their age or Eamon's condition. He wanted no stone unturned. That Eamon had messed himself under interrogation sounded to Coetzee like an old republican tactic.

The timing meant the aged Irish couple didn't witness their home being ransacked. It took place in tandem with the end of the assessment. Whilst Siobhan and Chas were arriving outside the private clinic Eamon was held in, a monster of a uniformed man was wielding an 'Enforcer' battering ram. He smashed the door of their home, tearing off a hinge, prising some of its frame from the brickwork. More police officers than could be fitted into the passageway at one time raced in screaming and shouting. Guns, laser sights and flashlights searched every nook and cranny in every room before the job proper could begin.

Nothing beyond the obvious was found in the gutted furniture or the demolished kitchen cupboards. Neither was there anything, aside from springs and stuffing, in the mattresses and nothing apart from water in the smashed porcelain of the toilet. Nor was there anything of interest under the carpet or the floorboards beneath it. Between the lath and plaster of the walls all there was was a gap. There were several copies of Clann Eireann magazines going mouldy in the loft, but they were from decades gone by.

On the drive home Chas searched for positives. He came up with things he had read about chocolate and purple veg that were good for the brain. It was good company so Eamon tried to save his thoughts for himself, but he couldn't keep it up. He started with saying the single diet he wanted was, "feckin' hemlock" and the only exercise was "feckin' walking the plank, or swinging from a feckin' noose". It went on right up to arriving outside the ransacked home. Siobhan had been concentrating on quietening him, so she wasn't looking out of the window. There was no room outside their house, so Chas had to pull over across the road.

When he parked, Siobhan took out her front door keys, thanked Chas, "as always" and chided Eamon to get his daft self indoors. Having exited the car, she waved to a departing Chas whose attention was on the road.

Siobhan hooked her arm in her husband's, glanced over and looked again. Chas must have brought them to the wrong house. It must be further down the road, left or right. Two police officers stood outside. Neighbours were on their doorsteps. Then she saw it was her curtains which were half torn, half down. Then she saw the front door leaning from its remaining hinge. Then she saw a set of drawers upside down in her hallway with one leg broken. The Waterford crystal that had been there lay smashed on the hallway tiles. She walked slowly and then dashed. At the beginning she thought it was the scene of a chaotic burglary. She screamed in the face of one of the officers. Gentle hands gripped her pulling her away while the other police officer drew his baton.

"Shush, shush, soft colleen. Nothing to be done here,"

Eamon wasn't so far gone that he couldn't read this. He hushed into his wife's ear, signalling to the police officers at the same time, that there would be no trouble. Siobhan in a fit of confusion wanted to call the police. Eamon told her to look around, she would end up in a cell, they both would, if she wasn't careful. She was outraged and was prepared to go there.

"You'll get nothing from a cell, darling woman."

"Surely I'll get a phone call and a solicitor."

"Likely you'll get something far worse. Either way you'll not be changing this."

It was reflex. This wasn't unfamiliar territory and Eamon knew exactly how to traverse it.

"Ring my old mate and get him back. He'll fetch us and calm us."

Within minutes of the call Chas was there to support them from the scene and take them to his house. The intention was they stay there until their own was made liveable. Chas was upbeat with them. Dealing with the insurance shouldn't be too hard, he would help them. He knew of terrific builders. What's more he already had it in mind to contact the authorities over Eamon's treatment at the Guild Hall.

One way and another it wasn't going to be an easy period, nevertheless. Anne thought Siobhan was a terrible prude and Siobhan thought her to be Godless and loose. A further reason, the major one, was that the move caused some disorientation in Eamon. Certainly, he struggled in finding the bathroom at night. Wheezing and gasping he did manage to find it the evening he was to be carted off to a hospital, having collapsed by the toilet. As they watched the ambulance leave with its lights flashing, the hugs the two wives gave each other were genuine.

C36

For a handful Covid meant making a fortune, for far, far more it meant hardship or tragedy. For Ned, helped by Sam, it was when he was promoted and saved from transportation. She created a record of performance evaluations, competence metrics, training programs, all excelled in, all tied to a role in the U.K. 'Promo', as he himself said, was nailed on.

"Bosses need pairs of sunnies, they think the sun is shining so brightly out of my bum hole."

For Billy and Sam it could have been a time to get close up and personal. Yet it wasn't working out that way. Sam remained sleeping on the settee. Billy thought that might be her preference. She liked Sam – a lot. She was quirky, bright and funny. She had invited her into her home to stay. Despite that Sam gave no sign of realising she was attracted to her – which should have been plain. Billy couldn't read her at all. There was no telling whether or not she was pleased, happy or unhappy. Sam gave little eye contact and spoke politely instead of warmly. At times she would simply sit down and fiddle with her games console. It was difficult to know if she saw herself in the flat solely as a guardian or wanted more than that. The end of lockdown had come. She guessed this meant Sam would be recalled to GCHQ at some point or take herself off there anyway.

Billy recognised things had to be moved on before they came to a complete halt. It was difficult because Sam was so different.

"Are you comfortable sleeping there, Sam?"
she asked. An answer that suggested anything less than 'yes' should have meant she could take an initiative.

"It's ok,"
was the reply. With advance warning Sam might have been able to give Billy a response that helped them both. In fact Billy couldn't tell if she was talking of being in the flat generally or spending nights on the convertible. It wasn't a response she could put to use. There was no sign of warmth

from Sam. Trying to cope Billy stayed out more. One vivid night a drunken Billy dreamed of Sam in her bedroom, dreaming she crept to her bedside and kissed her. Waking was excruciating. She couldn't take much more of it.

For Sam this was a period of bemusement compounded by frustration. The job she had told herself she wanted to do was done. Billy had been put in the picture and wasn't being spied on, although the pandemic might have seen to that anyway. In her heart of hearts she had hoped there would be a payback that was immense, that being Billy's champion might bring an embrace. Billy's yearning for her wasn't grasped by her at all. She took to the internet for help, went online to agony aunt sites and others. Nothing was like the situation she was in. There was porn that leapt to the sexual act without seduction. What it missed was precisely what she needed. Spring was over and nature had fulfilled itself everywhere except where she was. She didn't know where to turn. She was clueless. In not so many words she guessed her best hope was to be patient and follow any lead Billy gave. Should she attempt romance and stumbled to failure, it would be something she couldn't face. Sleeping feet from Billy was far better than that. If that was all there was, she would take it. She would stay with Billy as long as it took. In the absence of anything better the passage of time and the hope of good fortune were her sole strategy.

Sam did her intel job proficiently but with less enthusiasm than ever. All that was on her mind was Billy and it warped her judgement at times. There was a narrow miss. A phased re-opening of schools sent Billy back to work. Sam went and laid on her bed holding her dressing gown to her face. It became a routine. On one day in particular she fell asleep and woke up when Billy was coming through the front door. She mumbled an excuse about checking security which seemed odd, but Billy had become used to odd, quite liked it.

Unfulfillment climaxed in Sam losing control

completely. Billy came home late, drunk after a work do. It was the night she dreamt Sam came to her bedroom. She kicked off her shoes and clattered her way through the bedroom door to plunge on to the mattress and lay there on her back without the slightest movement. Sam was concerned and thought she should cover her over. Entering the room she gazed at her shoulders, her hips and buttocks and her the legs. She gazed further at her feet and toes.

"Exquisite,"

she whispered. She ached with it.

Ten minutes more and she remained gazing. Billy's eyelids were rapidly fluttering. Time standing there was no time at all. Nothing would ever be enough, but Sam knew she had to leave the room. She had come there to put bedclothes over Billy, so she did. With the last tucking in she was caressing hair from the side of her face when she suddenly lurched to kiss Billy on the lips. It was long, too long and Billy stirred. Sam jumped backwards as she opened her eyes. She was out of Billy's field of vision. Registering little, Billy closed her eyes again. Sam shot out of the room and went to the convertible for her breathing to slowly shallow out.

The kiss shocked Sam. Spontaneity avoided her, she was no good at it. Although it was late she rang Ned. She wouldn't regret it if he started in on 'doing the deed' – it was the purpose of her call. He on the other hand understood he wasn't to raise it in that way anymore. She had to tell him,

"Ned the deed's not been done – I, I don't know how to do it."

"Webo you think too much, you're making it too complicated."

That rang true.

"It's the twenty-first century mate, not Pride and Prejudice. Dive in or bail out. Christ I've seen lime scale build up quicker."

She would never bail out but hadn't a clue how to dive in.

"Don't be a galah. Alright she's a looker, but you're

not so bad yourself. You don't ask someone to a sleep over in your place without liking them – a lot…When you're still there weeks later, the only thing that's left's is ding dong and I don't mean wedding bells…she wants you."
It made sense.

"Look, one of the biggest turnoffs is when someone doesn't react. Carry on like this and you'll lose her. You probably won't want to hear this but there's a tactic…."
Oh, she wanted to hear it, alright.

"Get one of those deliveries – make it special for her and then blow the froth off as many cans as you can or vino, whatever – but not so much that it makes you chunder."

It was a long time since she and Billy had had a drink together and meals were eaten off trays in front of screens, often at separate times. They spent the bulk of the evenings vastly apart in different regions of the world wide web. As things stood she had little to lose other than the backache the convertible gave her.

Ned launched into a pep talk finishing with,

"Two things. The first one is difficult for you. Give her plenty of eye contact - you've got nice eyes you know. The second one is easy, be yourself and it's a winner, you're funny."

"Am I?"

"You don't mean to be, but that doesn't matter. With that and the meal you'll be home and wet."

Sam spent most of early evening the following day listening for the delivery. She heard steps up the path and before the courier could knock, she rushed to the door, putting her finger to her lips. It was the same story with the flowers.

Billy was doing her best to complete her school work for the evening, get it out of the way. It was unfinished when at eight o'clock she rushed from her bedroom. She was going to bring matters to a head. Her dream of the previous night meant she couldn't eat breakfast or lunch. Going to the lounge the smell of food made her hungry and her head swim. Supposing it was in the microwave she was stunned to see the table. On it was a heavily scented arrangement of flowers with place settings which she hadn't seen for a long while. There was also a small tray of chocolates. Wine was in an ice bucket with a white serviette draped on it. There was also what was intended to be a decorative salad starter which was a little dishevelled. She grinned and then beamed. The oven light glowed. Billy breathed in the fragrances so hard her light headedness almost turned to giddiness. She was dazzled. Classical music she guessed was meant to be romantic played, although a little too loudly. She dimmed the lighting. Laughing, she knew she was aroused. Sam saw the corrections Billy made and feared the evening was already in decline.

Prior to eating Sam raised a glass to belatedly toast the end of lockdown. Billy didn't quite shout, "amen, to that", but she tilted her head back and the glass almost vertical. Sam rehearsed more toasts which were difficult to refuse; nurses, then doctors, then the NHS. She would have added keyworkers, but the bottle was empty. The starters were yet to be touched. Sam fetched a second bottle knocking it against the fridge door, but Billy smiled and put her hand up to indicate no more toasting was viable. Once more, Sam wondered if she was wrecking the evening. Two courses down, in which neither diner ate much and Sam tabled a boutique ice cream they both gorged on. A dob of it lodged below her lip. She was mortified when Billy leant forward to coax it back into her mouth.

Thus far the evening had followed, roughly, the steps of a check list in Sam's head. She had told Ned no advice beyond this point was needed. But once the food was finished, she was at a loss. She couldn't leap over the table at Billy and walking round it to be beside her would be too clumsy, too obvious. The second bottle was sipped and the chat relaxed into exchanges about work. Billy initiated it, believing it could ease them into confidence in their relationship. Sam rued that this sort of talk was hardly going to lead to seduction. It was getting late for a teacher who had to work in the morning. Maybe this evening would simply be an increment in their friendship.

The flat mates cleared up and did the washing up together. It was domestic, not romantic. Sam looked at the wine left in the second bottle and readied to flush it down the sink. Billy enquired,

"What are we going to do with you Sam?"

It was a question Sam asked herself all the time.

"Sit,"

Billy told her laughing and patting the bed-settee for Sam to sit down beside her. She did it so heavily she see-sawed Billy into the air an inch or so. Once Sam was seated Billy got up and poured the remaining wine. They held the glasses up and chinked them.

"To us,"

said Billy. Neither of them drunk it. The wine had been out of the ice bucket too long and the temperature spoiled it. For Sam it was a metaphor for the entire occasion, tepid and unfinished.

"Oh Sam, thank you for this evening it was so nice."

'Nice'? Really? It had been that dull. This was worse than Sam feared. It wasn't a step anywhere other than towards a night of backache on the convertible once more. Billy yawned,

"It's getting late…"

Sam knew it was past Billy's bedtime. What could she do, what could she say? She had no hope of a liaison but an evening like the one she laboured over ought surely to have produced something. Whole minutes of nothing were going by. Billy sat static. Soon she would rise, bringing the evening to the poorest end. Any other attempts would have this night as their template.

Billy shifted on the settee. She put her hand down on the cushion next to Sam looking ready to use it to lever herself up in the direction of a night's sleep. Sam saw her gentle smile and despaired. Ned had badgered her to take forthright action.

"You're not giving yourself a fair shake of the sauce bottle. It's love, have a go, ya mug."

The last phrase he had used over and over. That sort of thing might have worked for him....

It wasn't spoken. Nor was it a whisper, a shout, or a scream. The lid of a voice box was sprung, jaws wrenched open and lips prised apart. The crazy thing was that the words that followed had not only been Ned's first to Sam but ones which were instantly rebutted.

"Any chance of a goodnight kiss darling?"

Billy looked astonished and then guffawed. It was easily the worst line she had ever been approached with, delivered in the worst way. No technology exists to cap a volcano. If it did Sam would have looked to it to avoid the eruption surely coming. She prepared for emotional annihilation. Billy's smile disappeared as she responded,

"A kiss?..."

Sam couldn't bring herself to repeat it, but Billy could.

"A kiss...goodnight? Just goodnight? The meal, the flowers. Surely you mean you want to sleep with me, don't you?"

Could that be the response Ned usually got? Whether or not it was she didn't know what to say. She lowered her head and then lifted it to look Billy in the eye.

"No..."

Billy's smile, worn most of the evening dropped. She wasn't expecting this.

"You don't want to sleep with me?"

"No...I, I want to wake up beside you."

Billy's hand pressed into the cushion beside Sam. She leant across, kissed her and waited to be kissed back. There was a pause, so she pressed a further kiss on Sam. Sam finally kissed her back. That night the convertible settee was unused. In the middle of the night Sam woke, looked at

Billy and believed no software, no computer, however powerful, could begin to count her lucky stars.

C37

"They rang me…told me I've got to prepare to lose Eamon."

It was in the middle of a temperate Autumn night and Siobhan was calling Chas.

"I'm allowed a visit, please come with me."

He didn't need to be asked twice. There was a problem with his black cab licence, so he drove in an old Vauxhall whose gear box housing rattled when he sped. The passenger side door couldn't be operated from outside, so he sprung it open. A weeping Siobhan had to be helped into the car. She urged him to put his foot down in spite of there being surprisingly heavy traffic. He didn't need to be asked. Speed cameras flashed and clicked while Chas raced by. The car leapt up and bounced back down as traffic calmers were ignored. The bumps sent the car left and right but Chas straightened the vehicle and kept his foot down.

Vision through the windscreen was made poor by the lights of oncoming vehicles and rain. This wasn't helped by the water in Chas' eyes. Flashing hazard warning lights and heavy use of the hooter made most cars give way. Those that didn't soon got the message when he drove inches behind their bumpers. One driver thought to challenge him but as Chas drew alongside him a glance at the state of Siobhan meant he decided otherwise.

Tyre rubber wasn't burning, a slip stream wasn't being created but the car was going flat out. Chas was alert looking this way and that, anticipating any difficulties. His concentration was near total. But that couldn't stop his head jerking sideways to look across the road, through his side window. As he did a man with a pram stepped out onto a pedestrian crossing immediately in front of him. Siobhan screamed,

"Chas, Chas, look out,"

Enough stopping distance didn't exist. Chas wrenched the steering wheel, the car skidding straight towards a row of concrete bollards. He glanced to see if Siobhan had on her seat belt. She screamed again.

C38

What obliterated Chas' focus and sent him tearing headfirst towards a pedestrian and pram was something extraordinary. Out of his side window he glimpsed two nurses on their way to work. He thought it was fancy dress until realised the black bin bags they wore over their uniforms were not light-hearted. It was protective wear. While Siobhan screamed, they were joined by a third in the same outfit.

The swerving meant Chas no more than scraped the car side and dented the wing. It was battle scarred anyway. A police car swung from across the road. Chas saw it but there was no time for that, so he sped off. To Siobhan it seemed like Le Mans but his car was no match for theirs and they drew across him forcing him to a halt. When he told them of purpose of his speeding he was verbally cautioned and then escorted to the hospital through red lights and junctions as fast as his vehicle could go, Siobhan gripping her car seat as they went.

Once the two were at the hospital, Chas expected he would be sent away, but they were given masks and visors and the staff let them both sit by the bedside. Chas mused to himself that a few days earlier Eamon had been to all intents in fair physical health and in a flash of lucidity, told his old friend,

"I don't want to reach the age where my name's on the cake and I'm blowing out the candles not having a feckin' clue whose birthday it is. You hear me, Chas?"
If anything, he felt sadder then than he did on this day, when his ailing friend lay on his front, tubes and machines everywhere, struggling for breath. Sitting there it crossed his mind that his wishes were coming true.

Chas and Siobhan were allowed to do shifts sitting beside the bed in the first few weeks. They were close to giving up, but the nurses and doctors weren't. Eamon was put in an induced coma and drugs just coming on-line were applied. After what seemed like an eternity to Siobhan, she and Chas came to collect him to take him to convalesce. Once he was brought out of the coma Eamon had surprised everyone, improving on an almost a daily basis. The guard of honour and applause when he was wheelchaired to the exit didn't help with his confusion.

C39

The care home, Sunny Meadows, Chas drove Eamon to was fifty miles from his own home and visiting inside the building wasn't allowed. Chas and Siobhan motored there regularly. The first time he came to the window placing his hands there and, insofar as chat was possible, he engaged. The following week in spite Chas of making daily visits Eamon remained sitting by his bedside when he arrived. Siobhan was spending time with her grandchildren and daughter who was having a difficult pregnancy so she couldn't make it until the week after. When she got there she struggled to get a response. She waved and mouthed sentiments through the window outside his room which he didn't acknowledge. When she got close enough for him to see her lips all that happened was the window steamed up. Seeing the state her husband was in she came back within twenty four hours carrying a white board and marker to write on but the glare of the daylight from behind her made it unreadable. On this occasion Eamon waved back but actually he couldn't even see who she was. Chas borrowed a large-screened laptop to show his friend football matches while the battery lasted but Eamon didn't so much as notice it.

On a day brown and gold leaves swirled around Sunny Meadows Chas and Siobhan were called to come, something unusual was happening with Eamon. Chas and Siobhan were the second exception made to the rule set for entering the home that day.

Bullied, the head of the care home had allowed access to Eamon by officials, who claimed to be dementia experts. For reasons of Covid, it had to be in the courtyard. Cheryl, the head, said they behaved more like interrogators. She raised this and was initially told it was treatment for cognitive decline. It wasn't anything like any treatment she had seen. When she challenged them two things happened. The C.E.O of the care company rang her insisting her career depended on cooperation. Secondly, she was threatened with the law. Eamon was to be sectioned under the Mental Health Act. She was refused entry during the examination but ignored this when she heard Eamon effing and blinding at the top of his voice. A few minutes and she was browbeaten into leaving the courtyard. When they received the phone call, Siobhan and Chas were already on their way. They had set off for one of their regular visits some time before. Once in their protective outfits Cheryl took them to the courtyard and entered with them.

What they saw there was Eamon livelier than for a sometime, holding his own with two people attempting to hector him. He had attempted to go back to his room and they had told him he was going nowhere fast to which he replied,

"That's exactly where I'm going and the speed I'm going at and yous'd better get out of my way."

The officials stepped back at that point and jumped back further when Cheryl, Siobhan and Chas burst in on them, Siobhan rushing to hug Eamon. Chas physically pushed away the officials further. One apparently recognised him telling the other,

"That's the taxi driver."

After a huddle in which they decided they were outnumbered, the officials left, knowing there would be other opportunities. Siobhan and Chas were allowed to accompany Eamon back to his room.

Entering Eamon's room Siobhan shed tears and Chas fumed. It was midday and Eamon slumped into a urine proof armchair sunken in the middle from the hours he spent there. Still in his pyjamas he stared blankly at a wall. He didn't fully recognise them in their PPE. When Chas tore his mask from his face, it produced little response. It was obvious what had to be done: they had to take him home. Cheryl agreed, saying he would make no progress there. She would have to consult the doctor who served the home and clear it with the C.E.O. That wouldn't be until the following day, but they could stay in an annexe which was unstaffed.

That would be Guy Fawkes Day which Eamon hated. Fortunately, he wouldn't be aware of the irony that he was to be released then. Come mid- morning the care head came with news of the second lockdown. She had been instructed that under no circumstance could she release Eamon. Siobhan was struck silent whilst Chas threatened his lawyer and his newspaper connections. Able to tell that this wasn't Cheryl's doing he relented. It wasn't in her hands and she herself was upset.

After that life was difficult for all in the building with Eamon out of control, barging into other rooms shouting at the top of his voice,

"Tokyo Three, Tokyo Three."

On the drive back to London Siobahn and Chas hardly spoke. She was bereft of hope and ideas whilst Chas was full of them.

C40

With the second lockdown finished Siobhan had lots of visitors. Her new grandchild was brought to her and her son came. He could throw no light on why his father was still incarcerated. He had made enquiries only to be told, sad though it was, this wasn't a police matter and it couldn't be helped. He was warned at one point that if he pushed things, it could make it worse for his father. Cheryl at the care home, however, challenged the nature of Eamon's examination. It turned out that there was no G.P. involved, nor was there an AMHP or psychiatrist. He wasn't sectioned although she was told he had to stay there as a matter of national security. Despite being warned she could not discuss the case with anyone she had let Siobhan and Chas know the state of play.

Chas' house also had had visitors. They were old friends who had been in scrapes and caused near riots in days of yore. They weren't past their sell by dates but if they were on supermarket shelves canny buyers would reach behind them to get the fresher stuff. It was their third meeting and details were settled, responsibilities allotted. The date was also agreed. New Years Day could be relied on as a time when every service from police to care homes had no more than skeleton staffs on duty.

On January first, outside Chas' house stood an ambulance. One of the old mates had worked at Elstree and this was straight from a firm which supplied the studios. Illnesses meant on the day they were down to five men. Chas was in the front in uniform and so was the man beside him. The other three were in the back in white with surgical hats and masks on. They were holding on to a wheelchair.

At Sunny Meadows they drove round the back and tried various side doors eventually using bolt cutters on one that was padlocked. One of them stayed outside because he was particularly vulnerable to Covid. He was to guard the exit. Inside the home the wheelchair was unfolded and Chas led them towards Eamon's room. One worker jumped to one side when they rushed past her and then rushed to the office herself. While Chas and company were trying to get Eamon to agree to use the wheelchair phone calls were being made.

Eamon took some persuading: they were going for a team drink up, they were going to a party, they were going to a ceilidh. He was ready to fight them until the new head of Sunny Meadows – the old one having been transferred – came insisting they should all leave and Eamon must stay.

The new head raced off to make more calls and the police were on their way. Getting Eamon up the ramp in the wheelchair proved beyond them so it was chucked to one-side while he and three mates had the rear doors closed on them. Chas had a fair idea of who was being phoned from the care home's office. He shot out of the grounds on to the road and after a brief search found the switch for the siren. Back in the office of Sunny Meadows the focus had been on making urgent calls, so the escapees use of an ambulance wasn't spotted.

Flashing blue lights accelerated towards the ambulance and then went by to be followed by an unmarked car. Rebel songs were being sung in the back of the vehicle when the journey was reaching its end. Chas dropped off one mate as he passed his home and then dropped the others where a car had been left to take them to their homes. They told Chas they had tried chatting with Eamon and got "little change", although he joined in the odd line of the singing. When the ambulance was returned Eamon remained very quiet.

The quiet continued in Chas' car as he drove off. All attempts to get Eamon chatting foundered on one and two word replies. The reality was Eamon had got used to sitting and being wheeled to and from the dinning-table, the toilet, the bath and his bed without conversation in an institution that was understaffed. Pulling up outside his house Eamon didn't budge. It seemed he didn't recognise it. To begin with Chas was at a loss but he hit upon driving Eamon around his neighbourhood in the hope he got the idea of where he was. Passing roads that should be familiar he couldn't help but say out loud,

"Oh Christ old friend, what's become of you?"

They had paused at a red light opposite a sushi restaurant to the right of which was a familiar pub. A man who had been bereft of words until then croaked,

"Take me there."

Eamon was pointing in the direction of the pub. Where would the harm in it be? Two pints of Guinness later, Eamon astonished Chas by going to the bar to order his third. He had stood suddenly and carried himself in an able-bodied way to the counter. Chas had hardly begun his second pint and ricked his neck twisting round to hear Eamon speak plain sense to the bartender. Had the alcohol flushed the clutter from inside his skull? He joined him at the bar to pay for the drink, assuming he had no wallet to find his wallet was shoved away. Eamon paid and then the pair sat down together.

"Are you back with me, old friend?"

"I'm not even back with me ownself – never feckin' will be, but what head I've got is clearing."

That was a little more like him.

Eamon drank the third pint more slowly.

"So do you know who I am now?"

Chas asked.

"You're the man, taking me to me home."

Chas had hoped he would say his name.

"Do you know where you live?"

Eamon looked at Chas like he felt sorry for the simpleton and answered,

"Jasus, at home."

Chas spirits sank, merely to rise, breach the surface and leap when this was followed with,

"Or are we staying at yours still, Chas?"

Siobhan and their belongings had moved back while he was in Sunny Meadows.

Eamon didn't want the rest of his pint – a first – and

Chas was driving, so he wasn't going to finish his either. Eamon asked him the time, to be told it was late evening, but he didn't believe him. In the home he had developed a thing about people and watches and clocks. He believed there was time for a walk, not too far and he knew where to.

"Stroll a while with me, me faithful old mucker. Let's see what's to become of me, where I should be put next."

Chas was delighted.

Two sides of a block later it was evident, Eamon didn't know really know where he was. Two more sides and they were back where they started. He was satisfied; he had found what he was looking for, the sushi bar.

"Peckish? You've had best part of three pints. You sure you can handle a meal?"

"You know me, I never like to eat on an empty stomach."

"Do you know what kind of food it is?"

The care home refugee claimed he did.

"Jasus of course, I know that, been here before."

It wasn't a lie it was simply categorically untrue.

Chas had driven two and a half hours, had a pint and a half and had had to manage his old friend, but he entered the restaurant with a will. A waiter asked if they had made a booking and Chas told him,

"I'm sure you can find us a table."

When they sat, Chas could see they were surrounded by diners half their age and less. Eamon insisted it was his shout, ordering an array of dishes without knowing what they were.

He didn't eat much, spending the majority of his time examining designs on the tablecloth and napkins and scrutinising the décor. Chas had to fetch him back to his seat after he got up to explore the texture of a woodblock print of a huge wave as it was toppling over. He ate a little more but then began to comment on the kimonos waitresses were wearing. It was mild and complimentary but too loud. Chas only succeeded in stopping him by getting him to look at another print – this time of a snow topped Mount Fuji. That was it, he pushed his plate away and was transfixed.

"Where is that?"

"Near Tokyo, Japan."

"What about the costumes the ladies are wearing, from the same place, Tokyo?"

More or less. He wasn't going to correct him.

Leaving there he responded in the same way with the other questions.

"The food, Tokyo?...The sea and the wave, Tokyo?...

Every time Chas agreed he could see his friend, concentrating and repeating the word, 'Tokyo'.

"I've been there, beautiful. We've been there."

Chas debated with himself whether to correct him.

"No, neither of us has."

Eamon looked at his mate. He wouldn't lie to him, but he'd slipped up here.

"You remember the drive to Cheltenham…"

"Ah to pick up that feckin' box, Tokyo something or the other…that's what the B specials grilled me on."

His recall here shook Chas. He couldn't understand how on earth he had remembered that. Murmuring during the drive Eamon constantly repeated,

"Tokyo, Tokyo, Tokyo,"

ending with,

"By all the saints… Beautiful…I want to go back there."

"You've never been within several thousand miles of that place…"

Eamon looked at Chas' face. He could trust him but once in a while the poor ol' cab driver got it wrong.

"For the last feckin' time. Once isn't enough, I must see it again."

In this instance Eamon merely wanted to go back to the restaurant. Once he understood this Chas shrugged and u-turned back to the restaurant. It was slightly embarrassing wandering back in there with him but no more than that. Hopefully this satisfied the wish to see 'it' again. Outside Eamon kept on repeating the name of the Japanese capital, followed by the word beautiful.

"No wonder, no wonder. Anybody, everybody would be fascinated by such a grand and beautiful place," he said at the end. Chas decided whilst it pleased his friend, he would humour him. He could be free to believe what he wanted. What harm could it do? After all it wasn't Hiroshima. He'd had his fill of that from his father when he was boy.

It was odd how Eamon could remember so little and concentrate on virtually nothing and yet hold on to certain things to the point of obsession. When Chas helped Eamon out of the car, he put his arm around him and was asked enthusiastically.

"Will you feckin' promise me, feckin' make me a promise?"

Chas believed he knew what was coming; he was going to ask him to help him kill himself. Chas would agree to anything whatever it was, except that.

"I love it there. It's beautiful."

The old friends searched each other's faces, one looking for a sense of commitment, the other for any sense at all.

"Promise me you'll take me there, Tokyo, before it's too late."

It wasn't possible for a bunch of reasons. Chas gave him the simplest one.

"There is no travel for now, least of all there."

"I'm not asking for the impossible. It's the one and only thing on me kick-the-bucket list. I can be patient for that. I promise you that if you promise me."

Chas didn't make his friend a promise, but he didn't say no. It should lead to nothing. Eamon could well forget this the moment his grizzled head sunk into his pillow. By the next morning the hope for Tokyo might be as far away from him as all other hope.

C41

Between the first and second lockdown Sam had to report to GCHQ. Her work on decrypting WhatsApp was going well. The meeting was relaxed which she put down to Coetzee's absence although she was to find he hadn't gone far or for long.

When a huge purple beach ball with protruding florets was a nightly image on tv Billy was yoyoing back and forth to work or otherwise running hybrid lessons. Once in a while she thought she was followed and Sam believed she could be right about the odd figure staring from across the road. Ned apparently had nothing to do with it. Come the second week of March 2021 Billy was back permanently at school. None of these ups and down impinged on their relationship. She and Sam were happy with the way things were going for them. They both liked to read and formed a book club of two. When they walked to shops it was always hand in hand. Ned caught some of it describing it as a bit of a "pandemic paradise."

In the bedroom Sam was a novice and was trying to learn. It wasn't that successful but when it wasn't Billy would laugh. Disconcerted Sam astonished Ned by asking for detailed advice. She didn't know what to do and during the act found her thoughts drifting. Not in a position to give a smidgeon of practical tips the best he could offer was,

"That's often how it is, some are in the engine room, others looking out the porthole. No wuccas, you'll be ok."
He added,

"I've not heard a whisper of Coetzee. No one seems to know where he is. It's worrying. Have you seen anything on the web?"
She hadn't.

"It would be better if you had mate, although the web's not usually the place he hangs out. We don't know where he is or what he's up to. He really doesn't like us and he's a vindictive bogan."

Sam worked wonders and cracked decryption of

WhatsApp but she wasn't sure she wanted to put that in the hands of GCHQ and told no one there. When she told Billy over dinner she praised her for being bright and principled. She was rewarded in turn with compliments about teaching. Cruising along on this smoothest of paths didn't prevent a pothole appearing. If left it would begin to gape. Over dinner Billy spoke of her long held wish to be a parent. She meant sooner rather than later and was hopeful Sam felt the same.

"What do you think? What do you think?"

Sam didn't think, hadn't thought of it, wasn't prepared for it. She didn't know what to think and knew even less what to say. There was a long pause. She had stopped stuttering around Billy, but it was back and Billy saw it straight away.

"I, I, I don't know."

It wasn't a no, but the tepid reaction hurt.

That night they went to bed in silence and when Billy left for work there was no mutual peck on the cheek. Sam was up before her and was absorbed in tapping on her keyboard trying to bury her achievement with WhatsApp. Billy came back late after an unscheduled drink with a friend. Sam was already asleep, so Billy got out the bedding for the convertible. Sam was shocked to find in the morning that she had slept alone.

During the day Sam had some worrying missives from GCHQ. Workers were being called back in stages. She was to be in the third tranche. She was doubly unsettled. She would fling her arms around Billy when she came in but she wasn't there by midnight. Sam had gone to bed tearfully believing if Billy didn't share their bed that night she no longer wanted to. Billy was by then being given a lift home by her Head Teacher during which she confided in her. The advice she got was that going in for a child was a huge decision for a couple. Her experience was that often the very best parents were slow to come round to it.

"You wouldn't rush your child into things, don't

rush another you care for. Let her come to it, herself."

Coming in Billy immediately saw that by the front door was a packed case. She hoped at worst this signalled that Sam had to report temporarily to GCHQ. Going to her bedroom she saw Sam sprawled across the entire divan asleep and smiled at the heavy snoring. Tomorrow would be Saturday and they would have time. She would do everything to persuade her to stay, put the issue of a baby into the future. Not to disturb her she once more used the convertible.

Waking early Billy waited in the lounge for Sam. Sam was distraught waking alone again. Billy wrapped herself around her the second she appeared, telling her the baby could wait. Sam gripped her close,

"I, I've always loved children but couldn't envisage myself in the role of a mum. It always seemed so unlikely."

She had spent the bulk of the previous day researching single-sex couple parenthood. It was more than possible.

"I want to be a parent with you."

The suitcase, she explained, was for a change of clothes for her recall to GCHQ shortly in the event she couldn't make it a day return. Preparing in advance was in her nature.

What would have been a joyful breakfast was tempered by her impending trip. A loud knock at the door sent Billy to unlock. She was there longer than normal. Voices were raised. Sam poked her head out into the passageway, to see a man point his finger and then jab Billy in the chest. Billy stepped back when he stepped forward. Sam bounded forward dipping by the radiator to snatch up the cricket bat still there. The man was short, his head was obscured by Billy's. He didn't see it coming or who did it. Sam smashed the bat down on his shoulder, making him shriek. He staggered off. Billy was stunned when Sam chased after him and cracked him over the head. Again he shrieked but this time he sprinted. Again she ran after him but missed with an outstretched third blow.

Billy hugged her as they went back indoors.

"You are never less than a surprise Samantha."

"To nobody more than me. We'll keep this there," she said placing the bat by the radiator. It was early but Billy put wine glasses on the table and popped the cork on a bottle of Prosecco. They toasted the future and being together, Billy adding,

"And a baby,"

which Sam corrected to,

"Babies."

While getting her breath back Sam got a call from Ned.

"You've sent Coetzee to hospital mate. Hope you enjoyed it cos he'll be madder than ever. It'll be blue until the end now, black and blue."

Sam hadn't stopped to think who it was, she had just hit him.

"We couldn't locate him but you did. Good news is he didn't spot you only the lump of wood cracking open his skull."

His attention had been on Billy and then on escaping a battering. He hadn't so much as glimpsed her.

Sam had hoped he was elsewhere. Actually, the day after the posting to South Africa came up, he boarded a KLM connecting flight and disembarked in the Netherlands. There he had linked up with fellow emigres in Rotterdam.

"He's back, has been for a while and active…Until you hit him over the boundary."

They had to move, Coetzee's worst suspicions about Billy were confirmed. He'd want to gouge and tear. Ned checked a text

"Christ, he's on his way. Go, go!"

"Where, to where?"

"Far away as poss', a coffee bar, anywhere. I'll find you" Ned paused to look at his phone screen.

"Go now. Now! He's with a bunch of heavies, two roads away, head bandaged all over. You've got hoods, keep them up and run."

C42

Billy had keys to an Oxfam shop not too far off, so she and Sam slept in the back on the floor for the night, no lights, no radio and hushed. Six o'clock in the morning the pair scrambled into the back of a camper van Ned had borrowed. It was dark and they were on their way to the flat of someone he knew that was empty.

"This place's sky high above suspicion,"
he told them. Jessica met them there passing over the keys. She preferred the Biltmore. They shouldn't be there for long.

"Don't move, don't even go near the window, be quiet in the dunny. Nobody can know you're here. He'll be scampering around high and low."
As things developed they had to move twice to other flats Ned had connections for, the last where its occupant had been admitted to hospital with Covid.

The marred idyll was punctuated, Sam was summoned. She had delayed and delayed going to GCHQ. Until then she had previously succeeded in arguing her asthma meant it was wisest she worked at home. The call came from her station manager who must have had a cold because she didn't recognise the voice. Her first thought was it was a late April Fool's Day prank, but he was adamant, she was overdue and they expected her. Sam had consistently given them the impression she was at her home in Cheltenham. That meant she should be able to report within hours if not minutes and this was what they expected. Trying to ring Billy who had nipped out to get milk was a no-no. A note was scribbled telling her she should be back by the evening and she rushed out. She was off-colour and wary of a journey on public transport, but it had to be less dangerous than not complying with the mandate to return.

On the train she wore an anti-viral mask and visor-like glasses. She was careful around her asthma, having been hospitalised several times when she was a child. In her rucksack she carried an oximeter to measure blood oxygen levels although it had been used less than half-a-dozen times in her life. She strived to keep socially distanced but ended standing in an area between seats in which most of the air available was second hand.

Upon arrival at the Doughnut temperature taking was obligatory. Sam's was fractionally raised but within the accepted range. Her station manager went over her work with her especially regarding the individuals she had worked on from the Tokyo Three file. The manager noticed Sam was perspiring but put it down to nerves as she all but cross examined her on her reports. When she was told there was to be no more working from home, Sam asked for a break to get paracetamol and went straight to H.R. hoping her medical history could get her an exemption. Once she was refused, she realised she must be under some suspicion.

Her station manager hadn't finished with Sam but soon realised she wasn't well and decided it was safest all round that she was sent home. The sensible thing was to head straight to her own place and to bed. Instead she was going to catch a train. It was Friday and she could spend the weekend with Billy. Her awkwardness had gone. She would fling her arms around her confident she would respond in kind. If she hadn't said it before she would try to tell her there and then she loved her, no matter how clumsily. Not all everlasting love got to be expressed in sonnets.

Sam didn't feel well enough to sit in the back of a cab. Walking to the station she stopped at an ATM. In the sunlight her eyes stung, making it difficult to see the screen. The machine twice refused her card but her third attempt worked. Moist fingers made taking the new notes a trial. Pulling them out led her to sway a little. She felt light-headed and her back ached. It played her up generally, but this was exceptional. At the ticket machine she struggled even worse than she had at the ATM. Supporting herself on the counter of a kiosk she asked for extra shots in what seemed a tasteless coffee. It was for swallowing more paracetamol. She knew something wasn't right but was clear it was too early to have symptoms of an infection caught on the train.

Ill or not Sam remained determined to make it back to Billy. Wheezing when crossing to the right platform she slumped on a bench to use her inhaler. Clasping the arm of the bench to stop herself flopping sideways she tried to ring Ned. Getting no response, she texted where she intended to go and that she might not be well. With some foreboding she did something she would never do if less muddled. Using her own phone and some of its diminishing data she messaged her parents that she was ill. It was a reflex. They had invariably looked after her when she needed it.

The train arrived, she rose unsteadily, making it to the opened door. Nothing was going to stop her from making this journey. About to step up into the carriage she realised her laptop was back by the bench. She twisted round to slowly stagger back. Bending to lift it she heard a noise she had hoped not to. The train was pulling away from the station. She fairly drooped back on to the bench and inserted a flash drive into a laptop port. Hand shaking, she tried to press 'enter' with no response. Running her fingers over the keys she pressed it again which cascaded sets of commands. With the other hand she let go of the laptop also letting go of herself. Sam slid from the bench, crumpling onto the harshness of the platform floor.

C43

The third lockdown had come and gone and there had been no attempts to re-capture Eamon. Chas believed his visit to the M.P.s surgery had taken care of that. The fact was at a level in intel quarters other options were being looked at. While that was happening, Eamon was getting no better.

"He's lost again?"

"No, says he knows exactly where he is but says he can never come home. He's been out for hours,"
Siobhan told Chas. Chas was ready to comb the streets however long it took. But there was no need, she knew exactly where her husband was. It was on the app she had put on his phone.

"I said I'll go to him, but he says he'll run off. He's making no sense."

Chas was on his way. It was walking distance, but he ran or as near to it as he could get. Eamon threw his arms around Chas the instant he met him. He looked bad, dishevelled with bruised knuckles where he could have punched a wall.

"I can't let her see me like this. I deserve to be put to rot in one of those feckin' homes. She'll want to wash her hands of me. Anybody would."
Unmistakeably he smelt of whiskey.

"She will if you keep on the Jameson's,"
Chas told him sharply whilst he swayed and gazed around weirdly. Eamon didn't think that was the problem. He only drunk at home when Siobhan allowed it. No, it wasn't that. He had known he wasn't right for a while, known his behaviour didn't go down well. Yet he had no clear idea of what he was doing wrong. Sometimes he thought it was her, even accused her. She could put up with so much and no more. He feared it was coming to an end.

"I know where I am, but it doesn't feel like it. Nothing looks the same."
Chas didn't know what to make of that.

"I've been imagining things…bad things. I nearly, I nearly, I nearly punched her in me sleep…"
He meant Siobhan.

"…Mother of God, I'd rather die. I'm…driving her up the wall …over the precipice. At the moment I feel less…less…less in feckin' control than ever."

Within a few weeks of the break-out from Summer Meadows he had picked up well, not back to his old self but better – much better than this. Chas knew he would get worse. He also knew Siobhan would stick by him above and beyond, no matter what. It was time to force Eamon to the doctors.

"It's your choice Eamon, medication or incarceration."

Another time Chas would have described care very differently. It would have been a mixture of a free house and a spa with saints for staff. Eamon looked at him with a grin. He didn't believe his mate would ever see him put back in one of those places. But the grin wasn't returned. There was not so much as a hint of a smile. This was for real. Chas had to convince him that something had to be done.

Chas told Eamon afresh of new drugs that were available and of drugs just coming off the conveyor belt. The minimum they could do was delay getting worse. There could be more, better, some recovery, a quality of life. And who knew during the course of that newer drugs might appear. They were working on it. He threw in for good measure that he had been working on the trip to Tokyo. It was true but a little misleading. He had made new enquiries but Japan was allowing no one from the outside Covid world in.

An emergency appointment was made at the G.P. surgery. In the wait Chas put plasters on Eamon's grazed knuckles. Eamon was sitting with him in a coffee bar being geed up, whilst oddly staring at his cup and saucer. He was still odd when Chas went with him into the surgery. The doctor had a batch of cognitive tests ready and was prepared to refer Eamon. but he didn't take either of these far. He was more concerned with symptoms of a preliminary examination. Eamon's muscles twitched and both his pulse and blood pressure were raised. He was flushed and above all his pupils were dilated. He also noticed that Eamon stared at items in the room for a pathologically long time.

"Have you been experimenting with drugs?"

Chas bristled at that. Of course he hadn't. It wasn't mind altering drugs that was the issue, it was a mind altering illness. Without breaking his focus on the sphygmomanometer on a desk, Eamon was clear that he had taken no drugs, steered clear of them.

"Hmm you have been drinking, though, haven't you?"

Eamon thought on this and replied,

"They gave it me and some paracetamol."

"Paracetamol?

the doctor asked.

"That's what they said it was"

They?"

Eamon looked blank as he attempted to recall. Then he burst out,

"They were your feckin' lot, white coats…Bless me, though, free whiskey, best prescription I've ever had."

He looked ready to rave.

"Feck me they were too mighty free with it…told them where to stick their questions…Me and my four associates, that is,"

he said rubbing his grazed knuckles. With that he was finished. There would be no more of it from him. He quietly cooperated with the doctor's tests.

On the way back to his home Eamon asked,

"What's happening? Is the game up with me. I don't know what's real or not?"

"Someone gave you pills and the whiskey?"

That he was sure of – and it wasn't in a bar. Chas' mind was working flat out.

"You had to punch someone?"

"The foreign one. He deserved it pointing and poking me. Doc had to concentrate on him then."

It wasn't a boast, the fool who poked Eamon already had his head in bandages, so he went down easily.

"Do you think this was real? Me head was spinning round and round like a maypole. It is May Day or thereabouts, isn't it?"

Thereabouts, it was. Chas was amazed he was aware of it.

"How did you get away?"

"Doubt I feckin' would've if they hadn't had to cart him off after I clouted him."

"Why did you go with them at all?"

"Bit dream like this…lime yellow and green checked vehicle. An ambulance, I think and that feckin' consultant with bad breath who saw me ages back."

"You said he was a quack."

"Did I? Oh, well I was right."

"What did he say when you were examined?"

To the best of his memory there was no examination, just drink.

"No questions, nothing?"

Eamon thought and then he thought again.

"Well not from the medical man."

"Who then?"

"The bandaged gargoyle faced man with an ugly accent… you could almost smell the sulphur around him – until I saw him off."

Eamon paused and added,

"It was Tokyo Three… Three, Three, it was."

Plausible though that was, Eamon was saying a lot of strange things, so Chas wasn't sure what to make of it. Was it medical or was that a ruse?

Chas put an arm around Eamon. His version of things had become difficult to trust. His friend may yet again have been put through a mill with spikes, or may not have been. The first chance he got he would take Eamon to the M.P. who seemed to be on their side. He would also use his local councillor, write to the prime minister and bypass the Herald to maybe go to a national paper or two. People in positions of power were misbehaving and their bosses should know about it. It was time to front them up. He would use every channel open to him – except maybe the police. In the meantime, whenever Eamon was to leave his house, it wouldn't be alone. He would be by his side

That night Eamon was still not right. He slept downstairs and Chas lay on the lounge floor beside him. Eamon dozed off and on calling out,

"Feckin' devil Tokyo…Tokyo. …volcano…"

In the morning a haggard Eamon belaboured Chas about the mooted Tokyo trip. It was never going to happen, but he humoured him waxing on that it would be golf at the foot of Mount Fuji. Verbally he summoned up a picture of it and spoke of all their old mates going.

"That South African devil asked me about it. D'ya think it's dangerous there?"

"Hardly, the Japanese are very peaceful. Small on bombs, big on manners."

As far as Chas was concerned any danger, if that was what it was, was where they currently were. Furthermore, they were going nowhere near Japan.

Day in, day out Eamon was plaguing Chas with Tokyo Three, Tokyo Three.

"You wouldn't lie to me Chas, would you? You never have. You wouldn't lead me by the nose up the blessed garden path, would you? I asked and you never said no."

How had he remembered that so exactly? Eamon put an arm on each of Chas's shoulders and held him straight staring into his face. He had Chas there trapped in the moment. There was a drawn out silence and Eamon shook the shoulders he was holding.

Chas swore he wouldn't lie, it was a promise. And there he was with a white lie transformed into a sworn oath.

It was a mountain to climb with a man strapped to his back. He had a commitment with no idea how to honour it. Bedlam not withstanding he would have to try to get to Tokyo.

C44

It felt awkward when Billy was moved to yet another dwelling by Jessica, she hardly knew her. Going to school and being alongside others would have been a relief from the misery she experienced at Sam's absence. Instead she was penned-in in this base for days on end with no company and no word from anybody.

Late on the day following Sam's departure Billy, despite all Sam's warnings, nearly rang her. By the second night of their separation, hearing nothing, one box of tissues wasn't enough to quench her tears. One day more and a shower became a downpour. Had she misunderstood Sam and their relationship? Was there something amiss? She believed she had done her best to make it clear that she wanted them to be together. Something had gone wrong. Sam was devoted to her, had risked so much to protect her. She wouldn't abandon her when she had clearly cared so much. It wasn't likely was it that their brief time together had blazed a firebreak between them? That wasn't how passion worked, was it?

A week went by, Billy anticipating every day that Sam would arrive. It became crushing. It carried on unaltered through to early summer. By that stage she knew she herself would have been suspended at work for unexplained absence. It added weight to her misery. She was reduced to wandering around a stranger's home watching tv during the entire day. The few and far between knocks at the front door were answered with an expectant smile. When an envelope fell on the door mat, her initial thought was that it must be from Sam, hugely unlikely though that was. While her colleagues were succumbing in legion to illness Billy was fit and well in her own isolation ward. Her belief was that any day she would find Sam on her doorstep, tearfully repentant or bearing an irrefutable excuse for absence.

Billy waited and waited. Denied going to school and helping in the Oxfam shop let alone meeting others in pubs or restaurants she was losing the battle against despair. Not only did getting out of bed seem pointless but it was becoming harder and harder. Minor tasks, including keeping clean, didn't seem worth it. She dwelt on the fate of those close to her, the demise of the old editor, Ashley's death and Sam's disappearance. When she was forced to shop, she became frantic believing she was followed. If her tv channels played up she feared she was being monitored. Once more she believed she saw shadowy figures gazing across the road from her dwelling.

Sam had to be dead. Not just Billy's dreams, not just her waking hours at night but her days were filled with images of Sam dying horrible deaths at the hands of the intelligence services. If she were dead, then Billy was utterly stranded. In her misery the most obvious thing that Covid could have killed Sam never occurred to her.

Billy contacted her doctor who prescribed another round of tranquilisers. The pills numbed her, but they also calmed her thinking. Had intelligence agents killed Sam it should have made the news, at least local news and there had been nothing of it on any channel. There was a chance she was alive. There had to be more to her disappearance. Whatever her own failings, Sam wouldn't have given up on her without a word. The note she had left didn't give the slightest suggestion of never coming back. Other reasons, powerful reasons had to be at work. Perhaps it was too dangerous for Sam to contact her, let alone meet up.

Billy upped her tranquiliser intake, so she soon ran out. Her doctor wanted her to have counselling and after a row refused to renew her prescription. Days after this Billy decided she had to use her mobile to do everything and more she had been warned against. She rang Sam. With no response, she began to bombard her phone with calls and texts. Without waiting for replies she simultaneously sent emails. Shortly after that she was putting appeals out on Twitter and Facebook and all other social media she could think of. She did get a reaction from Ned who ended up shouting she had to stop but she cut his call and blocked him entirely. That wasn't before he told her he was on his way round. Being off the tranquilisers was having an affect and she couldn't face him. Fleeing the flat she broke an even more fundamental rule by trying to ring Sam at GCHQ as she went. They curtly wouldn't acknowledge that Sam worked there. Looking one way and then the other she was sure she was being followed and not simply by one or two agents but a team, a crowd of them. She jumped on a bus and leapt from it into a tube station suddenly knowing what she must do.

Weaving her way back to her own locality Billy crept to the little Nissan still parked outside her own flat. It started first time. She drove with one hand, using the other to set up her satellite navigation. Heading to GCHQ she was going to march in and confront them. Should Sam not be there, she would demand an address and if that was refused, she would camp outside the entrance until she came into or out of work, regardless of what time that was. Glancing from the windscreen to her phone screen Billy repeatedly sent Sam a text,

"I am in absolute misery. What's happening? I am coming to see you. Now."

A final message gave the time she would arrive on the doorstep of GCHQ.

C45

Billy guessed she wouldn't be allowed to park close to GCHQ, so she found parking near to the town centre and used her phone app to guide her the roughly two and a half miles involved. It was a warm night and the walk was harder than she had hoped. She went part of the way around the perimeter, came to the entrance and asked to see Sam. She did not have an invite and she had not filled in the online form. Her tears were not acknowledged and she was turned away. Traversing a wide road she sat under a lamppost across from the entrance, glared at occasionally by its keepers. She constantly gazed up and down the road and over to the entrance hoping to see Sam arriving or leaving.

It was past midnight and dew was forming around her. By two a.m. she had been visited by police and told she had to move on. Nevertheless, they could see she was little threat, so they tolerated her still being there at eight o'clock in the morning. Crowds of workers were arriving and going into the Doughnut building. Billy could by no means make them all out, but she would have definitely been able to recognise Sam and she wasn't one of them. Thirst and hunger were making deep dents in Billy's resolve. A non-uniformed woman came over to Billy with a bottle of water a couple of hours later. Amiably she asked her why she was there. She wrote down Billy's number seeming to make heavy work of it, saying she would try to find out about Sam and would ring her with what she found out. The woman clearly wrote more notes than were needed for a phone number. In so doing she took a photo of Billy. Billy found out from her that GCHQ was around the clock and people in encryption and its like worked shifts. The morning workers were already in. Next would be an afternoon shift. If she did not see her friend in the afternoon, she wasn't going to see her. Dozing off and on Billy remained able to make herself alert enough for the next tranche of workers. With no sign of Sam, she finally despaired and staggered off towards a bus stop.

In Cheltenham she wandered into a brightly lit café and flopped down onto a ribbed bench. There was little choice but to return to London. Two flat whites, a miniature wash and scrub in the toilet and a fit of sobbing later, she went to a gastro pub to order the largest meal on their menu. She sat in a dark corner where they took payment before she had finished her glass of wine. Music of a sort she found comforting was playing. The music was much livelier when she was woken up to be told it was last orders. She had an espresso coffee and rushed out to find where she had parked her car. Her map app should be able to guide her there.

It was coming up to midnight and there were few people around. Billy's phone battery was low, but she had to keep the screen going to follow the route. Within a half a mile of the spot she hoped the car was the directional arrow spun round and then round anew and began sending her back the way she came. She tramped the streets, up and down trying to get a better signal or hoping to see something that would guide her. It was no longer possible to work out where the car park was. Eyes on a phone that had started to stabilise she picked her way through a litter of empty nitrous oxide cannisters, discarded blue Covid masks and a swamp of melted dobs of gum, narrowly avoiding a vomit splat the size of a pizza. Completing the mosaic were the remains of a wood pigeon set on by magpies and garbage from a dustbin raid by urban foxes. She cast around looking for some form of landmark, but the dark made it difficult, so she headed for the brightest spot she could see. Fifty metres and there were painted pairs of footprints on the pavement, along with warnings to maintain two metres distance. That should mean she was close to shops and hopefully the high street. She would find someone there who might be able to help her.

Once she was past some delivery alleyways signs of retail business tailed off. Bells sounded from a steeple whose utter blackness stood out against the dark sky. The subsequent silence was amplified. A church with a steeple of those proportions had to be somewhere near a major thoroughfare, so she walked in its direction. This took her left and then right, around a crescent and then another right. Shouting and screaming from a house sounded as though blows were ready to be struck. When she got closer the outline showed a pair of figures grappling with each other. The onslaught was passion of one sort or another.

The route was taking far longer than her phone had described. Passing a decaying old graveyard she went by an area in front of the church door in which a hooded figure leant into a recess. On the steps was a compressed huddle. There was coughing and a throat was cleared.

"Let's get fucking hammered,"
one voice croaked, followed by,

"Yeh out of our fucking boxes."
In the doorway itself another body lying in a tattered blanket was lighting up after adroitly spitting a huge phlegm globule onto the adjacent pathway. A car tore along, its tyres screeching as it rounded a corner. Flashing blue lights with a siren shot by in pursuit. Billy gazed after it, wishing it had paused where she was.

Accepting the truth that she was utterly lost Billy dropped her gaze to see a long rodent tail disappear down a drain. The breeze blew sewer odours her way and her eyes were watering. She tried her phone once more. The map was still stable and the direction was clear, although she was a long way from where she should be. Following the blue arrow, she moved steadily toward the town centre. She hurriedly passed by a tall man urinating in a bush. He soon became a large shadow cast from behind her. Speeding up she gained nothing and the figure was closing on her. She glanced left and right as she went. There was no one about and the few homes with lights on were sixty meters ahead. She started to run.

Within three steps the figure caught up and leapt in front of her. Her phone was out and she was two digits into a nine-nine-nine call when a hand shot forward, dashing the phone to the pavement. She reached for the pepper spray she kept in her jean pocket. It was jammed in there and her path was blocked. Would she be able to release it in time? It was out. She fired and missed, its spray drenching red brickwork several feet from its target who was now all but on her.

C46

Billy, faltering in the shadow of the spire in Cheltenham, saw her phone have its sim card flipped out and swiftly pocketed. She snatched a glance around but there was no help anywhere.

"Sorry mate, I'm being a bit of a dick but, you've got to stop using it the way you have. It's dangerous. It's how I found you."

She looked down at his flies in fear of what she might see. He caught it.

"The wild wee? A bit awks but I've been on the cans…look Sam must've told you of me working with her."

She had certainly let Billy know intel operatives could be thugs. One of them could easily know about her phone use and about Sam. She looked for help or a place to run to.

"It's alright, I'm a friend of Sam's …"

The tall man stepped back at the same time shushing and patting a tiny dog he had in a bag strapped across his front.

"She frets,"

he explained.

"You're looking for Sam. Me too. It's me Ned."

It was only the second time Billy had come across him and the first time they had been in a hurry.

"Look mate, I'm your best hope."

Now she registered the accent and thought she might recognise him. Sam had told her her tall handsome Aussie friend doted on his little dog.

"What's your dog's name?"

"I call him Dishlicker."

Ned extended his hand. It was holding a phone.

"Your one's got to be dumped. This one'll do the job, but no crazy things with it. Sam must've warned you against that."

Billy liked the dog and his affection for it. She shoved the pepper spray cannister back in her pocket.

"Where is Sam? Surely in your job you would know?"

"I know she caught Covid, but we lost her after that, except for a phone call which might have been her."

Ah, that was it, she had been ill and it had to be terribly ill.

"I thought you people could track anything, anyone."

"I'm using all I've got to find her, but there's nothing to go on."

"If you can't find her it's hopeless."

"Look mate, you've been on it all day…"

So, he had been tracking her that long.

"Come for a Maccas, I know an all-nighter. Let's talk, swap notes. We're missing a trick here."

By the end of sitting in McDonalds, Billy and Ned accepted that what they hoped would be an exchange of information gave no clues to Sam's whereabouts. Billy broached the obvious question.

"Do you think she's dead."

"I'd know if intel had got to her. If she is, it's Covid that's done it. …Can't be, no, no. I put people on this who are good. Had anything resembling her appeared almost anywhere they would have picked it up."

If Coetzee had her Ned wouldn't know but he didn't mention this. Instead, he said,

"Sam'll surface somewhere. She's alive, just not kicking that's all."

Billy was delighted to think that.

"Then what is going on, what is she playing at?"

"Some things in this game are hard to follow. She's as big a riddle as this Tokyo Three business that's got you in the crapper. But she'll surface at some point and I reckon you'll be the first to hear. Let me know."

Billy realised she would have to drive back to London in the dark, something she really didn't enjoy. While they were talking she Googled and booked a hotel. Ned's phone tinkled and she knew he had the information she had that minute created.

"You're limited this time of night but that hotel, well I wouldn't put my bum near it."
He knew the owner of a hotel. It was much nicer and he would get her a good rate. When she delayed, he offered,

"Or I can walk you to your chosen hotel. Would you prefer that?"
She looked at him. He must know she wasn't a candidate for his own bed. Of course, he did. She asked, indicating Dishlicker,

"Can I stroke him?"

"You can try, although this one's a bit of a marsupial,"
The dog was generally comfortable left alone in the shoulder bag. She stroked the tiny furry head and the dog nuzzled up to her hand.

"Strewth, I'll be stuffed."
The relationship was cemented. The dog liked her so he must and if he could look after a little dog like that, she was sure he could be trusted.

In the morning Ned narrowed down where Billy might have parked and at the second attempt they found her car. He would be in touch – "soon", he said. She should go straight back to the place she had been in London. If she needed to contact him, she had the phone he had given her and he was about to give her a bagful more. He knew being isolated must be hard for her. When she was desperate she could ring a friend or two. Once they had located Sam, then he would help her move on. In the meantime, Billy was clear, she would strictly follow the advice she'd had. After all, ignoring it had achieved nothing.

Knowing Ned was working on it, Billy's hopes were high. On a daily basis back home she managed to keep them high but as time passed it seemed unjustified. She did not hear from Ned. A single phone from the bag-full he gave her was left. She had used the rest to ring friends. They were concerned at her circumstances, albeit she could not reveal too much. Those who cared the most told her to forget Sam. She had to move on.

C47

After Sam collapsed at the railway station and Ned found out he immediately raced to Cheltenham General. It was bedlam there. He was told she would have been forwarded to the Nightingale Hospital in Bristol. When he got there, beds were empty and there were few staff and they assured him they didn't have her. After that he tried everything he knew to locate her. She was uncontactable, untraceable.

This was down to the way she prepared for the potential twists and turns of threats to Billy. She had set things up not only to wipe Billy from all files and give her a ghost identity but to sever any traceable relation she herself had to her. In the seconds before she was overcome, she completed the task, but she hadn't been clearheaded. Repeatedly dabbing keys, she also obliterated her own online identity. Data as basic as her NHS and national insurance numbers disappeared. By the time she arrived at the hospital she was a non-person.

Ambulances were in great demand. The one that eventually reached her had to take her to Cheltenham General in exceptionally heavy traffic. With so many emergency admissions it was mayhem. Having got her message, her parents raced there faster than they ever drove in their venerable Morris Countryman. Propping herself up on a trolley queuing with others in the open air, she spotted them parking up, dragged herself onto the paving and staggered to them.

They were a gentle Windrush couple in their eighties and lacked some modern wherewithal. They knew there was a virus, knew it could be serious, but didn't believe they themselves were vulnerable. Any danger to themselves anyway would have been outweighed by the thought their daughter was ill. They helped her into the back of their car and carefully drove off. The transfer to the Nightingale Hospital never took place and less than a smattering of paperwork existed.

Sam's family home was a terraced house a few miles from Oxford. It had been painted brightly but that was decades ago. It was festooned with photos, all of Sam except for one which was signed 'Claudia Cumberbatch Jones'. There, instructed by Sam, they left food marginally inside a bedroom door flanked either side by banks of her old trainspotting catalogues and Meccano sets. That was hard for them since they saw her rarely and always wanted to cosset her. Contact with the outside world was limited to food deliveries from a council run centre and the local Baptist church. Apart from that there was a landline telephone, 'Magic Radio', a tv with terrestrial programs and equally ancient neighbours either side.

There was no wi-fi there which wasn't helped by Sam having forgotten the lead for her retrieved laptop along with her phone charger. She would never use the landline because that meant her parents would be implicated. Within days, weak though she was, Sam took up her mobile to contact Billy but the signal there was hopeless. Being a non-person meant also she couldn't buy data. Paracetamol, sheer will and borrowing her father's walking stick got Sam out into the garden where the weather was poor. Her hope was the signal might be better. She used the last of her phone battery in an attempt to call to Ned but this failed. She shivered and then all but collapsed and had to be supported back to her bed by parents who tottered up the stairs with her.

After that she had to endure her parents ignoring her strictures not to bring sweet potato stews to her in bed. Her phone had become useless. She couldn't see texts from Ned of a number of addresses he had found for her and Billy to move to as and when. To make matters worse her asthma came at her more frequently and more severely.

While the pandemic proceeded in the household there was little drama except for the first lateral flow test. Seeing the red line by the letter 'c' on her testing strip Sam's mother assumed it stood for Covid. Late May the family doctor called to dispense a second round of jabs. While there she explained to Sam that she was dizzy and drained because she had 'long Covid'. There was no cure, she had to give it time. The way she felt she knew that to be true.

Sam slept most of the way through mid-summer and was as weak as ever but desperation gave her some impetus. She knew Billy must be isolated and under threat. She had to do something. Her parents refused her use of their car, but they relented weeks later when dressed and packed she threatened to hitch hike or use public transport. She was going to London to see Billy – if she still remembered her, if she still cared. Her father topped up the windscreen washer and checked the oil and tyre pressures. On the passenger seat her mother put a flask, sandwiches and an apple. Beside them was a stack of inhalers. They begged her not to go but she had to get on with it. Driving off she didn't turn to look but she knew they would be standing on the pavement in house slippers, arms around each other, waving with their free hands.

The drive was hard for Sam. Autumn meant the car windows were misting up. Mile after mile the temptation was to park up and doze. Twice she pulled into garages for coffee and part-charged her phone, although she was aware she wouldn't have a current number for Billy. Luckily there was little traffic and she arrived in one piece outside Billy's albeit mounting the pavement when she did. A glazed squint at the place told her it had not been lived in for months. Sitting behind the wheel she began to weep but stopped herself, knowing without moving around she would fall asleep.

It dawned on her that Billy would be in one of the 'safe houses' Ned arranged. She would try to ring him but checking her phone a text he had sent now appeared and she could see the three properties Ned had listed for her. The first was Jessica, so she knew it was likely Billy would have been moved by then. She calculated the second on the list would also no longer be in use. Trembling she checked for the route to the third property.

Pulling up Sam saw Billy's car outside but there were no lights on in the house. When she rang the doorbell there was no response. She couldn't know that its batteries had run out. She would wait – as long as it took. Constantly she switched between viewing in the wing and rear-view mirrors to see whether or not Billy was coming up the road. More than once she got out of the car and stood straining to spot her, all with no success. The time on the car dashboard was clear: had Billy walked to a local shop she should have been back by then. The standing exhausted Sam so she had to slump back behind the steering wheel despite knowing she had a battle on to stay awake. Within minutes she was snoring.

Yet Billy had followed advice, rarely going out and when she did she didn't go far. She was in, dozing herself with a book in the half-light and wearing a headset which she was no longer using.

C48

Billy leapt as the phone in her lap buzzed sending it flying across the room. By the time she had collected her senses and retrieved the phone the ringing had stopped. The caller was unidentified. She threw the phone onto an armchair from where it bounced on to the floor. She gazed out of the window and in the gathering dark hardly registered the Morris Countryman parked outside. The phone rang again and she scrambled to scoop it up.

"What's with you two? I know you like to take things slowly, but you should be stoked."

The accent was Australian.

"She's out there and hasn't moved for hours and you're inside."

"Is that Ned? Sorry, what'd you say?"

"Take a look out of the window."

Opening the blinds, she saw the usual dull scene, dark dwellings, the odd pedestrian and a heavily populated CPZ.

"Sorry Ned but it's getting late. I can't see anything out there."

"Sam. Sam's outside in a car that should've been put down decades ago. You can't miss it."

Billy raced to the door, ramming the key into the lock. She started opening the door as she snatched at the security chain, bloodying her finger. Sprinting outside she collided with the body of the car when she reached it. It was Sam. She was slumped forward in the car. Billy rat-a-tat-tatted on the passenger side window and while Sam was stirring ran round to her side.

There was no, "Where have you been? Where? Where?", "How could you have done this to me?", no anger, no resentment. She reached in with both arms when Sam finally and properly woke.

"Oh, oh, oh."

They both said it.

"Come, come."
Billy pulled at Sam's hand as she spoke. Out of the car Sam swayed a little and she could see she had been ill. It was clear she remained weak. The support Billy gave Sam became an embrace. It would be difficult to tell who struggled most to get through the flat's front door as they refused to separate. Billy, one arm across Sam's back and one holding her nearest hand, drew her straight to the bedroom where the teacher removed her shoes and tucked her into bed fully dressed. Back together at last though they might be, they were both shattered in their different ways. This night was for sleeping. Billy took a turn on the settee to ensure Sam got a sound rest. It wouldn't be used any more – at least not by either of them.

Waking in the morning, they believed not only had they found each other but that they could never be made to separate again. It was clear Omicrom wasn't the same threat that other Covid variants had been. The R number had bottomed out and was scarcely getting a mention. Wherever they stayed, wherever they landed, they were secure. Up to and beyond the demise of the pandemic they would be safe. Sam, after all was a non-person. In modern terms she hardly registered as existing at all. Billy on the other hand had been replaced by a ghost in a file of no interest to the intelligence services. No more risks would be taken, there was no need. The threat was gone, of this they were certain.

But they were wrong.

C49

"Saints preserve us Chas, he's driving me crackers. You've got to get him out of hisself."

It was winter and for a couple of weeks Chas had been preoccupied. Eamon all the while was brooding on the contrast between his wife's progress and his own decline. She had been getting bigger throughout their marriage. After their third child there was no mistaking it, she was outgrowing him, for sure. She was in charge at home as she was at work. It carried on up to her menopause. Then he wasn't clear whether she was exploding, imploding, a red giant or a white dwarf. Whatever it was it was big. She first bloomed and then she grew into a Sequoia. Years prior to his illness Eamon began to recognise she should be in charge of him. He didn't foresee to what extent that would happen of course.

In the months before Siobhan's plea for help Chas had spent a lot of time on Eamon's health. He went with him to all medical appointments and made sure he took the medication. Initially he was on Aricept. When each new drug was trumpeted Chas pursued it. Eamon ended up on a drug, the name of which he couldn't pronounce let alone remember, but there were real improvements.

During the autumn Chas believed matters shouldn't be left to drugs alone. Going with Eamon to cognitive and physical therapies gave him an idea: the London Marathon. Eamon couldn't, after all, lose his way on that. Covid had led to it being delayed, so they might stand a chance of getting in. He registered them confident they would get through the ballot. Locals were a mix of askance and impressed to see the two old boys, bending and stretching, huffing and puffing, leaning on brick walls and railings in between their shuffling along. Eamon took it with more than a pinch of salt.

"Think of the feckin' sponsorship we'll get. Best

costume ever, the first headless man to run a feckin' marathon."
Yet Eamon's entry raised questions anew about his mental fitness in intel circles that would have consequences.

Chas' back up position was to join the pair of them to a cycling club. That only lasted up to winter. On their final outing Eamon was sailing along. While other cyclists were working hard on their focus, he had nothing else in his head than pumping away on the pedals. Chas hung behind him so he could keep an eye. That didn't help down a narrow lane, however, when a car raced from a side turning. Chas shouted but with his helmet on Eamon didn't hear. On came the car, its brake pedal was slammed to the floor and the tyres screeched but it hit Eamon's bike.

Fortunately, it did no more than clip the back wheel spinning the bike round. That said Eamon was thrown to the ground and his helmet was badly damaged. Ostensibly he escaped injury, but it did in fact set him back and Chas felt some guilt. That was the end of the bike riding and their marathon application failed. Next year they would apply earlier.

Winter was colder and wetter than it had been for a few years. It was nature's lockdown for some of the old. It was more than that, nevertheless, that led Chas to see less of Eamon. His wife disappeared. Day one didn't bother him, she had disappeared more than once during their marriage. But she missed her birthday and that was unusual – she liked a present. Chas contacted her friends who were no less mystified than him. He tried the local shops and clubs and an evening class she went to. When they told him they hadn't seen her he assumed she was up to her old tricks. He had lived through that before, although she usually created a subterfuge prior to going.

"She went off in a posh limousine, blacked out windows and all,"
a neighbour volunteered. A limousine with blacked out windows? Enough had happened since the trip to

Cheltenham for Chas to accept that there were people, albeit a handful, that preyed on others. On the other hand it wasn't the first time she had gone off in a luxury car. He went through the motions of reporting her as a missing person. It wasn't taken that seriously but at least it was registered. He put up pictures of her in the local library and supermarket and pinned a bunch of the same to some trees in the neighbourhood. His best guess was she would come back when it suited her.

Chas was getting nowhere when Siobhan made her call for help. "Crackers", was her safe word meaning she'd had enough. With Chas' otherwise occupied Eamon was pestering about the delay in going back to Tokyo. Siobhan shredded his false memory, dissected his argument but didn't so much as dent the surface.

"It's like trying to slice water. Mother of God, Chas, he's driving me crackers..."

Anne would have to take care of herself, Eamon was always his priority. At his house he paused on the doorstep, steadying himself. Eamon's treatment was no longer working as he hoped and since the bike accident he was recognising him less and less.

Siobhan welcomed him,

"Come in, come in…he won't let it go. You've got to help. He listens to you."

Sometimes he did.

"Tokyo. Says you promised him."

Chas didn't bother admitting it.

"Says he's going back to play golf."

As it happened Chas had thought through the promise he made and it had grown on him. He had put out feelers. It would be somewhere between a fond farewell and a last hurrah. They used to go on drinkathons together and this could be the mother of them all. The Summer Meadows squad plus a couple of others all fancied a 'jolly' abroad. It would be like the old times. There was, however, a problem – his cab licence had been revoked, he wasn't earning and what should be a healthy bank account was playing up. He was certain he would overcome it but not sure about the time factor.

He picked up Eamon and went to see a travel broker. The broker left the issue of Japan's entry restrictions to another time. Matters seemed fairly simple. They would book flexible flights and for the hotel there was no up-front payment and no cancellation charges until the last twenty four hours of the arrival date. How could it fail?

Sitting opposite the broker it failed immediately for Chas. His credit card was refused – repeatedly. Eamon wasn't so far gone that he didn't understand this. On this occasion he understood it better than Chas who thought it no more than a blip. Tramping out of there in that spirit he at least left with brochures, print outs and the maximum number of images he could prise from the broker. He drip-fed them to Eamon who during several weeks poured over them time and again. Meanwhile Chas cast around for solutions to his money problems.

This took too long and Eamon moved on from pestering to harassment. Siobhan summoned Chas once more. At the bottom of his difficulty were questions raised afresh about bankruptcy. Looking into it soaked up weeks and he got nowhere. It was unfathomable with nobody and no company or firm with answers. In a last attempt he fired off details to the financial ombudsman although he fitted no criteria. He was told he would wait at least eight weeks for it to be looked at.

"Is Anne still missing?"

Siobhan asked. Quietly Eamon suggested to Chas that maybe his wife, Anne, was also growing and developing like Siobhan. That being the case, experience told Chas, the chances were it wasn't her wings that she was spreading. Siobhan had her own idea of where she was and what she was up to - a "fling", she surmised. Chas thought much the same. Yet something quite different had happened.

"Best to deal with what we can. Your best mate'll

make it nowhere else, he's past that. Take him – I'll pay for you."

Eamon had told her of the credit card refusal. Siobhan looked hard at Chas and he looked back at her without saying a word.

"Pay me back once you've sorted out the blessed business with the bank – which you're bound to."

Of that he had no doubt and he had a promise to keep.

"For the poor man's sake, you have to go."

It was an order, not a request. Insubordination wasn't possible.

Anne reappeared in the marital home, looking both the worse for wear and chastened – not a term Chas normally applied to her. She was troubled which was rare. She sought his company, wanting to talk. Insofar as he gave time to listen to her tale of abduction it sounded fanciful. Later, upon reflection, he thought it fitted in with the darker things which had happened to him and Eamon. To that extent she would eventually have got his sympathy.

It took a while to get an agreed date for the gathering of the old mates and then it was disappointing. One of the plus two failed to arrive sending no apologies. The other made an obviously bogus excuse. Notwithstanding that four came. Eamon's declaration,

"Jasus, I'm looking forward to going back to Tokyo,"

furrowed foreheads a little.

Unfortunately, the old crew were at an age where different parts of their bodies were fighting amongst themselves, often the immune system versus the rest. Chas was surprised at how hard he had to harry them to push the project on. When it came to the booking and committing two dropped out, the first with arthritis and the second because lupus meant he couldn't afford the travel insurance.

"Ah I remember him, lost his money on slow horses and fast women,"

Eamon quipped. Shortly after the other two dropped out.

One with a hip operation, the other with knees that had 'gone'. This time Eamon dismissed them with the riposte,

"They're not like you Chas, they carry on so old they should be carbon dated."

He added,

"Chas, it was always going to be feckin' just you 'n' me, Romulus and Remus, Castor and Pollux, Ronnie and Reggie…no? Luke and Matt then."

Chas wasn't lifted – he had heard it all before. He had envisaged the trip as all of them going as a bunch, all helping with the sole invalid. Instead of a team to carry the burden he was to be a one-man sedan. His dismay ended with him nevertheless concluding that he would cope, no matter what it threw at him.

Receiving the full deposit, the travel broker beamed and praised Eamon and Chas for having the get up and go at their age. He added it would be a life enhancing journey. He couldn't know it would be the opposite.

C50

Eamon's son rang him, spoke to him first and not Siobhan. It was unique so Eamon summoned up every iota he could to have some presence of mind for the chat.

"They failed me, Eamon."

His son never called him dad or father. Eamon couldn't work out anything this might refer to. He feared his son meant, "you failed me."

"I'm telling you it was unprecedented. There were far more people at my interview than was justified. Half of them were not police at all. There was a question mark over my background. When I pushed them on it, they were vague but it was current. It has to do with you."

There was none of the ire or angst of old in the son's voice. This was in spite of it signalling an end to his career hopes not to mention a blow to paying off his mortgage. Eamon was staring out a of window where snow drops and bluebells had gone and a magnolia was in full bloom. But he didn't see it because it was the blank stare of someone concentrating to their utmost.

"Saints preserve us, son you must be mistaken. I gave up all me memberships. Haven't been in touch with anyone for decades. What's more I never got within a country mile of the heavy stuff."

So saying he crossed himself.

"It's there. I've been a detective for long enough to know when something's there. They asked about you and the taxi driver and about your trip – Tokyo is it?"

A tocsin sounded in Eamon's head. He knew what this concerned. He didn't let on, he couldn't face telling his son. There was no point in underpinning the lad's dismay.

"All I can tell you is I never did anything illegal and still haven't. Jasus, these days I avoid that like the plague."

"It is there, Eamon think."

If his faculties and thoughts had been rounded up to be driven in the same direction, they were now bolting. He ummed and ahhed, helplessly.

His son took pity and moved the conversation on to family and life in general. It went on for longer than any conversation they had had in years. Before it finished Eamon was trying to remember how it was that his son knew he was going to Japan. He assumed Siobhan told him. At the end of the call Eamon's son shook him with the words,

"Enjoy it, holiday of a lifetime. Take care and keep yourself safe."

Eamon was lost again, managing little more than a solitary word,

"Er, er…goodbye."

And the son had gone.

Between them Chas and Siobhan managed to contain Eamon although some of her nervous energy was taken up by fulminating against the war raging in the Ukraine. Another month or so and Japan would start relaxing entry requirements, but all the while Eamon's medication seemed less effective. At one time he would have been able to say it himself; it was like sweeping up leaves in the wind. He grasped little except that he wasn't in a good way. Going to his house daily Chas was sometimes challenged on the doorstep. Eamon would declare this was a much older man than the one he knew.

In June he took him back to the travel broker. They changed their booking to a guided package tour to Japan which was all that was permitted. Chas was confident that they could use the official trip and then excuse themselves to go places at a pace that suited them. Eamon took most of it in although he let most out again.

Walking home Eamon's mood dropped as it increasingly did.

"You've got to help me top m'self. I can't keep doing this to Siobhan or you. I'm even bollocksin' up me son's life…If not you, who?"

Chas was having none of it.

"Aren't you forgetting Tokyo you mad old Irishman? We're set to go."

It had slipped his mind. Eamon studied him anew to make sure this was the truth while Chas went over details from a new set of travel brochures. Eamon brightened up.

In the build up to the pair's trip to Tokyo, Siobhan called Chas aside. He had to be aware of some realities.

"You're role isn't to give him a reality check. He's past that and it upsets him if you challenge him. Humour him, no more."

Eamon might be excused realities but Chas had to face up to them. He could hardly believe it. The dosette box, was ok but,

"Surely not."

Mercy killing his friend may not be in him, but neither was dealing with incontinence pads. He feared what Siobhan was asking of him was a degree of humanity he simply didn't have.

It got to a week before they were due to travel and Chas had Eamon on a new drug, Lecanemab, of which he was hopeful. Yet the single thing that kept Eamon's spirits up was laboured talk of Japan. Once when his mood had dropped yet again Chas got him watching a travel show on Japan. From the minute the program appeared Eamon was lifted. One section in particular, of a cherry blossom tour, had him ecstatic. He rose from an armchair and stomped around the room, yelling,

"Feck me. Feck me,"

but they were good 'feck mes'.

No sooner had the program finished than there was a knock on the door which he went sprightly to answer and then bristled. On his doorstep he saw uniforms where there were none – but he wasn't far wrong. Standing there were Foreign, Commonwealth & Development department officials. He made them repeat what he called a "mouthful", when he had actually heard them from the outset. On the third occasion they believed he was playacting. They had given due notice, they told him, that he had to surrender his passport. He explained brown envelopes and circulars were simply chucked in the bin unopened. He knew nothing of any notice. He was answered with,

"You all say that. Passport!"

"Ya gobshites, it's not click and collect, you know." Having left the lounge Chas was there by that stage and challenged the officials. They told him their next call was to his place to collect his passport. Failing that they would return with the police. In the kitchen Siobhan picked up what was going on. When she heard they were going to return with the police she went to fetch the passport, she had seen enough of what the police could do. On the doorstep Eamon was going from bad to worse.

"Me poor wife's just died in me arms and you come haranguing me."

The woman of the two officials, quietly said to herself,

"Oh dear, oh dear..."

Then she asked aloud,

"Died in your arms? I'm so sorry. How?"

"I feckin' strangled her."

It got laughs in the past but here it ended any sympathy. Siobhan appeared and handed over the passport.

Chas assured Eamon he would get it sorted but Eamon didn't believe him. His friend's daily fare was more pie in the sky than five loaves and two fishes. He grasped clearly his hope of an epic trip could well have been dashed.

C51

"It's all gone norks up…"
It was Ned.

"They've gone and done it. A truck load of shit is on its way."
Sam didn't understand. She and Billy had been moved from pillar to post but were grateful for it and had done exactly what was required. Ned had run out of places to move them to but had found them jobs as baristas in a boutique coffee bar with a studio above. Of course, it couldn't last forever but their next move, they hoped, would be their last. Some kind of work and a decent home were all they needed although it might be a long way off. To the cyber world they didn't exist. They were patient and careful. They should be safe.

"The taxi feller and his Irish mate…they booked a trip to Tokyo. They've seized their passports but that won't stop what's coming."
Sam began to understand and so to an extent did Billy who was able to catch most of the call. Sam put the rest of the call on speaker phone.

"So, that's begun to unravel some of the twists and turns of the defences I set up?"

"Bloody oath, it has. It'll be a shit shower if you're not careful. Get on it."
Sam raced up to the studio to a laptop and a heavily laden removable hard drive. Over the phone Ned cautioned her whilst she was on the move,

"You deleted yourselves mate but there must be links from the oldsters. You've got to severe those. Coetzee's on it…make yourselves safe…Don't think of the oldsters."

"You don't like them do you?"

"No. I'm head over heels with 'em. They're the best besties I've ever seen. But I don't think they can be helped."

Billy closed the coffee bar while Sam raced to get

on. It was no good repeating previous manoeuvres. Answers to those would already exist so it had to be of a different order. She would detonate an apocalypse she had modelled from the most malignant viruses. In essence she mined all possible files relating to Billy, Tokyo Three and to Chas and Eamon. Searches would set in train something dazzlingly obvious. It was meant to be seen that when redeeming the files was attempted, huge ripples would corrupt a hoard of files and if they carried on, it could spread incrementally in all Five Eyes establishments. With the flare created, her own place in it should be invisible. She had had time, it was prepared. Some minor additions and it was detonated. Finishing she rang Ned. He was checking her work on the screen in front of him. He burst out,

"Oh mate, what you did for the cabbie, a second prize. It wasn't wise but it's a beaut."

Sam thought so too.

"You two' are in the clear for the moment, the old feller's money problems are over and the Irishman gets his trip of a lifetime, but…"

"What? Be careful?"

"Maybe I'm looking at a gift horse from the crapper end but it may come back to bite us – bigger than a saltwater croc."

They were on speaker phone

"So we're not safe?"

Billy asked. Ned thought and replied,

"No, no…not yet, not quite. For Coetzee you haven't ceased to exist. I'm on it…something real serious has to be done where he's concerned."

Chas and Eamon got their passports back by special delivery the following morning. Shortly it would be announced all restrictions on travel to Japan had gone, including the need for visas.

C52

"Something's really badly wrong Ned."

Sam was ringing him after bounding out of a corner shop.

"Billy rang and she's seen Coetzee staring from across the road. He's left but from her description it was definitely him."

Sam was racing back through a shared alleyway at the rear.

"He's left four hulks over there and they look set to swoop."

"It's not working, Sam, somehow."

Ned was panicking, she could hear it in his voice. It was unique.

"Thought we were holding them back. There must be face recognition round there somewhere."

Ned took another call, gulped and told her,

"If you see them on the phone, that's the signal. Don't wait, you've got to go now."

"I don't understand. I did everything right."

"There's more than one genius amongst the Five Eyes. And Coetzee wants blood on his hands, a body count. Go, go. Now!"

He must have known the agents across the road had just got the call.

Sam rammed bolts home on the front door, grabbed rucksacks that were readied and screamed to Billy. The pair sprinted out the back and scooted down the alleyway with their hoods up. A bus and a tube trip later, they boarded a train for Oxford. Ned would have been beside himself had he known. Sam had to see her parents before she left on what might be a one-way trip. Fortunately, her parents wouldn't be at home.

A taxi ride paid in cash brought them outside a church when it was emptying. When her parents emerged, Sam introduced Billy and they understood more about their daughter. She was leaving. Her explanation was brief and barely understood. They knew their daughter was never melodramatic so with hugs and tears they were resigned.

Lots of prayers would be said.

A taxi back to the station was paid for from their small pool of cash. The train and tube led to a tourist rickshaw in Covent Garden where they paid a fortune to be taken to an out of city train station. After some toing and froing they were in an anonymous two star inn in a people forsaken Kentish village. Ned was sent the address on a phone that was then destroyed. They had left behind all other devices but for Sam's laptop and two more phones. They would be used the once – when Ned contacted them.

Taking a room with a double bed Sam and Billy hadn't been welcomed with open arms in the hotel. The proprietor looked them up and down and took her time in booking them in. When they looked around, they could see why. Everywhere there were crosses and religious paraphernalia. Above the reception desk were two huge, framed pictures. One was of Billy Graham and the other of his son Franklin in full flow.

They had booked for one night, having no idea of how long Ned would take to come back to them. It daren't be long. They couldn't use their cards and had been told they must pay up front. It took a lot of the remaining cash they had. There was only enough for one more night. If he didn't ring, then they would be sleeping rough.

C53

"Shame, heard one of 'em joined the three commas club, life was looking up for him."

It was straight from Langley, although not quite accurate. The reply was in a South African accent.

"That Premium Bonds win looks suspicious to me. They're better connected than you think. No matter, it's got to be done."

"Some here don't buy that. It should be a last resort."

"You pushed us to get this done."

"We didn't envisage the scale of your plans."

"There is a team behind them – look at the way they snatched the Irishman when we had him locked away. Uniforms, emergency service vehicle, bolt cutters. It's definitely a team."

"That was Keystone Cops style."

"Except they got their man. Well planned and well executed – they're pros. They're a pair of slippery giyns."

The American had a think. The Boer was hugely experienced. He was there in amongst it and would have a finer grasp than he himself did. There was too much at stake to be sentimental.

"So be it. Japan's more and more important. Too much to lose. We've done the math. We'll give you all the resources, all the assets you need for this to be done cleanly."

"They'll be alone. That or they'll be in a spot where we make sure they're isolated. No evidence will be left. With the right resources it'll simply fly away."

"Are you definite the two old guys deserve this?"

"I doubt the taxi driver did much more than take a fare but he's in the mix. It's on him, he made a bad choice of friend. This way it's definitive. No doubts, no loose ends. Clinical. It's gone"

"I'll make sure it's ok from this end. It's agreed. Everything you ask for. Wrap it up.

C54

"We've been here two days. We need to be out of here."
Ned had rung.

"I'm working on it, but you need to do something for yourselves now. Mate, the great Gus Gorman, right?"
Sam was baffled.

"Unless …that Ernie Bonds manoeuvre …can you do it for one last time?"

"No. The only reason it went through was because they've still got so many staff off with the virus or working from home. That and that it could have discredited the whole scheme. We won't get away with it again."

"Thought so. Gus Gorman it has to be then."

"What?"

"Richard Pryor, mate, Superman Three. You seen it?"

"Ned, what are you talking about?"

"Just answer me!"

"Alright. Yes, it was funny."

"Right, you've got to do it, the same, cream money off the top of huge accounts. You're going to need it."
Ned explained and moved on.

"I said Coetzee bypassed all the cyber stuff. Probably got an old filing cabinet and written notes in it with photos. He'll know everything."

"We've booked the one more night here but we're out of cash."
They needed to be taken out of there.

"I've got a few probs with that. I'm working on it."
The problem was no registered cab firm and no hire car firm could be used and all the intel cars available had tracking devices with recorders on them. He didn't say but it was proving nigh on impossible to get them a vehicle.

He moved the subject on, remarking that Sam could pass for a Portuguese and asking,

"Billy teaches Portuguese, doesn't she?"

She taught Spanish in the school where she worked, but her degree was in Portuguese. They would be going to Heathrow.

"One way or the other this is finishing. You can't ditch your last phone, we may need to speak again. If they identify it, we have to hope it'll be too late."

Sam's original job at GCHQ was tracking money laundering. She knew the accounts least likely to detect siphoning off of funds and those unlikely to protest. It couldn't be as Gus Gorman had done but it was in the same spirit. Cyber transactions took place, funds popped up and then liquidated themselves. Notional losses were made so HMRC interest would be minimal. She transferred funds to Jersey, then to the Caymen islands, back into London and then to Panama. She and Billy became seriously wealthy.

"It's not happening, Sam, not for the moment." Ned meant getting transport of any order. Again, he sounded panicked. He was getting nowhere with it. This wasn't a job he should get his mates on. Often there was a delay, Sam knew that well, but he had never failed on a commitment before. While the call was ongoing he was making one last attempt.

"I'm not sure. Maybe I can't do this…Got to run." It was the first time Sam had ever heard him say "can't do". It was a hundred miles to Heathrow. Using her phone for a cab, could be a disaster. She hoped Billy didn't hear it. Billy however had got the drift of it and whispered.

"Oh, we've had it."

Sam expected tears. Instead, Billy came and stood beside her and said,

"We're in it together, whatever it is."

Past hope was what it was. Intel would soon be upon them. Sam stood knowing there was nowhere to turn. Billy went and slumped on a chair.

Sam's phone rang.

"Give the man a coconut."

Sam looked to the ceiling. What on earth? It was Ned

calling.

"I've done it, got us a driver – not ideal – and got us a wagon. It's no fezza but it's on its way."
Apparently there was no other option. Was it another contact of his? He had faith in them all but sometimes it wasn't justified, sometimes they simply let you down.

C55

"Five minutes away. Time's tight."
It was Ned. That could mean an hour or more, but Sam was taking no chances. She and Billy leapt upstairs and leapt down again with minor luggage and double checking they had their passports. At the reception desk the hotelier surfaced with a printed bill for the third day she said was due. It had not been met and she was on the verge of ringing the police. In her hand she had the landline phone. A vehicle could be heard parking at the front.

Coming outside Sam half-feared seeing a pony and trap or its like but it was far worse. She looked at the vehicle and then looked for another. It was a white Rolls Royce, straight from a wedding still with white ribbons on and a trail of rattling cans. Billy stood unable to say anything. The pair looked to Ned. He shrugged. Sam shouted at him,

"We wanted to escape notice, not command it."
Billy giggled and then changed to crying. When Jessica stepped out of the vehicle Sam added,

"It's a five-seater and there's six of us. The second the police see us, that'll be that."

"No, they'll never stop us in this, lovey. If they do, we'll just say it's two lots of newlyweds, me and my mate and you and yours. They'll wave us on."

It was the driver who now looked to Billy and asked,

"Some getaway car, eh? Recognise me dear?"
Billy did. He was the old taxi driver. She turned to his mate saying,

"I recognise you too, don't I?

"As what, Jasus?"
It was the former teacher from her school. Chas explained he'd had a wedding job that morning but had to have the vehicle back by the weekend.

Two more bags were squeezed into the boot and Eamon waved Sam and Billy forward with both hands. Sam remained standing there. Chas came over beckoning her.

Sam looked at Ned. How could he do this and how could they all get in? He merely curved his arm, hand out indicating she should get in. She ignored his gesture and walked off towards the back of the car. There she tugged and snatched at the string holding the tin cans until they ripped off, damaging the bumper at the same time. For one second she considered throwing them at Ned. Chas helped her into the Rolls, shoving her up against Billy, who was already tight against Jessica. Jessica had got in momentarily before, having gone to pay the hotel bill.

Ned had done his best. There was nobody else. He knew Chas and Eamon were going to Heathrow, on their way to Tokyo. He took the risk of going to Chas' and offered him serious money. Sam did her calculation and thought the whole ride was risky but not as risky as staying where they were any longer. Eamon constantly glanced backwards to make sure they weren't being followed. Ned was confident they weren't, but that all changed when he heard a police siren. They were pulled over by a police car that was unusually full. Three officers got out, checked around the car, whilst the fourth was on a link, checking the vehicle and its owner. Torches blinded Chas and his passengers while one by one they were scrutinised.

"This may be a wedding but there are too many passengers in the vehicle."

It was uncompromising. Blue lights were flashing into the Rolls' interior, distorting objects and faces. Chas rammed his hand over Eamon's mouth, who was ready to deliver some home truths from across the Irish sea.

Particulars were checked by one officer. The boot had to be opened.

"Stay in the vehicle, madam."

Jessica ignored it and two uniforms closed on her. The officer who had remained in the police car ran over. Jessica had been on a link herself. A brief conference between the police took place. Snippets could be heard:

"…it might not be on the number plate…but it's

from the top… it's not for us, lads."

An officer with sergeant's stripes came back to Chas, ignoring Jessica, whom he clearly disliked,

"You're free to go, sir. May I suggest you stick to the speed limit?" There was shock and awe in Chas' car when Eamon shouted out,

"Feck off."

The sergeant caried on walking as though he didn't hear.

C56

Upon arriving at Heathrow Eamon came out with,

"Is all this about Tokyo, Tokyo Three?" There was silence until Billy said quite simply,

"Yes."

Chas was told to drop his passengers on the road by the short stay parking he was heading into. They wouldn't be catching the bus into the terminal. While the two old men parked to catch their shuttle, Jessica led the others off.

What now? There had been little opportunity to explain plans in confidence. Picking their way to the terminal Ned told them,

"You're going from Heathrow to Tanzania."

"Where? Why?"

Sam asked.

"You're going to the Serengeti."

Billy was appalled by the idea of a safari.

"You'll be killed and your bodies destroyed."

That wasn't funny. Billy gripped Sam's hand, while she fixed Jessica in a stare. She responded,

"Lions'll kill you and hyenas destroy what's left."

"All arranged I've got mates who're gameos there..."

"Mates", for once wasn't reassuring.

"Best we can come up with. It's the sort of thing that's happened in the past, its plausible. We'll fix the reports. Don't worry you'll be safer there than you've been for a long while."

"While your death is confirmed you'll fly/drive to Guinea Bissau,"

Jessica told them, prior to demanding,

"Passports!"

They passed them over to her and were issued with two new ones each. She insisted they walk more quickly.

From there they would fly to Lisbon.

"You'll be in a place 100 yards from the terminal, mate. You won't be staying and no beds, I'm afraid."

"Where are we going to end up?"
Billy asked.

"The Azores if we get everything right."

"And if not?"
It was Sam.

"Don't, just don't mate."
For Sam the reality could hardly be starker. She asked,

"What about you, are you coming with us?"
It was heartfelt.

"It's not for us, we'll be covered,"
he said nodding towards Jessica. On the tip of his tongue Ned had

"Don't forget, mate, we're only ever a keyboard away."
But he swallowed the words. He was certain and he knew Sam would know it, that risk would never be taken. Both knew they would never see each other or even speak to each other again – online, anywhere.

They were taken through the diplomat's entrance avoiding normal scrutiny. Prior to boarding Sam asked,

"What will you do?"

"We'll put the blame on you – seriously."
Jessica was blunt.

"You should come with us."

"Don't worry, Ned's taken care of. This is your chance – take it."
Sam studied her, the tied back hair and the suit.

"Are you in danger?"
she asked Ned. Jessica replied,

"Don't worry, he's safer than you – a lot."
As she looked at Ned he added,

"No worries. I'm like a coin in a nappy – I always come out shining at the other end."
He leaned forward and hugged Sam. She patted Dishlicker farewell.

"Where will you go?"

"We'll be safe. Failing that we'll go boldly where

no one's gone before – that or the land of the long white cloud,"
he laughed. It was all set up should they need it.

As they separated, Ned held up his hand and gave Spock's Vulcan farewell. It was the nearest he could get to a valediction. Sam tried to respond with,

"Live long…"
but she choked on the sentiment.

"…and prosper. No wuccas"

Ned took Jessica's hand and the pair receded. As they did, he looked back to wave goodbye mouthing the word, "Besties."

C57

About to drive off to pick up Sam and Billy in the Rolls Royce Chas' parting words to Siobhan had been,

"It'll be hairy,"

He meant the trip with Eamon, handling a foreign language alongside a man to whom everything had become foreign. He had done his homework, read up on Japanese culture and bought a phrase book, mastering half a dozen phrases which he thought should get him by. He also had got Eamon on a new drug Aducanumab which seemed to be having a positive effect.

On departure day when Eamon said goodbye to Siobhan she looked vulnerable to him, more a sapling than a mighty Red Wood. Was she afraid he might have forgotten her by the time he came back? His memory was shedding names daily and soon none would be left. Before long hers would go but faces remained - for the moment.

"Soft lass, will you look in these eyes. Are they crossed or squinty or spoiled with disease? They've seen your face and have a memory of their own. They'll always know you."

Walking to the car, Eamon had his arm around Chas. It had become a habit which in the end Chas didn't mind that much. Sometimes when there was nobody around, he would put his own arm around his old friend. Driving to pick-up their last minute passengers, Eamon called him, "Bob" and was slow to correct himself. It troubled him less than Chas. In the Rolls Royce he had bemused Sam and Billy with his comment,

"You know I'd like to be the undertaker's next pay packet?"

They had heard stranger things – just.

Siobhan had eased paths at the airport, doing all the forms online. She also obtained a doctor's letter testifying to Eamon's condition. It came in handy in duty free where he unscrewed the top of a bottle of Jameson's and took a swig before Chas could stop him. Chas paid for the whiskey.

Money was no longer a problem and he was pleased in the end to be able to pay for his own trip. He was a hundred thousand pounds better off thanks to the Premium Bonds win Sam had rigged. He had long believed the jackpot would come his way in spite of having one solitary ticket.

Queuing, in the lounge, at check-in Eamon constantly commented on other people's appearance. Chas squirmed when he stood in front of a group of men carrying golfing equipment repeatedly looking them up and down. Chas dragged him away, but his friend wasn't abashed telling him,

"Instinct, says they're not right. There's something evil about them."

At the security area Eamon ducked under the zig zagging bands with Chas throwing his hands in the air, unable to follow him.

"Feckin' unhand me,"

he told burly police armed with automatics. Lights were flashing, alarms going off and more personnel sprinting to the scene. When Eamon was pinned to the floor effing and blinding, he challenged one and all to a fight. He calmed down when Chas got there. It was evident Eamon was more like a drunk than a hijacker. Chas' explanation that he was on drugs, along with the doctor's letter meant it was himself who was warned on any further misconduct. He intended to keep within inches of Eamon after that. This didn't prevent him from saying to the men he had already scrutinised when he passed them,

"Who the feck d'you think you're fooling. I know you."

While Chas apologised Eamon wandered to a group of roughly a dozen women. He asked them if they were sisters. In truth they did look alike with lips, cheekbones and foreheads all having undergone the same procedures. He winced when Chas dug him in the ribs to shut up, but it didn't stop him.

"Either the poor things've got a feckin' syndrome or

they're the world's first dodecahedlets."

It was said quietly but not quietly enough. He was silenced with a harder dig which winded him. One of the stewardesses understood some of what was going on, so she had the women phalanx down to unoccupied seats at the back. The minute the opportunity arose Chas put a cup of tea on his tray. Eamon didn't want one and immediately shot out down towards the women. Chas expected to see stewards drag him back to his seat but there was no need. Even a diminished Eamon was far from being cruel and he grasped he might have offended. He 'helloed ladies' the women and bought them a round of gin and tonics using all the U.K. currency he had. Then he proceeded to entertain them. Chas took his head out of his hands. He had seen it many times, Eamon could be very winning. He had a skit from days gone by. It was of a clueless husband who bragged that his wife said nothing was too good for him, asked God what she'd done to deserve him and declared he should get everything that was coming to him. He had the women in hysterics. On his way back he stopped and stared once more at the men he gave a hard time earlier. Now they looked back. Each recognised the other, predator and prey. By the time Eamon reached Chas and sat down he had forgotten what he had just seen. Chas knew his friend had stopped to stare but it was something he was used to. In years gone by Eamon had antenna for villains. That was, however, long ago. Chas glanced back at them and saw nothing to be concerned about. He got him a whisky and insisted he took some of the tranquilisers Siobhan had supplied. He was soon in airplane mode himself, nothing getting through. Before long he dozed off.

In the Tokyo terminal Eamon told border guards he was looking forward to the Yakusa at his hotel, by which he meant jacuzzi. While he and Chas were being frog marched to a side room the taxi driver wondered whether he might have done this for the hell of it. It wouldn't be unique. On the other hand, it was surely not a big enough issue to warrant being interrogated. Passports and their luggage were checked once more. Chas was too intent on handling Eamon to notice one of the passengers he had scrutinised briefly enter the room. While he got on his mobile Eamon was leaning first to one side and then the other. His face was close to vacant. Anyone should be able to see he wasn't entirely with it. Spotting sets of latex gloves readied on a bench Chas stood close to Eamon hoping he could stop him from kicking off. He pressed the doctor's letter on the border guards only to see it brushed away.

The old pairs' belongings were shaken from their cases and poked, medication examined and then all flung to one side. A phone rang. One of the border guards held it out for his colleagues to hear. To begin with it was in English with an American accent. The message was confirmed on a computer screen. An interpreter appeared and told Chas there had been a mistake. The border guards looked baffled at the orders to let the two old travellers go. As they went Chas explained to the interpreter that what was meant was jacuzzi not Yakuza and she laughed.

In a taxi bound for their hotel Eamon remarked,

"At times I'm not deliberately making a joke." Chas looked at him and smiled.

"You still make people laugh."

"But I feckin' don't know why."

The hotel check-in saw a similar faux pas, ending with Chas losing his temper – and then regretting it. There was nothing to be gained by it. In their room Eamon took Chas' hand telling him,

"I know, I know I'm nature's fool. I don't blame you for getting angry."

"So, old friend, you forgive me for all the scolding?"

"Always. You know you're special to me. Piss on the carpet and it'd be holy water on hallowed ground for me."

As Chas unpacked for them, Eamon told him,

"I'm interested in the quality of death. This is the

land of Hara-kari, isn't it?"

"Cut out the Japanese, please Eamon. It'll cause trouble."

Up to a point Chas got it. For a while he had been having difficulty in coming up with an argument against the ending of Eamon's life.

Looking at their room it suddenly dawned on him the travel broker had made a mistake, it had one bed alone albeit queen sized.

"How on earth are we going to sustain three nights of this".

"Feckin' easy…"

said Eamon,

"You on the left, me on the right."

Chas clapped him on the back, handed him a pair of swimming trunks and said,

"Here stop pestering and go and enjoy yourself in the Yakuza."

They both laughed.

It was a good job that their travel package involved tour buses because the course was rained off. He told Eamon the arrangements.

"Yep, I remember,"

he lied, also asking,

"Did you hire the blessed clubs yet?

Chas had.

"Should I oversleep tomorrow stick a tee in me ear and see if you can blast it with a three iron…"

Chas laughed. It would be a comic stroke from someone with his handicap.

"…and then finish the job with a hefty great driver. No air shots two or three attempts should do it."

Club him to death? Not even Eamon could want an end like that. It was light-hearted so he didn't tell him to leave out the morbid stuff.

Chas was concentrating on packing a few things for himself and Eamon in a rucksack. He recoiled at a pack of incontinence pads in a draw. Eamon shook his head,

“Siobhan worries too much. I’ll never allow meself to sink that low. You’ll never have to deal with that.” Chas breathed out, as his friend strolled off in his trunks and dressing gown. Eamon shouted behind himself,

“I’d rather be blown to pieces, cremated alive.”

C58

The start of the bus tour wasn't the nightmare Chas feared, but there was an incident when Eamon didn't restrain a monster fart.

"Freeing trapped wind."

he declared as though it was an act of emancipation. Chas did his best to ignore it as did everybody else. The bus was half full and they were able to sit, earphones plugged in at the front on top. The third time they exited, they stood for a long time on a stone bridge in the grounds of the imperial palace, Eamon staring at the water flowing underneath. He thought he saw his face stare back at him wanly from the riverbed.

"Have you ever gazed at fast water and considered jumping in for the feck of it?"

He caught the look in Chas' eyes and knew he should shut up. He had got to go to the toilet. Chas went to accompany him, but Eamon shooed him away, insisting to his relief that he could handle it.

"A bit of blessed dignity,"

he said ambling off and following signs to the toilets. Chas watched him go, keeping an eye out for his return. A group of tourists looked lost, so labouring with a bus tour map Chas volunteered to help, finally sending them in a definite direction.

A full twenty minutes and Eamon hadn't reappeared, so he went to fetch him. He angered occupants as he checked every cubicle, but his friend wasn't to be seen. The old cabbie scampered high and low, left and right and up and down. Accelerating from a trot to a sprint he double and triple checked, going round and round. Remembering the bridge, he raced there fearing his friend had jumped but there was no crowd of onlookers, so he knew before he got there that Eamon wasn't being swept off in the waters. There were many other bridges, but he would have chosen the nearest. Chas recalled reading in an English language paper in their hotel that the number of missing person cases in

Japan had reached a record high a few years earlier. It remained at more than seventy seven thousand. He rang Eamon's phone fruitlessly. If so many Japanese could get lost what might happen to a man whose mind itself was lost? There was no choice but to phone Siobhan, dreading her response. She was relaxing on a spa day and calmly reassured him.

"You know Eamon he's on a wander. You'll find him, the app on your phone works abroad too, you know." She added,

"Remember, what I said, it's pointless having a go at him – he's beyond that. You're there to soften the hard facts not shove him up against them."
She goodbyed him and put the phone down.

Before he could try the app his mobile rang and extraordinarily it was from Eamon's device, although it wasn't his voice,

"Bring money,"
he was told gruffly in a Japanese accent,

"for friend."
Missing person's maybe, but the article the old cabbie read said nothing about kidnapping and ransom. He demanded to speak to Eamon.

"They've dragged me in here into this bar…"

"Should I get the police?",
Chas whispered,

"Just say yes or no."

"No! Police? Jasus, no. Don't let them near this. Just bring your wallet, no police. It'll be fine."
He never wanted the police involved in anything. He sounded alarmed.

"Are you being held."

"I'm being held up alright, feckin' definitely. I've pushed the boat out and now I'm all at sea, up to me neck."
The phone was evidently snatched from Eamon and an image with the bar's frontage on it was sent.

Eamon was in trouble. Chas hailed a cab, showed

the driver the image on the phone. In broken English, the driver asked him if he knew this was a "Yaks bar". Chas nodded as though he did and the cab was on its way. He understood he was heading for a Yakusa establishment.

Close to his destination the cab came to a halt in a street jammed with crowds. He jumped out and hurried forward on foot. Over twenty five yards he buttocked and barged onwards. A European shoved him back hard and he bashed his shoulder on a wall. He forced his way ahead along a main throughfare full of bars and eating places, its buildings a vivid orange and white. He searched for the image he had on his phone.

At the far end of a dark alley he saw the sign he needed. Nobody from the crowds was interested in going there, the alley was empty. He was in a hurry yet found himself walking cautiously to the bar. When he got there his entrance was blocked by two huge square shaped men wearing crisp white shirts. They bowed and he reciprocated. Through the shirts he could see their bodies were covered in tattoos. He had read of tattoos like these, done using bamboo tips. One of the men looked at him and said,

"Gaigin?"

mimicking a deranged face and pointing to the stairs. Chas understood. Wise or not he was going up there. Before he went, he was given a white cloth to wipe his hands. They bowed and he again returned the gesture.

The stairs up were steep. He breathed in and steadied himself with a hand on a wall covered in a design of double rhombuses, lines running down their middle. Like CND semaphore he grasped these had a serious meaning and a sort of warning. He peeked into the room where Eamon was at the bar wedged-in by younger men either side. There were others and Chas thought two of them were the men Eamon didn't like the look of on the plane. He edged back down the stairs. He tried the Japanese he had practiced,

"Herupu..."

"Herupu."

The two doorkeepers didn't move. He rushed repeating it in all the ways he could, but they simply shrugged. His phrase book wasn't helpful. They watched while he typed on his translation app finally showing it to them to read.

They grimaced and followed him upstairs. When they appeared, the men either side of Eamon sprang back. The man behind the bar, however, was snarling and holding up his left hand to point. Chas saw the top of his small finger was missing. One of the door keepers held up his thumb and forefinger rubbing them together. Chas got it. Siobhan had put a low limit on Eamon's Monzo card and it was exhausted. Eamon called out,

"Feckin' small beers here, I tell you Chas, me kingdom for a wallet."

Out came his own card, the barman bowed and took a payment. Eamon called out,

"I pay me way, no matter what the company."

His round honoured Eamon offered the two doorkeepers a drink. They declined but liked him for it. They took care to escort the two old men down the stairs and stood side by side blocking the exit as they went. In the bar and on the stairs there was a shrugging of shoulders.

Chas and Eamon were quickly cabbing it back to the hotel.

"How did you get there with them?"

Eamon struggled to recall. Slowly and with gaps it emerged he bumped into two of them when he got lost wandering off from the toilet. A drink? Yes, he was up for that. Soon after, he told Chas, he was banjaxed.

"Why did you go with them?"

"Hmm…They knew me. I couldn't remember one fecking' way or the other…Knew I'd been to Cheltenham… An invite to a drink, that's friendly enough, isn't it?"

"What about the guys from the plane?!

"They turned up in the bar."

"I thought you didn't like them."

"They bought me rounds of drinks, had 'em lined up

on the bar counter. And then it was my round. Nobody feckin' gets away without me getting my round in...Call it drinkin' with the enemy."

For Chas this could be just one more of the scrapes he'd had to get Eamon out of throughout their adult lives. But the men from the plane turning up there specifically for a drink when there was such a huge choice of bars? That was an almighty coincidence. He reassured himself they were a continent away from the difficulties they had had back home. The security people had surely finished with them. After all was said and done, they'd been able to leave the bar without much difficulty. Who'd be interested in two old duffers like them?

These thoughts didn't stop him constantly looking behind while they travelled, checking wing mirrors. Leading to their hotel he saw clearly the road behind them was empty. That was until the last mile when two cars in convoy appeared. He kept an eye on them but by the time they arrived at the hotel they could no longer be seen. He did wonder if they had simply gone elsewhere or were trying to allay suspicion. In the hotel Chas couldn't stop himself from berating Eamon

"You were supposed to go to the toilet and come back. I had to ring your wife."

Eamon was full of drunken remorse.

"The pair of yous are making regular commutes to the blessed ends of the earth for me. I get it, I do get it."

Finishing dinner, they went to their room to watch some tv. The air conditioning was on maximum and it was cold. They slept in their dressing gowns curled, facing the same direction, left and then right. In turn they each tucked themselves around the other.

In spite of lights from the hotel grounds breaching the room curtains, Chas slept well. All the drama was behind them. When the weather finally permitted and they eventually played he thought the sole threat he would encounter on the golf course would be to his ego. Eamon was by far the better golfer. That said the taxi driver knew should he end up threshing about in a bunker at the foot of Mt Fuji Eamon would literally stand by him.

C59

Boarding the plane for the last leg to Ponta Delgarda Sam's phone rang. She hadn't expected to hear from Ned ever. She was thrilled until he said,

"It's real bad news mate."

"Are we in danger – imminently?"

"No that's taken care of, no, not you. Jessica's on it but it's too late. There's nothing she can do for the oldsters."

"What is it? Is there something I can do?"

"I don't think any of us ever could. I thought about booking a flight, but I'd be too late, mate. Anyway there'd be nothing I could do."

"What is it?"

A team had been sent.

"It's Mossad style, only instead of tennis outfits and rackets, it's golf gloves and clubs."

Sam recalled an assassination in Dubai a few years earlier.

"So Chas and Eamon are at risk."

"No mate, they're cactus, goners. Owed it to you to tell you."

"I can get another flight. There must be a sterilised pc or laptop somewhere. I can intervene."

"You're not listening mate. This is Coetzee's doing. The world wide web doesn't include him. It's all but done. If you could send the oldsters to a cyber twilight zone or wrap them in body armour it still wouldn't do it."

"Can't we ring and warn them? I'll phone – I'll take the risk."

"Think of Billy. You might as well put the gun to her head and your own and you'd have thrown everything away and for nothing. Calls'll be monitored and what's more blocked. I'm sorry Sam, I loved the old fellers, but it's done, it's fucking done. Catch your plane."

"Coetzee. I want you to do something about him."

Sam knew exactly what she was asking.

C60

The second day in Japan Chas made sure the hours were filled. There was a different bus tour but they never left the vehicle, so it was the next best thing to not moving out of the hotel. He believed whoever the men in the bar were, they had been given the slip. He ordered sushi for their meal, but Eamon wanted a burger instead. They were brought complementary wine but stuck to drinking whisky. It was to be an early morning, so the two sleep-mates took the lift to their bedroom. Eamon had spent a chunk of the day looking over his shoulder and didn't stop now. They hadn't drunk that much yet wobbled in the lift. Going to their bedroom they wobbled more. Each had to put a hand on the wall to make it to their room.

Booked into the same hotel were four men who came on the flight with Chas and Eamon but who kept themselves out of sight. In addition to golf equipment their luggage carried restraints, instruments for clinical asphyxiation and bags for body parts. Four others, two men and two women had joined them with guns and sights. No chances were to be taken. Those from the U.K. were Coetzee's men. The others were sanctioned by Langley. The wine Chas and Eamon declined was more sedatives than alcohol. It was intended to make things easier all round. It was early. They wanted Chas and Eamon asleep. Hours would pass slowly. Anticipation was all consuming.

Inside their bedroom Eamon put the security lock on the door and stuck the back of the chair under the door handle. Chas let him do the same the previous night. This time Eamon went a big step further and insisted on taking the bedclothes under the divan to lie under them there. Chas didn't argue even when his friend insisted he joined him on the floor. He accepted Eamon was too troubled and just got on with it. There was carpet and thick underlay, so it wasn't too bad, except that Eamon fidgeted and was fitful. Chas played a song from his phone that Eamon claimed was by an Irish girl. Siobhan found it calmed him. Putting in earplugs

Chas pulled the pillow around his head which didn't quite work. He was set to lower the volume but changed his mind because Eamon was singing along,

Lay me down gently,
Lay me down low,
I fear I am broken and won't mend I know
There's one thing I ask when the stars light the skies,
Who now will sing me lullabies?

Songs were one of the few things his memory was still good for.

The room was warmer than the previous night, but the two old friends still dozed close to each other, Eamon soon placing his arm around Chas's waist. The old cabbie wriggled it off. Later when it came back, he left it there. One o'clock in the morning, in pairs the killers strolled talking loudly of the local golf course. Some were wearing elaborately pimpled golfing shoes, some carried golf bags. One feigned being drunk. One woman had on a Nike Tiger Woods tee shirt. Cameras recorded her roommate practicing her golf swings along the corridor. Yards apart, some pairs knew each other, others apparently not, as they entered separate rooms.

Two o'clock, the cameras were down and the team were edging towards Chas and Eamon's room with a set of keys. In the old pairs' room the bed shook and Eamon half woke.

"Did the Earth move for you?"

he asked Chas. Chas was less awake than him but when Eamon said in jest,

"Hold me tight,"

he did. Hearing noises outside their room Eamon hit his head on the underneath of the bed trying to sit up. Hearing it too Chas got out from under the bed, deciding,

"It'll be room service, they've made a mistake."

"Don't touch that feckin' door,"

Eamon hissed.

By the time the last of the team was assembling by

the bedroom door, the same tremor that woke Eamon had made them ever more alert. Gloves were on, nylon restraints and plastic bags at the ready. Hypodermics were in hands and tasers were out just in case. Loaded guns with silencers would be a last resort. The keys were tried but the door wouldn't open. One of the women took them, tutting, but her hand trembled with the key, as the lock rattled. It rattled because the door shivered in its frame, the wall that held it quivering. A hallway mirror shattered when it fell, followed by a painting crashing down. The assassins looked to each other as the floor beneath them shook. Suddenly off balance the biggest of them sent another flying into two more making them tumble together. A taser went off and a syringe snapped. Alarms began.

"Stop, stop."

C61

Alarms were going off more and more. They were sounding in buildings nearby too. The hotel assistant manager had appeared and was clear, they could go back to their rooms, there was no need to head for the emergency exits. He repeated,

"Stop, stop. Only shindo four point two. It happens all the time. There are thousands a year. It is safe."

The armed guests in the corridor, tools of their trade tucked away, weren't convinced. The assistant manager added,

"The hotel is built for this."

Everyone should return to their rooms. Constant checks would be made. Staff came to clear the shards from the mirror and painting. The assassins would re-emerge within hours. They reconvened at four a.m. They were even more alert and ready than they were earlier. Time was short. They had to be quick. Everything was at the ready. They could despatch they two old men several times over within minutes. The key was in the door lock and this time it was working. It was opening centimetre by centimetre. The second it was open wide enough the team rushed in. The bed was empty. The bathroom was checked, then the wardrobes, then the window ledge. Pillows were missing and at least one cover from the bed. With hand gestures, no words, one assassin was stationed by the door, as one pointed to the bottom of the bed. He lifted the sheets, slowly ducking down to see a duvet with two bundles in the foetal position lying underneath. He beckoned and three of the operatives were positioned either side of the bed. A hand crept down and ripped the bed sheets back to reveal the underneath of the bed. Weapon holders dropped to the floor to strike. They duvet was torn back and the bundles heaved out. Thumbs were on syringe plungers, tasers and guns primed and plastic bags gaped ready to suffocate. Containers for body parts were ready.

C62

The hotel Chas and Eamon slept in was a stone's throw from where the B29 dropped its bomb in the summer of 1945. The golf course and one bunker in particular were exactly where it burrowed below ground. But the course was closed. Previous bad weather and the tremors saw to that.

The assassins found nothing under the bed except for two pillows, two discarded dressing gowns and a duvet. Chas and Eamon were at that moment snuggled together elsewhere in another double bed. Chas had persuaded Eamon that sleeping in the bed would be ok in their new room. After the noise in the corridor, he had collared the assistant manager, revealed Eamon under the bed, blamed the light entering their room and succeeded in getting an upgrade.

A few floors from there the assassins weren't going to give up. These two should be the softest of targets. A quick reassessment was all that was needed. The one day left would more than suffice. Exigencies had been planned for.

Come the last morning of the trip Chas rose to see a lump on Eamon's forehead. The explanation was his friend had walked into a toilet door in an unfamiliar room. Chas knew it wasn't so. He had heard the bang an hour after sunrise and a cry that wasn't in pain but anguish. Was it the new drug? There was something different about Eamon. He seemed more lucid.

"Forget the feckin' game Chas, we should go home."

"You're the one who insisted we came,"

"There's something wrong here Chas. I know I can see and hear things but there were people outside our room last light. I just don't know that we should be here at all. Someone put a key in the lock."

"Of course they did – the manager. It's a fine day for it, I'm playing golf and you are too."

And on it went, Chas' optimism versus his friend's doubt.

Since part of this doubt was self doubt Chas was always going to win. It took longer than it might, however, and it made them late to breakfast where Eamon couldn't face eating but had three cups of coffee.

"Privilege of the condemned man,"
he announced. Now he had won the debate and they were definitely playing Chas hoped there would be no more of Eamon's morbid talk. He answered Eamon's comment by saying

"Look, for most of us life's not all it's cracked up to be you know."

"Mebe but death feckin' is. It's untroubled, unbroken sleep."
Chas wished he hadn't responded.

"Look mate when we enter the final straight, we'd all like a good run in but for most it isn't that way."

"Mebe but don't tell me when we're ferried over the Styx we're all in the same feckin' boat, because we ain't."

Neither of them noticed the breakfast hall and most of the hotel were empty. Residents had all had notes under their bedroom doors that due to conditions the golf club was closed. The news sent most of them on a variety of trips out. Going back to their room to get their golf bags Eamon and Chas passed a huddle of residents who were not taking a trip. Eamon bristled. If he recognised them, it was more as a type than anyone he recalled seeing before.

"Jasus why did you bring me here, Chas?"
Instead of leading off on how he had been nagged into it incessantly Chas simply said,

"It's beautiful here, as different as could be and you love a game of golf."
No matter what Eamon's mentality there was no answer to this. They were staying and going to play golf and enjoy the craic.

Although in Japanese terms it was a small quake there was movement in the building where local buses were housed. Bricks and concrete were blocking its exit doors.

At the hotel fewer staff had made it to work but it shouldn't have been a problem given it was largely emptied out for the day. This forced Chas and Eamon to lug their own equipment into the lift and to go down. At reception was an unfamiliar face who informed them there was a taxi waiting to take them to the course. Taxis were not normally allowed right up to the hotel steps.

"No problems with the course, after last night's shenanigans, then?"

Eamon asked. No, the club was open like normal and the taxi was complementary. That wasn't usual nor was the vehicle either which was, as Chas commented, "a cut above". It was a Range Rover with blacked out windows. Going to the revolving doors Eamon grabbed Chas' arm and speeded him past the huddle of residents still there, apparently waiting.

Getting into the vehicle, Eamon told Chas,

"We don't have to do this you know,"

to which the reply was,

"Oh yes we do."

Insofar as he was capable of making a clear decision Eamon did there and then. He would cease bellyaching; it was getting nowhere. Did he have the presence of mind to carry that through? It would all depend.

Minutes after the old friends were on their way two full vehicles left the hotel car park. Each was identical to the one supplied for Chas and Eamon. They were also on their way to the golf club but hung back out of sight.

While Chas and Eamon were arriving at the club grounds the last signs saying it was closed were being removed. They noticed nothing. Eamon wanted to get some tees but the golf shop was closed. There was one person alone on the reception and she seemed to know little including where some extra tees might be found. They were told systems were down so receipts were not available. Their passports were taken to be held. They had seen this in hotels but never at a golf club anywhere. Chas wanted photographs of the pair of them in the club house and out by the tee but that wasn't allowed. Unusually it was club rules to not have mobile phones on the course. They had to be left behind the counter. Eamon protested,

"This ain't feckin' right."

Chas couldn't see the harm in it, but Eamon pressed him,

"We should get out of here,"

Chas decided to interpret that as meaning they should get on the course and led them out to the initial tee. There Eamon's mind moved on to the matter of golf.

In the car park the other two Range Rovers with blacked out windows drew up. Their passengers slickly dismounted and collected equipment from each boot. It was the eight who had tried to enter Chas and Eamon's bedroom the previous night. They mingled, checked and double checked their equipment with some rehearsing. By then the person behind reception had disappeared and there were no staff in the club. One of the women in the troupe placed the closed notices back up, locked the entrance and switched off the lights in the reception area. Following the rehearsal half were to gather on the raised area of the first tee once it was empty while two pairs were to separate and station themselves in bushes either side of the fair way. In the spot chosen maps were clear; they couldn't possibly be seen there from the club house, actually from almost anywhere.

Standing at the tee there was nobody in front of Eamon and Chas. Eamon swung and hit a fine stroke on to the fairway. Wherever their balls went Chas would be sticking close to Eamon. With effort his ball landed not too far away and the pair of them par holed. At the second tee Eamon was struggling to remember the golf grip he had used for decades. Chas reached around him from behind and coaxed his fingers into a simple wrap. As he did so Eamon pecked him on the neck. They both laughed, at the same time Eamon looking around. He caught a glimpse of two of figures going left into the rough ahead of them and straight away saw two more go to the right. They shouldn't be there, they hadn't played a ball. Eamon's swing suffered a bit from his unfamiliar grip. He looked to the sky and then up the hill behind him.

"Can the latest clubs look a bit like feckin' rifle barrels?"

he asked. He was unfamiliar with modern new fangled clubs. Chas shook his head and then returned to concentrate on his swing.

"Can they have attachments that look like sights to guide their strokes?"

Eamon saw Chas' irritation and shut up so he could complete his stroke. It landed near his friend's but when they strolled forward, Eamon darted off to a bunker way over to the right. He had forgotten to take a precautionary pee prior to leaving the hotel. He had also dismissed Chas' suggestion he used the toilets in the club house. When Chas caught up with him, he was set to piss in the hollow of a bunker on the next fairway from which a ton of sand had been shifted by the night's tremor.

"D'you think a leprechaun might have put a spot down there for me to aim at?"

He looked at Chas who looked back at him shaking his head. Of all the daft things he could come out with this was one of the daftest. Eamon's tone changed.

"Something big and silvery down there. I'd say it was a feckin' fin…and I think I've seen its like before."

A closer look or a poke with a club might have confirmed for both men that the chunk of metal they could see was a small part of something far larger. Chas wasn't set to indulge him.

"Leave it out, you can't pee here, people have to stand in it. Go over there by a tree…give us your club, I'll be waiting by our balls.

"No need, it's gone off now."

There was nothing to be gained by arguing.

That hole completed, at the following tee Eamon wanted to know the distance to the next. It was the hole with the bunker where he attempted his abortive pee. It was the shortest on the course. Chas fetched him a glove and a five iron and put both in his hand. Eamon stared at him.

"Ah …"

He delved but couldn't dig out Chas' name. Finally he did.

"Chas, Chas, feckin' Chas…"

He was chiding himself.

"…no man in all the blessed world could have a better friend".

"Likewise, mate."

Eamon grinned hugely, turned, addressed the ball but paused to say,

"You know some of them have gone ahead and disappeared."

Chas simply told him,

"Play your stroke."

At the tee behind them where the ground was higher a woman was lying flat with a high-powered rifle. It was aimed directly at them. A man in the group produced a tripod from his golf bag, propped a rifle on it and was adjusting its sights. The remaining two were holding the handles of trolleys on which were a mechanical saw and body bags with the zips undone and ready.

Eamon hit the ball badly, so it plopped into the bunker he had not long stood over to pee. Chas hit his ball every bit as badly and it landed beside his. Eamon looked at him with suspicion and then they both roared.

Back up on the higher ground fingers were on triggers and trolleys were already on the move. In the bushes to the left and right, rifles were put to one side and handguns out. Still laughing Chas and Eamon raced each other to the bunker. The rifle of the sniper laying flat had to be re-trained. The tripod and its rifle were shifted millimetres. Mobile calls were made to their fellows in the bushes. The opening strike remained the snipers' prerogative. Eamon won the race and by the edge of the bunker dropped his trousers. Chas reached him and dragged him into the hollow of the sand. He was resigned to Eamon messing there. When he had finished he started to pull up his trousers.

"Whoa, whoa."

Chas shouted. He popped up to his golf bag to fetch a cloth he used to clean his club. Up the slope there was frustration and re-adjustment of sights. Chas told Eamon,

"Touch your toes".

Like a child might, he obeyed. Chas did a half decent job of wiping the cleft between the buttocks that faced him. With that he again popped out from the bunker to fetch plastic bags to collect the excrement. There were sparkles from the direction of the first tee reflected from gun sights. Simultaneously two triggers were pulled. At that exact moment Chas was flattened, not by a bullet but by a tremor bigger than the previous night's. The sound of ground cracking overwhelmed the noise of the gun shots. Back up the hill it was chaos. People there were thrown to the ground and were still clinging to it. Mobile calls were made and assassins with shouldered rifles left the bushes with guns in hand. The final element for disposing of the bodies was minutes away.

The excrement bagged and stored with the rest of his equipment Chas leant down to give Eamon a hand.

"Fine feckin' show this is."

They looked upwards from where a deafening noise was coming. A helicopter was hovering above them.

"Mother of God, can you just see what that is?"

Eamon meant not the blades whirring overhead but the atomic bomb which had been laying there since 1945. The last tremor meant it was now completely revealed. Chas at first thought he meant the helicopter and shrugged. Once he saw the exposed bomb, he murmured to himself,

"Oh Christ…Is this what you meant dad?"

The two sniper's rifles behind them had been packed away and four automatics were coming down the hill. Assassins from bushes left and right were almost upon them and the helicopter landed ahead of the bunker, blocking the remaining escape route.

In different ways the old friends accepted one way and another that the game was up. Calmly their attention was on an image of a faded angel in black and grey with the signature 'Cassidy' on the bomb in the bunker. Near it was the handlebar shaped detonator which was still in good condition. The first of the four agents from the bushes reached them. His gun was within a third of a metre of Chas' back. As the trigger was being pulled and in the instant before the bullet sped from its chamber, Eamon threw his own body across Chas'. The bullet tore away a chunk of the left ventricle of his heart and carried it on through his friend's ribcage where it fused with his own. Rounds of bullets followed and Chas slumped forwards whilst Eamon twisted and dived. If his mouth could still function, he would have been screaming,

"Back to hell, the feckin' lot of yous,"

as his skull connected with the detonator.

C63

While Sam and Billy were fleeing aboard a plane, Ned was standing outside a bar near Millbank. Hours after his last call to them he had walked in all directions back and forth around the area, looking in every nook and cranny. Alleyways there were cramped and dark. If Jack the Ripper ever left the East End it would have been for there. The spot was in shadow and the location was devoid of cameras and passers-by were rare. He was at Jessica's side wearing a white outfit head to toe that complemented hers. A security light had had its bulb removed. The pair were waiting as Coetzee stepped out of the bar. He stopped, saw the white suits and recognised Jessica and all but stood to attention. He was drunk and wanted to sneer that they looked like extras from Saturday Night Fever. Instead, he smiled,

"Good to see one of the old brigade, someone who knows how it's done, hard choices and all that."

Spotting Ned with her he couldn't resist,

"All you need is a Hazchem mask to go with that."

"Covid's still around. Not a bad idea. Can't be too careful,"

Jessica responded, holding an involved mask she had in one of her gloved hands. He was tempted to say he didn't like the company she kept but decided he didn't dare. He contented himself with the thought that the Australian's downfall wasn't far off. He was going to ask,

"What brings you here?",

but this was pre-empted by the presentation of a gift.

"Your work has been recognised. Call it a token from across the Atlantic,"

Jessica told him. Coetzee took the gift bag with its heavily wrapped contents. Flushed and perspiring with the effort he tore off the wrapping and then struggled to prise apart a plastic container. Inside the container was a welded polyurethane bag which he ripped open to uncover a pack of Montecristo cigars. Someone had done their research. He was delighted.

“In recognition of my service, eh. At least someone gets what I do.”

“Couldn’t have put it better myself…just put the plastic rubbish in here, the environment and all that,”
she said, holding out the thickest of rubble bags.

“We’ll bin it for you. All part of the service.”
He obeyed the order and the bag was clamped. He was never able to delay his wants. He bit the mouth end from the cigar, lit up and luxuriated in the smoke entering his lungs.

“Tobacco will be the death of me,”
he coughed.

“It won’t be smoking that kills you,”
the American assured him.

The cigars were excellent quality and insofar as any tobacco product is, they were harmless. But the box he unwrapped wasn’t. Coetzee never recovered from the mystery illness he rapidly went down with.

EPILOGUE

On the flight home from Palomares and Nerja Chas Senior read his son a note he had written for him the previous day. It was forgotten by the time the son was in his thirties. That said he had kept the single sheet. It was the note that moved him when he found it upon returning from the mortuary to his marital home. It read

"Dear son always remember:
almost every war is a proxy war,
launched by those who never fight in them,
coffers flung open by those who never experience the privations that arise from them,
exhorted on by those who never suffer the agonies of ordinary folk caught up in them."

After passing the note to his son Chas Senior briefly took it back to add a postscript,

"Today there is, no place flung far enough, be it desert or island to go unscathed in a modern world war."

Would he have included the Azores in that? Almost definitely.

Not long after finding a rental apartment that suited them, Sam and Billy heard of an explosion in Japan that wasn't pinpointed at first. There were suggestions of Russian and Chinese aggression and counter accusations. All were eventually dismissed. When the dust had indeed settled local media blurred news of a quake with an accident transporting waste from Fukushima. For the international media it was hardly an event at all. Nevertheless, fleets and squadrons in different continents had been on maximum alert, missile silos readied and hotlines at melting point.

That notwithstanding Sam and Billy believed they were safe. They had few doubts and could answer their own questions. Could a life on the outskirts of Ponta Delgada be fulfilling? Could it be that two young lovers might stroll the hills and shoreline of the volcanic archipelago holding hands in its quiet and its peace? Could they be unmolested, unthreatened and free to enjoy the calm and beauty around them? When they asked each other, the answer to their questions was yes.

They had hope. They hoped that when they climbed Pico da Vara the 'V' formations they saw would be of wagtails, shearwaters and bullfinches, not the triangular geometry of lethal squadrons stealing across the skies. They hoped when they boarded a glass bottom vessel, they beheld shoals of ornate wrasse and other fish, not a conning tower in the depths. And should they go whale watching they hoped it would be creatures with blow holes they saw breaking the surface and not missiles storming off into the stratosphere.

These weren't quite all their hopes when they looked to the future. They wanted a child, children. Sam grew to be sure the pair of them would cherish and nurture them. She did her research. Where they were living, this might be a struggle. For adoption Porto and Lisbon were possibilities but for them Chile and Brazil were safer bets. Better than that there were various forms of donation as well as IVF. Under her new identity Sam swung it for Billy to have the children they wanted.

"Did I hear Ned?"

Billy asked. Sam lowered the tv volume.

"Surely not, he was so tired I didn't think we'd see him until morning."

"Hmm, he seemed out of sorts."

"It's been a long day, maybe it's that and no more."

"Poor thing. You could be right, but he's been in a mood which is unusual for him."

"True, he hasn't been chilled like he normally is. Perhaps he's coming down with something."

"If it was anyone else, I'd say he was upset over this or that, but you know him..."

Billy finished the thought for her,

"Not much puts him out and when it does, he's relaxed about telling you."

They were both extremely fond of Ned, devoted in fact.

"He's so lucky. He was born like that. I'd loved to have that easy way, instead of feeling so awkward with everyone."

"Not with me you're not Sam. Anyway, it's gone quiet, let's not disturb him. Do you think he's put on weight?"

"Bound to, isn't he? I think his hair's got darker too."

So the evening went with the tv volume on low. It meant they could listen out. This was intermixed with chat of Ned and how he had come to them and how he got on well with their six month old baby.

A while before Sam and Billy's bedtime Ned appeared rubbing his eyes and yawning at the lounge door opening. He was as naked as the day he was born. The two women burst into laughter. He coughed and went and sat between them. Sam took his temperature while Billy fetched him a glass of water and told him,

"Nothing wrong with you mister. Your temperature is normal. Now go and put something on."

Ned was honest that it wasn't that he was feeling unwell. Simply he was awake and wanted some company. The two women let him stay. Half an hour later he was still between them. Both had an arm around him. Bedtime came and together they tucked in their four year old toddler. Billy kissed him goodnight, whilst Sam gently shushed him.

"Ned, remember your little sister in the cot…"

she said pointing across the bedroom.

“We don’t want to disturb her, do we?”

Were Billy and Sam and indeed their two children as safe as they hoped? As safe as anyone can be in a world armed to the teeth. Did they survive? It’s too early to say, isn’t it?

In memory of the Kiritimati communities exposed to radiation from the bomb explosions on ‘Christmas Island’ 1957-8 and of the servicemen made to sit, hands over eyes & backs turned, just 30 miles distant.

In awe of the veterans who have battled for recognition for more than 60 years.

Milton Keynes UK
Ingram Content Group UK Ltd.
UKHW011848091123
432282UK00001B/14